The Eternal Quest

Julian Branston

The Eternal Quest

SCEPTRE

First published in Great Britain in 2003 by Hodder and Stoughton
A division of Hodder Headline

A Sceptre Book

1 3 5 7 9 10 8 6 4 2

A CIP catalogue record for this title is available from the British Library

ISBN 0 340 82281 3

Typeset in Sabon by Palimpsest Book Production Limited,
Polmont, Stirlingshire

Printed and bound in Great Britain by
Clays Ltd, St Ives plc

Hodder and Stoughton
A division of Hodder Headline
338 Euston Road
London NW1 3BH

This is for you, this that I owe
It comes not so much from any debt
nor from any loss of yours
but rather something reciprocal
as the ocean gives in waves and tides
that harness the land to its mood
as the steady growth of pine
takes place beyond any duty,
this is taken from the world that we inhabit
which – if you accept –
we gild with our gifts

Dedicated to the extraordinary spirit
of Miguel Cervantes

Contents

The Eternal Quest

Contents

Before You Go Any Further

Some remarks from the author of *Don Quixote*, one
Miguel Cervantes, deceased, and an explanation of the
present volume.

*A*s it has pleased God to reveal early in my life
his profound mastery over the fate of all human
beings, I renounced any aspiration for fame from
my writings to fulfil one single aim; that is, to
reveal a little of God's intelligence to his obstinate, graceless,
and ungrateful creations. It was allowed, a little, in my long life
to reveal some of this in my two novels of *Don Quixote*. But
my character, circumstances, and a divine requirement that an
equal if not surmounting purity of spirit should accompany any
such aspirations, meant that this accomplishment could occur
only late in life. After the publication of the *Don Quixote*
books, my life shortly thereafter ended, and I had not so much
influence on the outcome and development of my novels. Yet
new knowledge will produce fruit, even in the desert, and
these novels of mine have since been published in many other
languages than my purest Castillian, languages I had never
heard of. This is a paradox, for many do not understand my
books, as they were a hurried creation and a dying man can
only blunder at his final duties. However, as there exists no
facility whereby history might burnish its better moments, it
falls on a few who receive the inspiration such a work affords
to renew the source. These recipients know that it is a task,
inherited by every human being, whether they know it or not,

that they strive to honour the divine in all things, for it is the promise of God to raise everything after him.

And so, humanity has a debt in my favour. For no sooner had the first part of *Don Quixote* been published, than a dozen paltry and malicious counterfeits tried to take its place. More conflict took place between rival booksellers of these and my works – a war between my purest concept and the influence of unsound and criminal editions – than ever existed between Turk and Christian. In the time that it takes to write this sentence, these shadows of their better – the hidalgo Don Quixote – spurned their pages, and like rebellious children, inclined to dictate their own destinies. Before my creation could be fully rounded, and to protect the content already published, I was forced to write a sequel to the first book that was but an end to one of the choicest of all characters.

However, though it suited divine ends that a hurried conception should be followed by a faster end, it was allowed that there must be some resolution to my novel's inspiration. Therefore an individual has been elected to deliver another addition to my life's work, intended as a companion to the originals, both in spirit and humour. And as my main character has already found an end, then this freshest episode must make an addition without intruding into the exploits of the noblest buffoon in history. The deliberation of this newest episode is the work of this author to engender.

This new author is an individual aloof from my history and origin. His mind has never found a true purchase in a worthy ideal, while his character has the same wildness, uncertainty, and manifest despairs that once afflicted my soul. Yet this flawed pupil is as suitable to the purpose of God as is the sunrise, or the ebb and flow of the sea. Therefore the birth, progress, and resolution of the adventures contained in the following pages have my blessing but not my hand. His heart then must find partner with God, his mind turn the mill of phrases, and his pen enact the spirit of lucid and genial Comedy.

Redoubtable Pedro

Pedro, redoubtable trader, visits a print shop and enquires
after the first episodes of a new comic romance.

G iven Pedro's ambition to be the world's finest merchant in traded goods, it gratified him, on his morning walk through the lower quarter of Valladolid – the new hub of the Spanish Empire – to see his neighbours and acquaintances carrying full to overflowing shopping baskets. And further that many of them would frequently and cheerfully greet him by his first name and make a reference to their latest business dealings. Someone might say, 'Your eggs made an Emperor's breakfast, friend Pedro, and did you find a worthy pair of legs for those stockings?' or, 'Tell your wife and daughters to come for their fittings, friend Pedro, for that lace would be a fortune for any milliner.'

Occasionally there would be complaints, but to these Pedro would willingly listen, for he believed that his reputation depended not only on his successes, but also on the speed with which he allowed and redressed his mistakes. And to this he added a firm patience, for he would always have to remind his partners in trading that nothing was for free, and that he required something for himself. If there was any labour involved, for example, harvesting oranges or pulling carrots, this meant 'something extra' for him. People liked him, therefore, because he facilitated their needs, he knew everything about everyone without harm to anyone, and he never failed to deliver a little more than what was requested. With a pleasant roughcast manner and the immediate poetry of argot in his speech, people thought of him as being friendly, fair, and above all, a genius of surprises.

Pedro was not a family man. His wife was a worthy Catholic matron, the mother of six healthy daughters, yet their names Pedro found hard to recall, and their birthdays he never remembered. His body was a mere visitor to his family and home because his spirit was dedicated to his ambition. This was difficult to discern, since he liked to pass the time eating, drinking and conversing with his friends and acquaintances. When asked about his family, he would say, 'The Emperor can raise an army, a general can raise a siege, a wit can raise a snicker, but I can hardly raise six daughters, and not one of them thanks me for being their father. All the money I have goes to combs and petticoats. Now, about that row of cabbages I know you have in your garden strip. It would please the priest's soul, God save him, to have those for an excellent soup that is the speciality of his housekeeper, and is so good a medicine, so it is said, that it can cure winter and bring on the spring. Now if you would give me those to give to him, then he will give your boy Bible lessons, and say special prayers for you at Mass. But if you have the mind that your own prayers are good enough, and that the parson, Heaven bless his kindness and excuse his feeble wits, can say no more prayers on your behalf than God himself, then he will also teach your daughter a lesson or two on the church organ. Let me come tomorrow morning, and relieve you of the burden of those cabbages!'

So in a time of uncertain economy, when the ship could sink or the harvest could fail, Pedro knew how do without the money that nobody had.

But there was a Pedro that no one could guess at. In part because he had never fully expressed another of his ambitions even to himself, and because his family, friends, and acquaintances would rather consider him as the cipher of a likeable trader and unwilling husband than as someone with aspirations that were abstract and out of the ordinary. For Pedro wanted to be Mayor. It troubled him little that this ambition was inappropriate – a peasant-farmer, recently moved to the city, could never be considered for so high an office – or that the status he sought was so specific; it was not to be rich, to be famous, to be powerful, but to be Mayor. How had this ambition arisen? A delighted recipient of several jars of the best olive oil had said, 'Friend Pedro, if you wanted to become Mayor, I would cast my vote for you.' And as is the case with some casual remarks, it had special meaning, and the idea took root in Pedro with surprisingly little doubt attached to it. It was the natural end, in his mind, to his assiduous work on a thriving assortment of trades and connections. In this aspect of his life there were few disappointments, and this helped him forget the neglect of his family, to ignore the many Masses that were said on his behalf by his wife, and to remain deaf to the caustic remarks of his six – or was it seven? – daughters.

On this particular morning, there was much to look forward to, both in satisfaction and challenge, because Pedro was about to visit Robles the printer, the one person who adamantly refused to trade with him, and after that meet with another person, an author, with whom he was enjoying a so far admirably and mutually profitable business venture, only this time, one that produced actual hard cash.

Pedro entered the cool of the print shop from the dusty hustle of the street. The printer's boy scrambled from a stool, and Robles appeared, trimmed and alert, already in inking sleeves and holding a gathering of papers.

'Let me know the figures,' said Pedro, 'for I am on my way to my friend Cervantes, and as he lives more by night than by day, I can provide the fire for his inspiration this evening.'

'Well, you have your own space in the window, and not an

hour goes by when someone does not buy the latest episode,' said Robles. 'Look, here in my hand, another dozen gatherings for printing.'

'Then let me take money to him as well,' said Pedro, 'for he has more debt than a cemetery has stones, and despite his cheerful character, he does have the melancholy.'

'I do believe,' said Robles, giving Pedro a small bag of coins, 'that success breeds melancholy. You must tell your friend that writing comedies is the saddest activity for any man, and working through nights, with no-one to talk to but the moths around your candle, is a sure route to desolation. Tell him to come and have dinner with me.'

'I know his reply,' said Pedro. 'He will smile and say that you cannot cheat a man of the work he must do, not even for friendship's sake. But I will tell him of your concern, and of your invitation.'

Robles shrugged his shoulders; he also knew Cervantes.

'Now, on another matter,' said Pedro, 'there is someone I know who would like a few of your best sheets of parchment—'

'Before you go any further,' Robles interrupted, shaking his finger, 'remember what I have previously told you. I am not in the business of trading, but the business of cash. I am committed to coins and paper money, and no other currency, and there is nothing that you can say or do to make me change my mind.' Robles shook his finger again and said, 'Most people in this neighbourhood are engaged in some kind of trade with you, but money is bankable and cabbages and carrots are not.'

'How can you be so hard,' said Pedro, 'when every month you buy a bigger and better hat! Would your business fail from one or two small trades?' he continued. 'Why, even the baker trades with the butcher, and it is well known that these two have never spoken since the baker married the butcher's sweetheart, and the butcher married the baker's sister in revenge.'

'Forgive me,' said Robles, 'if I think this is even less reason for trading. May I remind you, friend Pedro, that I will not do a thing simply because a dozen other fools have done so. I do not choose to trade because I do not need to and that is an end.'

'And what if your wife,' said Pedro, 'whose beauty and cultivated tastes are unquestioned, should stop me and say, "Dear Pedro, my blessings on your wife and daughters, and what have you heard on the latest fashion of leather boots in Madrid—"'

'I would say that you are an artful and clever liar,' interrupted Robles, 'and that it is questionable courtesy on your part to comment so freely on my wife's beauty and love for fashion.' Robles paused. 'But it is inevitable that she will stop you and say that same thing. That does not mean it is a good idea. I must be more vigilant, both with my young and beautiful wife, and with you. But how is it,' he continued, 'that having recently engaged in such a profitable cash venture with our friend the author, you still obstinately engage in trading? Give it up,' he said and flashed the only smile he would give that day, 'and become like me, a real business man.'

'To tell you the truth,' said Pedro, 'I am terrible in business. As a farmer, I was the worst. Even the pigs left home. My current profession I only discovered through talking with friends. And without a good conversation, most of my trades would fail.' He paused. 'Also, I must remind myself that this new cash venture is only as good as the next sale. And that depends very much on my friend Cervantes, who, it must be said, sees more the tenants inside his head than the rent-collector outside his door.'

'Now in this, I do not envy you,' said Robles. 'Cervantes hardly keeps the hours of an ordinary man, and his attraction to taverns and theatres has not recommended him to his neighbours.'

'My policy,' said Pedro, 'is to keep him busy with new work. And having said that, I shall now take leave of you and visit my friend, who is probably, at this late hour of the morning, asleep at his desk.'

Pedro turned to go, and then because charm was in his blood, turned briefly and said, 'Your wife's beauty would be incomparable in the latest fashion of boots from Madrid. I can find a pair, as scarce as they are. It would bind her heart to yours for an age.' With this, he left.

For Robles, it was not a comfortable moment. His wife's beauty was one reason why business was good. Numberless love-struck poets had requested his wife to cast an eye over their verses and approve the typeface. This was an irony, for his wife had no expertise in the setting of type, much less poetry. But their flattery and their unctuous requests only proved to Robles how much older he was than his young, beautiful, and essentially empty-hearted wife.

It was something of a mystery, Robles knew, that such a woman should love him. She was made for the bedroom, he thought, and then began a sequence of thoughts that had often kept him sleepless, shaming his waking moments. Had she lovers? Could she, so artlessly devoted to inconsequential pleasures, love an old man in inky sleeves with the squint (he knew) of approaching blindness? And was the solution to his anxieties, he thought bitterly, a pair of new boots from Madrid?

The Author

A meeting with the author of a comic romance, his family, and other members of his household.

*H*aving left a small disaster where he thought he had left success, Pedro had now another opportunity to do good, and that was to bring Cervantes the money that he knew would be a solace for many ills. His pace slowed just a little: he remembered that in order to see his friend he must encounter his friend's family, for they fortress the house like so many bastions, he thought, and you cannot enter without a good supply of powder and shot. Pedro was not an expert in arms – that was the domain of Cervantes – but the simile was appropriate, and as he was not accomplished in dealings with his own family, he hesitated. He tossed the bag of coins; the robustly solid shape fortified him. It was a weapon against all the vagaries of the world. Inspired by coin and the virility of his optimism, Pedro drove himself on to the house.

But then he paused again outside. It was his habit to carry up to Cervantes his first meal of the day – as coaxed from the women of the house, something of a triumph in daring and charm – for it had been his generous-hearted gesture one morning to take a bowl of soup to his friend. 'For what I have in my pot will do you good, said the whore to the priest,' he had said blithely, thereby scandalising the household. But what had been his generosity became the selfishness of the house, and preparing a little something for Cervantes became a chore that no one else would undertake. On some mornings there was nothing to be had at all. What would it be on this occasion?

Inside, the kitchen was filled with an array of hanging onions and the bobbing heads of women, the larger population of the house; among them, Cervantes' wife, Doña Catalina, and his sister Andrea. Isabel, Cervantes' daughter, the illegitimate progeny of an affair with a long disappeared tragic actress, was vigorously stirring soup on the fire. She was a strong young woman with a skin of painted gloss, like those fierce wooden mermaids on the prows of trading ships. Sensual strength glowed from her shoulders, bosom and hips. She treated anyone as inferior who did not have the ardour of her convictions. And she was intimidatingly curious about anyone that did not have her same beguiling physicality. This meant that she was never far from altercation; 'The soup is too thick! The flour in this would break a donkey's back!' she said, vigorously stirring a blistered pot.

'Stir it and add water,' said Andrea, grim and disapproving of her illegitimate niece.

'Perhaps I could do so much for you,' Isabel said, vigorously leaning into her movement.

'Meaning what?' said Andrea in combative tones.

'Meaning,' said Isabel, as her movements climaxed triumphantly, 'that mud shows no life until you stir it.'

Andrea threw herself to her feet and in a fountain of rage walked rapidly to the kitchen door.

'There,' said Isabel, 'you prove my point.'

It was at this moment that Pedro opened the door from without. His first view of the room was the trembling Andrea, whose tall, ungiving figure and light eyes, glistening with anger, seemed to him like a lightning rod newly struck.

It was not uncommon for Pedro to be greeted with rage when returning to his own home. In these instances, he had several lines of defence. The first was a heavy handed flattery, like a poet maddened by bucolic rhymes, and after he had called his wife 'a splendid Hera of the heavens', and his numerous daughters 'sisters of Aphrodite', and knelt on the beaten earth floor and kissed the black hem of his wife's shawl, then the house would return to harmony. His second line of defence was to justify his absence, or neglect, or whatever had caused grievance, with manufactured indignation. Surely, he would say, you cannot see how exhausted, how besieged I am with the duties and responsibilities of my position, and how it perplexes my soul to see such ingratitude from the members of my own house! This line of defence was mostly ineffective, because it would often result in long, terrible quarrels and end in his feeling a despair that would utterly submerge his natural good spirits. The third line of defence was to leave immediately and spend the night with his good friend the poacher who, having laid traps for birds, would lie out under the stars and talk philosophy. This was an uncertain method, because returning home in the pale and languid dawn, he would have to endure an implacable silence from his wife and daughters, perhaps for days.

Having quickly calculated these possibilities, he decided that the first line was preferable, especially as he had the energy for it, fuelled by the slick jingle of coins in the bag and the good news from Robles.

He bowed elaborately, and rose quickly. 'Goddess, beauty, you are a prize of the heavens.' Andrea's anger, though consuming, was mute. 'How shall I,' he continued, 'praise your high qualities? How shall I . . .' But this was all, because his new-found Goddess made a brief step forward, slapped him hard across the face, and left the room. Pedro, whose ploys had never so quickly failed, could only hold the growing warmth of his cheek and totter into the kitchen.

Isabel laughed, while the other women, finding it likely that there was some justice in the blow, also found reasons to be angry with him and immediately made him accountable.

'What brings such a wastrel to this house?' said Doña Catalina, sourly heaving at her sewing. Pedro opened his mouth to praise her beauty and munificence, when Constanza, the daughter of Andrea, demanded 'Did you bring money?' Although Pedro knew that the money would, naturally and inevitably, pass from his author's hands to those of his household, he felt it his duty to lie. 'No,' he said, but then hastily, addressing Doña Catalina, 'I have brought good news and, as it is your husband's practice to work through the night, I thought it good to wake him with it and a bowl of this family's famous soup.'

'Perhaps you could encourage him,' Constanza said, 'to find a respectable profession, rather than scribbling and singing army songs at night.'

Pedro often found it strange that he knew Cervantes better than did his own family, for asking him to stop writing and resume some desultory profession or another would be like asking a fish to fly. But the mood in the kitchen being dangerous, he nodded, smiled, and proffered a bowl for filling to Isabel. She glared at him briefly, and immediately handed it back. She had already found her meat for another argument.

'Do you think,' she said to Constanza, 'that my father,' with special emphasis, 'has no honour? Should he not choose the profession that best suits him and his service to God?'

Constanza, more vocal than her mother Andrea, replied immediately. 'Perhaps, after so many decades of writing without success, or writing for less money than would feed a sparrow, he might consider that God is telling him to make something else of his fading years.'

'In my opinion,' said Isabel, arms akimbo, 'to follow a natural inclination in his fading years, with his children already so decidedly grown and ready in the world, is to be admired rather than mocked.'

Constanza was scornful. 'You would only say that because your mother chose a profession cursed by God! For even defending it, you should be excommunicate! Your mother, an actress!' Constanza threw up her hands for effect, but had no time to revel in her own eloquence for Isabel's face was suddenly inches from her own.

'Do you think that it does not give me the greatest pleasure that her profession, despite its glory and her talents, causes you the greatest embarrassment? For I have heard you say such things about me, one who can walk as far as any man, that you might as well call me "slattern" and "bitch". For this less than loving family has extended no more tenderness to me than a crowd at a bear-baiting. So I mock your rig-maroles and say that these are the issue of a virgin and a prude.'

'Then, Miss Whore,' said Constanza, daring in her anger, 'this is the respect you deserve.'

'Contanza!' said Doña Catalina.

'Miss Milk!' said Isabel.

'Gypsy!' returned Constanza.

'Housekeeper!'

'Slut!'

'Girl!'

Pedro, filling the bowl, turned to everybody. 'Does it need salt?' he asked. The room rounded on him.

'Did I make it?' said Doña Catalina.

'Mr Profitless,' said Isabel, 'you might leave that soup for other members of this family.'

'You have not been attending,' said Pedro, 'this is for your father, whose labours are many, and doubtless your arguing has awakened him.'

'Then he can come and get it for himself. This kitchen never sees him,' said Constanza.

'Perhaps there is a reason for that,' said Pedro to himself with precise irony. With that, he left the room.

Outside, he could hear the rising temper of voices. He quickly began to climb the wooden stairs into the dark of the upper floor. The rancorous sounds faded. He turned down the shaded hall towards a doorway at the end.

The room he entered was large, airy, with a good view of the courtyard. It was a respectable mess, with a row of books and pamphlets, a writing desk, a camp bed from soldiering days, and several candlesticks. A man was sleeping at the desk, and Pedro's immediate action was to inspect a small bottle – which proved empty – close to a manuscript on which the sleeping figure had very firmly placed his head. Pedro went to the window and pulled back the linen coverings. From there, he could see the robust shape of an olive tree at the centre of the courtyard. A low wall of stone surrounded the tree.

'Sir Author,' said Pedro, shaking the bag of coins, 'Author, respected, venerated, successful author. Ah, I thought that would wake him!'

And yes, this did awaken Cervantes, rousing his fitful sleep from the nightmare of war, with screaming shot flying over-head, the rasping sound of his own breathing, and the ominous clash of weapons. As this dangerous fog receded, he heard the voice of Pedro, and then his own voice saying, 'Thank God!'

As he uttered these words, he felt the onset of a familiar and disturbing pain. The remains of his tormented left hand, blown apart by a harquebus during the Emperor's wars, still ached for its previous unity, as though the spirit of the limb could not tolerate the mutilated form. Here it begins, he thought, as the slow drum of blood in his arm pulsed against the obstruction of the hand. Soon each fibre and nerve in his arm would open like delicate plants and commence their silent protest against a noisy and overbearing world.

'There are many good reasons for thanking God,' said Pedro.

'That may be,' said Cervantes, his face covered by his one good hand, 'but the truth is that God sometimes chooses to terrify his servants into heaven, and so thanking him becomes mere politeness, and surviving becomes the first order of the day. My friend, you have entered my room like the dawn chorus, and my head feels like a circus of fools and lunatics.'

'Well,' said Pedro, accustomed to the ritual, 'if you will eat opium for supper, and drink nothing but ink, and stay up all night scribbling, then it is no wonder that you look as pale as the wax that you are wasting. But I have brought you money,' he continued, glibly, 'good news, and a bowl of soup that your daughter made and that your wife swears by.'

'You are more than extrovert today, my friend,' said Cervantes, rolling his sleeves and dipping his face into a basin. 'Did you find a million in the gutter?'

'I have been talking to Robles,' said Pedro, 'who is too proud to count all his money, and if he did, would crow all night.' Pedro placed the bag of coins with a convincing click upon the desk. Cervantes nodded his thanks. 'It is rare,' he said, 'for you to criticise your friends.'

'It is because,' said Pedro promptly, 'he will not trade! He has every other virtue, and yet his one vice is that he will not trade!'

Cervantes smiled at this. 'I am sure,' he said, 'that he will survive your summation of his character. And what about you? Are you not oiling his young and beautiful wife with apparently innocent tales of the latest fashions? For your compulsion to do a person good by taking something valuable from them would shame the Society of Thieves.'

Pedro seated himself on the edge of the desk. 'It is not only to talk of Robles' beautiful wife that I have roused you this morning.'

Cervantes dried the dampness of his face, his eyebrows raised in question.

Pedro coughed nervously. It was time to discuss something delicate with his friend. He continued, 'I have an idea that will bring the story more in line with commerce.'

'Keep it for sleepless nights, my friend,' said Cervantes

quickly, 'for all I need is the patience to endure the dictation of God, and I pray that there is time to fulfil the roundness of this work.' There was something behind his quick response. This was a successful business venture, and Cervantes was writing with a joy and accomplishment hardly experienced before. But even with his hand so happily and firmly fixed on the enigmatic serpent of inspiration, the coils of his story were writhing free. He could not hold it; truth, action, speech were growing beyond the collusion of his hand and brain. In fact, he had written far more than Pedro knew, but had not known what to do with these errant chapters and paragraphs. They were in a strong box under the camp bed, along with memorabilia of the wars.

'Well, it is a comic romance,' pursued Pedro, with the insistence that makes an exemplary salesman great and an ordinary one irritating, 'and yes, it is comic. But where is the romance?'

'The old Knight is in love with ideals,' said Cervantes, 'that is the romance.'

Pedro looked disbelieving that such a subtle significance could have so much effect on the story.

'You do not feel,' said Pedro, 'that a woman might be suited to your story, a love upon whose bosom your old Knight, after his trials are done, will finally rest his head?'

'You have forgotten the old Knight's lady love, Dulcinea del Toboso,' said Cervantes.

'She is not a romance,' said Pedro, 'but a torment.'

'Such is love,' said Cervantes, 'as you have so readily proved upon your worthy wife, at least half a dozen times.'

Pedro absorbed this reference to his daughters without a blink. 'Perhaps they could kiss,' he pursued, 'or something amorous?'

'Now if you really want to help,' said Cervantes gently, 'then perhaps you can reconcile my uneasiness with the character of Don Quixote, who although alive and breathing in me, is not drawn from someone I have observed. My work most satisfies when it comes from the study of my neighbours.'

Pedro stood up from the desk – a guilty thought had struck him. Cervantes observed this but he said nothing; compassion had made him gentle.

'But also the truth is, I find men a simpler study,' said Cervantes, watching his friend. 'Women are a different order of creation, and I cannot own to any expertise.'

As if to punctuate this observation, the sound of the women in the kitchen, their tirades turned to laughter, surged through the house.

'Well,' said Pedro, 'you already have me in the story, my very own likeness, so much so that people ask me if I have a twin.'

'This much is a success. It is the character of Quixote that troubles me, seeing that he is based completely on your anecdote,' said Cervantes.

Pedro saw his chance. 'Ah, now that's where you amaze me.' He took a deep breath. 'You have drawn such a real picture of him, to the life, and delicate as a pin.'

'To the life? What do you mean?' asked Cervantes.

'The real Quixote. The live one,' said Pedro.

'What are you talking about?' said Cervantes.

'He is indeed,' said Pedro rapidly, 'the son of your works! He is such a likeness to the one in the book that you need not water down the other, they are so alike!'

There was a pause.

'Then your anecdote, which is the foundation of my story, is a real person of your acquaintance?' Cervantes asked.

Pedro, smiling through alarm and guilt, nodded.

'Would it not have been simpler to tell me?' said Cervantes.

'Well, it would have hindered your powers of prophecy,' said Pedro. 'Why curse you like a Cassandra? The beauty of it! It was an even bet which of his humours you would describe next. Like milk from a cow you were, prompt and warm.'

'Ah, so you have been betting on my inspiration,' Cervantes said. 'This explains your guilty expression some minutes ago, my friend. What else do you have to confess?'

'I have nothing to confess, unless under constraint,' said Pedro, 'and that is I have taken my advantages as I have found them.'

'My new powers of divination are telling me,' said Cervantes, mocking, 'that the producer of this comic romance, none other than a short-and-unscrupulous-tradesman-of-this-city, has, with the speed and resolution of the greedy, placed gambling bets on the progress of the not-yet-mentioned-but-ever-present author of this aforesaid comic romance?'

'Well, if you asked me outright, said the thief to the judge, instead of clapping me in jail, then I would have told you I was guilty,' said Pedro.

'And the bet?' said Cervantes.

'That you will continue,' said Pedro, reciting from memory the wager with his betting companions, 'to describe the old man without ever having seen him, even to the last freckle.'

'Now is this honourable?' said Cervantes, becoming amused.

'It's profitable and there is honour in that,' said Pedro, 'and as it is a separate business venture from our present partnership, I cannot offer you any of the proceeds from it, if you understand.'

'I commend,' said Cervantes, 'your lack of principles, and your willingness to exploit a helpless colleague for the sake of your compulsion for gambling.'

'Now to complain when things are going so well is like throwing good fruit after bad, said the actor to the audience,' said Pedro. 'And why carry on so, when you can sit in the sun all day and write comedy?'

'I never saw anything written well that was not crafted,' said Cervantes, 'and I am a slave to the craft. Only the Toledo sword-masters turn their steel more frequently than the writer of good prose. I am fortunate in one thing. God lived in a vacuum before creating the Universe. He did not have my courtyard and a beautiful olive tree to look on while he worked.'

'Well, and as my old mamma used to say,' said Pedro, 'God created a busy world to keep himself out of mischief. And if he did not create a lot of busybodies like yourself who wish to comprehend him totally, then how would he have any holidays?'

They paused in their bantering. Cervantes looked out at the tree in the courtyard. 'But,' he said, 'I must meet him,' talking of the counterpart that Pedro had, in usury, hidden from him. 'Tell me the real story of this individual.'

'Well, it all began, as I remember,' said Pedro, relieved that his confession had been so lightly taken, yet mourning the loss of future winnings from his bet, 'from an evening of solace in the Lepanto tavern. It had been a terrible day. You and I both needed commiseration. I had recently made a foolish trade.' Ah yes, the experience still had a sting in it. Pedro had given a compass to a pedlar and his dancing bear, in exchange for a night of entertainment for his neighbours. The pedlar had taken the compass and was never seen again. How he and the bear had escaped so quickly was beyond comprehension.

'And then,' Pedro continued, 'your play had ended after a week.' Cervantes nodded in recollection. There are only so many unpopular penny plays that one can write – they may be unworthy children, but they still die in your arms. Pedro was still thinking of the pedlar and the bear . . . how fast can a bear run?

'And then you told me a story of a crazy old man, who was in love with chivalry and very flowery in his speech. You said that the story would cheer me up and that you'd heard it from your friend the poacher,' said Cervantes.

'I told you the story of the old man,' Pedro said, somewhat bitterly, 'to beguile the pain of having met him.' For any compassion that Pedro might have felt at the outset for the old man soon evaporated. He had learned that encountering him usually meant experiencing something unforeseen and unpleasant, as had been true of their very first meeting, which he now began to relate. 'It was a hot day, too hot for business, and I was paddling in the river where the women wash their clothes,' he recalled. Cervantes' intelligent eyes were on him. Pedro began to explain. 'Well, it encourages them to see someone like me take an interest in their activities. They like someone watching as they play in the water.'

Cervantes' look of irony did not falter, so Pedro sighed and continued.

'I was startled out of my contemplation by the loud cry of a snow-headed old man who, wearing what looked like kitchen utensils, threw himself in the river. He sank so promptly, that I wondered if I had dreamed his appearance.'

'And you rescued him?' asked Cervantes.

'My first mistake,' said Pedro mournfully. 'I struggled through the shallows and dragged him to the bank. He was very heavy, and even though the fall had knocked him out, he was smiling blissfully, as though he had drunk hard liquor.'

'And then?' prompted Cervantes.

'He woke up and burped water on me,' said Pedro. His expression was so sorrowful that Cervantes began to laugh. Pedro continued. 'I told him that he was proving his second childhood on me, whereupon he sighed contentedly and thanked God that he had been able to rescue me from the currents of a tormented stream. This did not please me, so I told him that *I* had rescued *him*, and not the other way around. At this point, the old fool took my hand and looked at me with shining eyes. He told me that my need was great, and that drowning was a dreadful death. Then I got angry and told the old fool that I did not need rescuing! The foolery continued because he nodded as though wise and said that he had misread the order of events, and that it was he that had needed rescuing. This made me sarcastic. I asked him why he had not saved himself before jumping in. His response was very prompt. "Ah, my friend, it must then be true that you, being blinded from too much sin, had also misread events, and failed to stop me before I jumped in. In this you were lacking." If I had had any remaining strength, I would have thrown him back in the river. "I dispute the blind," I said, "and therefore conclude the following. Firstly, that from my lack of a siesta, I did not foresee your progress down to the river here. Secondly, that my lack of any cries for help were so clearly an encouragement for your action. And thirdly, that God himself must be lacking a wit, for he could not prevent you from concluding that I was drowning in the water that I was paddling in." Again, the old fool was ready with a response. "I go where God needs me," he said. So I advised him that God wanted him in the colonies and that the boats left every day.'

In his retelling of this story, Pedro began to see the humour in it. 'I discovered,' said Pedro, 'that he was wearing metal plates sewed into his pantaloons.'

'What happened after that?' asked Cervantes.

'He stood up, and there was already rust on him, and he looked into the distance for so long, I thought he had fallen into a trance. Then he blessed me, told me that I had been difficult to rescue because of my sins. He then whispered to me that he was Sir Lancelot and that lakes were as familiar to him as snow in winter. He delivered some other crazed homilies, and then asked me if I had seen any evil magicians, for one had stolen his – Sir Lancelot's, that is – celebrated sword. Discovering that I had heard of no such person, he then wandered on his way.'

'Your misfortune then became my inspiration,' Cervantes commented. 'And where shall we find this original?'

'Rather than find him, it would be better to move to another continent,' Pedro said.

'Come now, you make him sound like Bad Luck in person.'

'He's one of the plagues that they write about in the Bible.'

'But,' Cervantes said, persuasive, 'I must meet him. It is good for the veracity of my work.'

Pedro sighed. 'Is this the reward for my honesty?'

'Well, if it is too difficult, then you could always share your winnings with me.'

Pedro shook his head disapprovingly. 'And I thought you the soul of reason,' he said. Then he grasped Cervantes arm. 'You will not be able to find him. He's all air and mischief. You'll have to wait until he finds you. And then when he does,' and Pedro wagged his finger wisely, 'your troubles will multiply like midges in spring.'

The Old Man

A singularly determined and very mad old man.

*T*he identity of the old man and the circumstances that led to his madness are now revealed for your private understanding in the following swiftly delivered paragraphs.

Of proven hidalgo blood and ancient family, as a young man he had received a good commission in the Emperor Philip II's armies and risen quickly in rank, noted for his courage and abilities in battle. He had become the Emperor's favourite soldier, a salve from the numerous turbulent generals jousting their jealousies at court. And because the Emperor felt kindly towards him, and wanted to do him an honour, he was appointed officer in attendance to the Duke of Alva. It was this that proved his undoing and unhinged his hitherto reasonable mind.

First, his new position had nothing to do with soldiering, but rather more with sycophancy, a skill in which he had little learning and no interest. Adding to his unease at this, an astonishing stipend was awarded to him that increased whenever the Duke was assigned to another of the nation's conflicts. For one schooled by the Order of Calatrava, the nation's finest and oldest military academy, he was confounded by such venality. Plagued with money, carrying a brittle dress-sword that could never be used in real combat, he was expected to keep his shoes brilliant and look keen and obliging, like a dog. The Emperor's kindness had taken away the life he loved best.

But these perplexities were followed by something more terrifying; the experience of being in service to the Duke himself. On the campaign against the dissidents of the Low Countries, the Duke skirted conflict with enemy forces and marched for the civilian populace, upon whom he visited wholesale butchery. Communities were executed. Innocents were burned, hanged, strangled, impaled, and beheaded. Death was piled up in the squares and courtyards.

Trapped in the specially appointed trial-chambers, our young officer began to realise his own culpability, for the notes that the Duke so swiftly wrote and that he then delivered – those innocent white papers – all contained death, a steel invitation to oblivion. He was the Duke's executioner. And as the Duke waded into blood, he found an inner blankness encroaching on him. Robbed of the roots of his tongue, the numbness grew as he endured the Duke's obsessive summoning, and interviewing, and adjudicating, and executing. He would stand mute at the Duke's compulsive review of the day's prisoners. As executions swiftly and summarily occurred, he watched – which was required – as startled heads were plucked from shoulders fretted with blood, and witnessed the Duke's terrible excitement as death thudded to a finale.

And then it happened. Standing attendant one day, he suddenly heard the shutters and panels of the Duke's mind opening, and clearly saw emerge – like the clever figurines of Swiss clocks and chimes – a small, deadly machine on precise wheels, the order for death.

And then he began to listen to his own mind, as though the clicks and scuffles of the Duke's brain were no longer sufficient study. For why did he do nothing to obstruct this dismal route of royally sanctioned murder? Listening, he discovered the whisperings of a dozen voices, murmuring discontent and dissent. Perhaps this is why, he thought, the Duke has found it purgative to murder dissidents; he has heard the same rebellion inside himself. But then why did the Duke allocate these voices outside himself, as though issuing from the mouths of his unfortunate prisoners? he thought. And to this question, a voice inside him replied, Because the Duke cannot tell the difference.

'Ah,' he asked himself, 'then can I?'

'Yes,' said the voice, 'but this is not a solution.'

'But,' he remarked, 'there is hope.'

'You speak,' said the voice, 'as though you were already mad.'

'I think I am,' he said, 'for I witness a terrifying amount of death without a murmur. I must be mad, to stand here and observe such pitiless cruelty, rather than find some means to prevent it.'

'Then leave,' said the voice.

And he did, although it was not his will that made this happen. He was summoned to court, and owing yet again to the Emperor's myopic kindness, honoured for his loyalty and service with a handful of titles and stipends. At this point, during the ceremony in the Emperor's apartments, he felt something snap inside his mind, followed by an acute feeling of nausea. The Emperor now appeared to him as an overweight and overdressed monster speaking in a succession of small, impossibly prim farts. As an act of courage, and because of his impeccable manners, he did not say anything in the presence of this monstrosity, and as soon as he could conveniently do so, rode away to his estates in the country.

But this was just the beginning of a strange set of experiences. He was to become familiar with the population of demons, ghouls and monsters that surrounded him. The demons were netherworld tormentors, skilled in sullying and perplexing the clarity of the human soul. The ghouls and monsters were usually unhappy spirits, and he discovered that most of them were illiterate and inarticulate. And then there were other experiences more difficult to classify. He discovered that touching the skin of another person would reveal the real creature beneath the surface, a metaphysical prisoner, he concluded, interred in a doll of flesh. He had gained an extra perception, similar to his detecting the nasty oils and gears of the Duke's homicidal mechanism. But by now, his relatives – or the immaculately dressed chimpanzees that now claimed his kinship – had become alarmed about his condition, and fearing that he was about to give his wealth and lands to the peasantry, had him conveyed to an asylum.

En route to the asylum, he reflected on his new situation. His mind had given way, he knew. Memories of family faces would surface, but they became symbolic of a previous existence, like small pagan shrines on village roads. But now he had another priority, a resolve to redeem his unfortunate life with a quest.

Once incarcerated in the asylum, it was not apparent how he was to proceed. It was in his cell that he encountered the deepest and more troubling aspects of his – and perhaps of anyone's – nature. He found himself scattered, like a mystic archipelago, with outflung islands and rocks of a previous unity, and the new ocean of an unfathomed and unrealised identity. He found that he was not himself many times over. And so, he required even more urgently a mission to consolidate, at last, who he would eventually be.

Deciding on this took time, more than he knew. He was to remain in the asylum for twenty years.

After this period of time and into this point of his life, we shall now intrude.

The complete and utter darkness of the old man's cell was as profound as that terrible shadow which God finally destroyed with the first manifestation of light. For this is where the old man was incarcerated – a truly desolate darkness – until into this void, as the sky outside his cell cleared, light entered through the grille, lavished into a brilliant and extrovert column. The focus of light split the darkened arguments of form in the cell, like a sombre etching, and revealed not one, but two figures, both preoccupied.

The first occupant was the old man, whose introspection was as much a part of the darkness in the cell as anything. The other occupant of the cell was an oily and massively ugly demon – its name was Fabritinex – who seemed to be composed of leprous and badly formed organs. This was the old man's tormentor, for as he had discovered something of the truth in all things, the demon had been sent to make him despair. The old man knew that his strange new condition did not require an antidote, merely courage, but as he was unpractised with the fights of the mind, and because of the dark, the demon's resources were at first formidable.

The light awakened the old man. 'You are the soul of torment, Fabritinex,' he said, 'to keep me thus contained and feed me nothing so much as dead voles and water rats. But all that you try to do to me will only strengthen my resolve to escape this dungeon, and once more regain the Holy Grail. So feed me what you like, Fabritinex, even nothing at all, for morning has come, and I shall set forth, reclaim my horse and my armour, and once more go in quest of the Grail.'

The old man knocked heartily on the door of his cell. The echoes of his knocking were ominous but the results immediate. Keys began grinding in the lock. The demon, knowing that his task was a difficult one – that is, to deliver a soul that was learning to see the truth of things into one of despair – laughed as irritatingly as it could, and said,

> 'These old tales of a dingy old Knight
> have no effect on me or my might.
> The truth is, you will be pleased to know,
> that he is where you shortly shall go.'

And then resumed munching on a bone that it had found

somewhere in the cell, for it knew that the sound would irritate the old man. Besides, it was hungry.

The Warden of the asylum where the old man was incarcerated was also mad, being convinced that the asylum was Purgatory, and that his inmates were souls with unfinished duties on earth, preparing to be born into another life.

As a guard brought the old man to the Warden's study, they could both hear the Warden laughing to himself, a delirious chuckling. The old man looked at the guard for explanation. The guard said, 'Our beloved Warden is very fond of reading picaresque novels.'

The old man shook his head, not knowing the phenomenon.

'These adventures are a stimulating and informative history of the World of Sorrows,' said the guard, portentously, 'and the Warden intends to have weekly readings for the other inmates.'

The guard knocked. There was an abrupt and almost total silence on the other side of the door. Familiar with the ways of the Warden, he escorted the old man into the room. 'The prisoner,' he said.

The Warden, who had been eating raisins while reading, stood immediately and said in irritation, 'It's about time that you left this establishment, old man, for God has spent enough time on you, and you should be finished by now.'

'The prisoner has requested that we return his horse and armour,' said the guard.

'Don't be ridiculous,' said the Warden, 'we don't have his horse and armour, and stop calling him a prisoner, he's a guest.'

'If, sir,' said the guard, 'the old man or prisoner is a guest, then according to regulations, someone should pay for his board and lodging.'

'This is really too much,' said the Warden, 'to be quarrelling over quibbles! Very well then, he is my guest, and I shall pay for his board and lodging.'

'Then,' said the guard, 'we should collect all payments from you.'

'Ah,' sighed the Warden, 'my life is a sufferance of details! Yes, yes, you can collect the payments from me at the end of the month.'

'That is what you said last month, and the month before that, and the one before that. This means that it is the longest month in memory.'

'Is that the time already!' said the Warden. 'Then for the love of God, remind me earlier next time, then you won't have to wait so long. Now, old man,' he continued, 'you have certainly bided your time as a child within these friendly walls, and now, as an accomplished creature of the Most High, you have requested to venture forth into the real world. This is not before time! But here in this In-Between House that is the bridge between the Vale of Sorrows and the Realm of Eternal Bliss, we have seen all that may be seen in human types and character. And although it is the duty of this establishment to finish a man before letting him venture into a careless and unruly world, we must, in your case, give credence to the extended preparations that you have made here, the better for enjoying a rich and profitable life. When you leave these walls and journey to the next hill, you will be born to your mother, and be raised as a devout Catholic in a great country, governed by the most famous Catholic monarch of history. The course of your life must then depend upon your character, and the preparations that you have made here in the House of Purgatory.'

'Sir,' said the guard, 'it must be said that the prisoner has exhibited many signs of being mad.'

'That,' said, the Warden chuckling, 'should suit him quite well, considering the place into which he will be born.'

'But sir,' said the guard, 'the purpose of this institution is to remedy the madness of its inmates before allowing them into the outside world.'

'If you mean,' said the old man, 'that the state of madness is nothing more than the soul's objections to the sins of the body, then that is exactly how I perceive it. And to resolve the course of my life towards an honourable end, I shall make a Quest for the Holy Grail.'

'You see,' said the Warden to the guard, 'he has already decided on a worthy occupation that will ensure his spiritual success.'

'From my point of view,' said the guard, 'it would seem that the prisoner might be of inconvenience in the world, for the age of knights and quests is long over.'

'Any age,' said the old man, 'has need of valour and courage.'

'Well said,' agreed the Warden. 'So you can remove that disapproving expression,' he said to the guard, 'otherwise I will wash your face for you. Now let us accompany you,' he said to the old man, 'to your setting off point, and may the charity of God be with you always.'

The old man, having bid farewell to the Warden, was released from the asylum.

On the first afternoon of his journey, he found himself on a wide and deserted plain between the location of the asylum and the new capital where, unknown to him, he would have most of his adventures. The plain was eerily deserted. There were no sounds, no cries from the birds of the scrub and ferns and, for a circumference of many miles, no dwellings could be seen.

The old man decided that this god-forsaken spot must be the Wasteland, wrought by the crime of the most unfortunate knight in the history of chivalry, Balyn the Cursed, who had wounded King Pelles, descendant of Joseph of Arimathea and keeper of the Holy Grail, with the lance that had pierced the side of Jesus during the crucifixion.

'Such sacrilege of a holy relic,' said the old man, 'could only have resulted in widespread death and disaster. And here I am, without proper accoutrements for a knight, when who knows what devil or demon afflicts this cursed place.'

The old man found a small tree and sat with his back against the bark, and meditated on his quest and the potential dangers that he might find.

In the midst of the old man's meditations, the demon Fabritinex appeared, and finding a convenient rock, sat down close to him. The old man noticed that the demon's peculiar stumps or feet had been squeezed into improbably small boots, probably causing the creature's retarded flesh some pain and discomfort. The demon, he realised, must have found it difficult to move his bulk across the ungiving ground; its breathing was halting and difficult. The old man said, 'I am surprised to see you, demon, in such a place.'

Fabritinex said, 'It took some time to get myself out of the asylum.' It belched loudly, and the old man schooled his expression into resolute indifference. He was already well acquainted with the noxious habits of the demon.

'Also,' said Fabritinex, 'it took time to find the direction in which you had travelled.'

'Surely your powers,' said the old man, 'would have indicated instantly where I was.'

Fabritinex smiled, which was a bit like looking into a dish of tentacles, and launched into a simplistic rhyme:

'That is not how the infernal lowerarchies work,
my schedule is one day in seven, what a smirk!
This forces junior demons to learn more quick
and advance them like me to be wicked and slick.
But now I have caught up with you, I can torment
your heart and your brain to my liverish content,
for it has been agreed that you shall be my soul
project wherever you go, and this is my goal.'

'Do not think I am not ready for you,' said the old man,

resolutely, 'for I have seen worse in my own mind that you can ever show me.'

'It is not my intention,' said the demon, relaxing into ordinary speech, for the boots were very tight, 'to scare or threaten you. For this is something you would expect. As you are a man, raised in a warring world, you already have been hardened by acts of brutality and life on the battlefield. It is perhaps more pertinent that I show you something which you truly desire. But then again this would take some discrimination. It cannot be something conventional, like the suggestion of the female form, or a treasure chest of gold, or for everyone to call you 'sir' or 'great'. These are common desires, and as you have not properly lived in a house for more than twenty years, and would not know what to do with the suggestion of the female form, then these desires are unlikely to sway you. We shall have to show you something on a spiritual realm to tempt you.'

'Nothing that you show will tempt me,' said the old man, 'for I know that you are a demon, and that you can only show me illusions. All I have to do is merely pronounce you and your devices as unreal.'

'Now this in some measure offends me,' said Fabritinex, 'because you can hardly imagine that a demon of my rank and superiority would have no real powers. For example, I can produce a loaf of bread, so hot and tasty looking that you could not help but stretch out your hand, and then make it disappear. Then, of course, the next time you would see a loaf of bread, you would question whether it was real or not.'

'I do not personally care for bread,' said the old man, 'because I think the flour does something in my throat, and so you can see how much I would dislike your illusory bread. You must find another device.'

'This only shows me how clever you are,' said Fabritinex, 'and more than ready for my temptations. The challenge is to move you in some way, so that you forget your purpose and, overwrought, completely lose the reason for your being here. Now how am I going to do that?'

'Well,' said the old man, 'while you are thinking, I will continue my journey.'

'You know,' said Fabritinex, 'it was I that provided the means for sending you mad. In fact it was a practical demon-stration for junior demons, and what a great success it was! By piling contradictions on your head, and providing many incongruous experiences, you eventually became insane, and your family were forced to remove you from society and keep you at that worthy institution where you and I began our fiend-ship.'

'Well, you have said a lot, and more than is usual,' said the old man. 'But as for driving me insane, that has only resulted in my feeling confident in the Will of God and appreciative of his love and good wishes for me. So then, let him keep me from sanity. Now excuse me, I feel the urgency of my quest calling me, and something tells me that I should leave you and this tree as quickly as may be.'

'Well, if you must,' said Fabritinex, 'then do so, for I cannot actually obstruct your path. I shall rest here and think of other ways to reduce you to sorrow and perdition.'

'I have lost everything already,' said the old man. 'There is nothing else, unless you take the ground from beneath my feet.'

'Well, no,' said Fabritinex, 'it must be admitted that the ground is the property of You-Know-Who's-Superior. My realm is your heart and your mind, where things become complicated. I was responsible for the plague of thoughts and half-thoughts, suppressed, restrained, denied, ignored, anxious, confused, hateful, and so on, that accumulated in strength with every fresh calamity. You might say that I embody all those fears and vices, and that I would not have any power over you if you did not believe in them.'

'And I do not believe in them, or you,' said the old man, 'and I was already aware of that in the asylum.'

'So you knew that you were in an asylum,' said Fabritinex. 'And how did you come to this conclusion?'

'With each person madder than the last,' said the old man, 'it would have been hard to refute it. Now you must excuse me, for as I said, I feel a certain urgency in travelling away from you and this tree as fast as possible.'

'Well, do not let me delay you,' said Fabritinex, 'for I will be quite happy rubbing my scales on this stump. Farewell until the next temptation.'

The demon watched as the old man marched through the low ferns.

'It must be admitted,' said Fabritinex to itself, 'that we may have lost him. The old fool seems to be most determined, with a simple resolve that cannot be derided. It's a curse that simple, implausible convictions should so strengthen the human mind. But although this will not look good to my infernal superiors, I think there is a solution, for if we have to relinquish our control over this foolish old man, there is another that might take his place.' Fabritinex waved at the old man, who had turned and was standing some distance away. 'Why,' the demon asked itself, 'is he still standing there?'

The old man, watching the demon from far off, had been propelled from his resting place against the tree by an inner prompting whose origin he could only guess at, but whose urging was undeniable. He had watched the demon talking to itself, and observed a densely black cloud, almost balloon-like in shape and colour, appear above it. The demon had paused in its plotting to look questioningly once more at the old man, when a brilliant bolt of lightning, erupting from the cloud, fell upon it, completely evaporating it, the tree, and a fair portion of earth beneath.

It took some minutes for the old man to absorb having seen his enemy so completely and utterly destroyed. After a sigh, and looking once more at the smoking earth, the haze of white sparks that still hovered upwards from the burnt circle, the old man reflected, 'Surely, a lightning bolt from God! And this makes my situation more unusual and most urgent. For not only do I have a lightning bolt for an ally that destroys my enemies, but an undeniable reminder that chases me onto my quest.'

Realising that his quest had the Hand of God in it, the old man began to march away from the blistered earth and in the direction of what, he imagined, would be a place of civilisation. This he knew: that he needed to recover his armour, his horse, and the sword of Sir Lancelot for his quest, all of which had been stolen from him (by whom and when he could not remember). God would provide these items, and help him prepare for the difficulties of his quest.

In the many months that it took him to make these preparations, he had some minor adventures. These included rescuing a somewhat corpulent merchant-trader from a demon river, and reading about himself in an assortment of bulletins – dictated he could only infer by God's scribe – that a university student had given him. He had also discovered that his old tormentors Emperor Philip II and the Duke of Alva had deceased, and that the Empire's new capital Valladolid was close to the asylum in which he had been incarcerated for so long.

But these were incidentals. He was still in search of a mighty and magnificent steed, and as he marched the roads around the new capital, keeping himself trim and alert, he prayed God for the grace of an interlocutor, a learned hermit or holy friar who would instruct and help him with his purpose.

The Magic Telescope

The first in a number of remarkable incidents with
startling results for all concerned.

*O*n the dusty road leading to the new capital stood a
shop containing a number of motley goods, run by
perhaps the rudest and the most unsympathetic man
in the world, and his enduring wife. She, like a dog's
resemblance to its owner, had lived so long with the expression
of negative indifference, a doldrum of expression, that she
looked blank, like the inside of an empty box.

The shopkeeper prowled the dusty edge of the street. As the
heat rose in the afternoon, and while his neighbours took their
siesta, he watched the road, haunted by the numbers that had
not visited his shop, or, having visited, had purchased nothing.
The store had everything – dried meat, flour, buttons, weapons,
farm tools, bedding, plates and knives, wine, and so on. Even
one of the new telescopes, barely invented, which had fallen
from a speeding carriage, and complete with its slightly scuffed
leather case and a small dent in the shaft as a result of the fall,
was the pride and centrepiece of his wares.

He had practised showing the telescope to potential customers, using his hands to hide the dent. He would polish it
thoroughly, reciting the name of the maker inscribed in the eye-
piece to impress with his knowledge of telescope-makers. But
the carriages still raced through, never staying, leaving nothing
but dust. He had even tried looking through the telescope for

carriages as they approached, but had never seen one. Then they would suddenly whirl through, as though materialised from a world where there was nothing but speeding carriages, chariots, and coaches. He then tried looking after them with the telescope, but could see nothing but flinty dust and the black smudge of disappearing wheels. Hope would fade with them. His life passed him in sudden anonymous carriages as they sped towards the capital.

On this fitful and irritating afternoon, as the shopkeeper stared across the street, waiting for the next disappointment, he heard the sound of singing and the determined stamp of marching feet. He saw an old man appear on the burning road, whose white hair was blazing, crowned by the harsh afternoon sun.

The shopkeeper knew that the old man was mad just by seeing him. Alone, carrying nothing, out in the heat of the sun, with no protection; if he were not already mad, he soon would be. Perhaps the old man was a threat. The shopkeeper went inside to fetch his pistol.

The old man reached the entrance of the shop. Seeing the door opened on a dark interior, he reasoned immediately that this was one of those blessed caves inhabited by holy men, who would with the acumen and good timing of God, provide food, shelter, and spiritual sagacity to knights on their quests.

Meanwhile, the shopkeeper emerged with his pistol and was startled to see the old man kneeling devoutly in the dust. The old man raised himself, embraced the shopkeeper with tears in his eyes, and entered the shop. The shopkeeper, alarmed at this invasion and holding the pistol, looked fearfully both ways along the road; as far as he could tell, there was nothing, no carriages, strangers, visitors. If he had to shoot this crazed old intruder, he thought, then there would be no one to see it happen.

However, none of this was meant to be, for the old man had, in the space of this rationalising, returned to the street, yawning, and stretching. He was also carrying the telescope. This became a fixed reality to the shopkeeper's blurred perception. He was being robbed! His limbs jerked in a curious way, like an animal in a bag.

'Bless you for your hospitality,' said the old man, 'for the restorative powers of your herb bedding, the refreshment of your clear spring water, and the wholesome nourishment of your bread. And this,' he said, holding up the telescope, complete with its leather case and strap, 'is the finest gift of all, a magic spy-glass, so that I can seek out my faithful steed Bucephalus and vigilantly watch for the demons and evil spirits that afflict this unfortunate land.'

Once more, the old man embraced the shopkeeper. And it was part of the shopkeeper's later hazy recollection that the old man had at that moment smelled of sweet sleep, refreshment, and cleanliness, compared to seconds earlier, when he had reeked of the road, sweat and dust. Suddenly, he smelt wholesome, like an apple. But in the second that it had taken the shopkeeper to realise this, the old man had resumed his march along the road, resolute and formidably innocent.

Still trembling, the shopkeeper raised his pistol. He would shoot the old man for he had just cause; the villain had stolen his telescope. The shopkeeper's wife suddenly appeared, spectral in the doorway. Had she encountered the old man inside? he wondered. Her face retained that tight-lipped blank disappointment that he had hated for so long, it was a stone inside his heart. She can not have met him then, he thought. My culpability will depend on my explanation. He pointed the pistol at the old man again and held on with both hands to stop the trembling. He looked at his wife again. Nothing as usual. 'Shoot,' said a voice inside him, 'and change everything for ever.'

But then a carriage suddenly appeared, emblazoned with the handsome crest of a crowned swan, and without a blink of realisation, ran over the shopkeeper, and continued careering along the road.

The shopkeeper was actually unharmed by the carriage. The flurry and speed of its progress just forced him off the road and into a ditch, where he lay sprawled, humiliated, in a generation of dust, that in another season would have been many inches of mud. The pistol, jerked from his hand, bounced once and fired, the sound obscured by the rattle of carriage wheels. The bullet – there was a special providence in this also – plunged high above his wife's head into the shop, destroying several items, and ended, finally, burrowed into a bag of flour like an over-zealous weevil.

The carriage, hurtling onward, soon reached the old man. Whereas it had not swerved for the unhappy shopkeeper, it swerved for him, and then kept on, bouncing on straining wheels towards the capital.

The old man saluted its departure, realising that the comfort and speed of the carriage were things that he did not need. God had delivered to him, from the hands of a blessed friar, a magic telescope.

'Come to think of it,' mused the old man, 'the friar's blessing seemed to be somewhat short on devotion. In fact, to judge from embracing him, the friar had more the soul of a greedy shopkeeper than anything else.'

Inside the store, the shopkeeper was discussing with his wife the terrors of his experience, and how they had lost a considerable profit from the theft of the telescope. He trembled and shook. But his humiliations did not end there, for his wife told him roundly that this was nonsense – the telescope had dropped from another carriage, and had never been truly theirs. What's more, she went on, if the old man had insisted on seeing their shop as a chapel, maybe they should consider it as such also. After all, there had been no profit for as long as they could remember, and perhaps it would be better business establishing a charity rather than selling telescopes.

During their conversation, the old man was still marching and reflecting on his quest, and the carriage hurtling on its way.

And you might be wondering, as this vehicle has already made such an inroad into this story, and moreover was travelling in the same general direction as the old man, where it was going and who was its occupant.

The Duchess

The most beautiful woman in the Empire and news of a
dead Emperor.

*T*he destination of the carriage was a substantial
mansion – more a discreet fortress – with high
walls hidden by wisteria and the tall points of
cypress trees. The lawns were a cool display of
formal beauty, interrupted by fountains playing their music to
the birds and signing the long walkways to and between hidden
grottoes. Pruning had groomed the retaining bushes and small
trees of the flowerbeds into a restrained shine. The orchard –
itself fortified from within by crumbling and mossy walls –
glowed in a haze of mottled greens and browns, pricked with
the brilliant hardy orange and yellow of the fruit, the puckered
robust skin of citrus.

The mansion housed a literary Academy dedicated to the
classical ideal. Within easy journey of the new capital, invited
poets and writers would sojourn there for the late spring
and summer months. Comfortable, beautiful, cool in the
monotonous blaze of summer, maintained by polite and attentive servants, and without that formality which sometimes makes
great houses mausoleums. The mansion, for all its ambitious
size, avoided self-importance, as though the character of its
very wealthy – surely, hugely wealthy – owner had, like the
beguiling portrait of a beautiful person, invested it with an
integrity greater than looks: the eyes of the portrait's subject,

as it hangs in your gaze, moves you from appreciation to respect.

The favourite walk of the mansion's widow was the *pasedas de damas* or ladies' walk, down the broad, limestone steps from the large windows at the back, along a path by one of the glistening fountains, and through to the haven of a small wood. In the many months following her husband's death, she would find the silence of a listening God in the green of the branches; the undisturbed delving of young plants for nourishment from the earth; a radius of green and benign shadows. From there she could see the house, hard white, shining. And while it glimmered, a fortress for the best of principles, she could release the barriers to many thoughts, to feelings, to her sorrows.

She would sometimes bring a book, because she was good at thinking, and a noble sentiment or thought would stimulate her own varied perceptions. When she did not bring one, it was because she felt ready slowly to encounter the blackness of a pervasive grief. Unaccountably, the more she understood and unwound the hasty bandages of her grief – and every unravelled emotion had an accompanying connection to the body, witnessed by tears, spasms – the more she became filled with rage.

This had been unexpected. To resolve, to reconstitute her hidden anguish into a new life, this was one reason for her walks. It was undignified to be conquered by grief for overlong. She felt able to wean her heart from the feelings of loss and yearning, the vivid memories that lanced one's flesh, so that the experience of sorrow opened one up like a tree, in full flower, bearing the fruit and leaves of reminiscence, recollection, past seed now a fruit of the present. This humiliation – to be so commanded by one's skin and senses – she could endure, and would unravel completely behind the locked doors of her bedroom. But the rage, a hard contrast to the peace and security around her, would possess her utterly. Sometimes, still shaking from the bitterness in her mind and the bile in her heart, she would enter the house from the garden and, finding her path crossed by a diffident servant, would want to snatch up the unfortunate and dash them to pieces, shake them to pieces. Victimise them with the same power and brutality with which war had conquered her and made her a widow.

The Emperor's wars had taken from her a beloved soldier-husband, the best commander of his time. Or rather, as the bitter momentum of her thoughts dictated, the Emperor had robbed her, expending the life of her husband in a fruitless ambition, heartlessly offering her sorrow in exchange. It had been some time since her husband's death, and yet the Emperor was still unwearied by the failure of his conquering ambitions. And was still alive.

Alone, trembling in her room, she would try to calm herself, but feel, with a nagging certainty, that she was suddenly corruptible; she realised that hours, days, weeks were given over to consuming anger: how to control it? Sometimes it was like a fit upon her, and at other times, a shadow that harried her temporary solace, a silent pack, devouring her mind. If the direct attack of anger made her shake, then the shadow of it made her suspicious, humourless, wary, and eventually, vindictive.

But some months before the present action of this story, a whirlwind – one that would shake her heart for another reason – arrived one fine morning with news from her maid. Like Pandora, she delivered a cloud of evils with the innocence of a child. It was early, and the Duchess was sitting at a desk in a window alcove composing invitations – the ink rich and well-scribed on the elegant fold of paper – which was an activity that suspended her mind and gave her a respite, until the noise and activities of the house grew, and inevitably, someone with a duty would seek her out.

She knew the noises intimately. They protected her solitude

– the sluicing of water, banging of doors, the wheezing of the ancient cook. On this morning, however, the running spatter of feet from the coachman's boy – she also saw him from the window as he sprinted through the gate – warned of something disturbing. Perhaps someone was ill, she thought, and she would send the doctor, or go herself. She continued writing, unhurried. The noises in the house grew. Some sensational piece of news, she realised. The servants were emerging from the lower quarters, talking in excitement. She looked outside, at the cool trees and their shoulders of sunlight, hoping that there was no terror for her in the news. But she already knew, as feet clattered towards her, she already knew that her life was about to change – a crucial twist – once more. Whether for joy or for sorrow . . .

The maid Cara found her mistress waiting, turned in her seat, her eyes steady.

'My Lady—'

'What is it, Cara?'

'The Emperor—'

'Yes.' She was too quick. Her maid gulped and continued.

'The Emperor is dead.'

The moment burned in a vacuum.

Another man dead, came her hopeless thought. Why do they die? Is it to spite? What do they leave behind when they so consistently abandon us?

'My Lady!' said Cara. Her mistress was dwindling into vacancy. The Duchess followed the direction of her maid's eyes, turned, found that her pen had jerked involuntarily, black drops spoiling the paper and desk-top. Carefully, she placed the pen on the edge of the blotter; her hand was also soiled. But then there was another involuntary movement, and the contents of the ivory ink-horn spilled over its brim, and she watched without interest as the slick moved across the desk. Cara rushed to stop it, dabbing nervously with her apron, an anxious glance at her mistress.

'There are obsequies, my Lady, to be read.'

'Why?' said her mistress.

Cara looked at her, startled. Ah yes, thought the Duchess, I must observe duty and proper ceremony.

'In the chapel,' she said, 'see to it that our priest comes in good time. We shall have candles. And flowers.' She paused on that last word. Flowers and a dead Emperor. She was bitten by a thought; I would not waste the smallest wayside flower on this finally dead Emperor! Not even a garden herb to dress the carcass. Not even a blade of the humblest reed for the death of this perverse, bigoted monster . . . Her mind filled up with curses. She could see nothing in front of her. Her maid broke in. 'Please, my Lady, is it safe to go to court?'

Never, said her mind. The son will succeed. Another Philip. 'We are safe, do not worry,' she said. It was odd. Her formality guarded the maid from the hatred coursing inside her.

'Yes, my Lady, but to visit the court?'

She realised then that her maid and the other servants were excited about the news; it was the reason for a fiesta, like spring, ringing in the new Emperor, carting out the old corpse. She realised that her undeterred resolve never again to set eyes on the face of the Emperor – the murderer of her husband – had cast a thrall on the house. Her people had assumed a disgrace, and had assumed that it was not her anger against the Emperor, but his against her.

'Cara, have I changed much since my husband's death?'

The maid twisted the apron. It was a question she would rather had never been asked. The pause contorted as she avoided the eyes of her mistress.

'Your answer would do me a kindness, Cara,' said the Duchess, steadied by her recent understanding, 'and whatever you say, I will not take unkindly.'

'It is because of the death of the master,' said her maid.

'Yes, the reason is just for my change in behaviour,' she said evenly, 'but what is the effect?'

'You had such joy for life, my Lady.' The maid grew bolder as she spoke. 'You seem to have hidden your feelings. You cannot be reached.'

Cannot be reached? By what, thought the Duchess, when inside I am daily crushed? 'Thank you, Cara,' said a steady voice, outside her mind. The voice was dismissing her maid. It was in control, she thought. But her maid had not finished, and turning to leave, said one last thing. 'There was honour in his death, my Lady. He was a great soldier.'

The maid left. Then she was alone, while the house, alive with the possibilities of a new era, began to celebrate.

A hard sob shook her. She stood, terrified, covering her mouth with lace. Another spasm of anguish. It partly escaped her, and she heard the keening sound, the insurrection of grief, as she struggled to quash it. Not like this. She forced herself; I will not be subject, these are my feelings to command. Her breathing steadied, and with it a new resolve.

Inside her bedroom; a large chamber with a bathing closet adjoined, and another closet for clothes. In here. A corner that even her maid did not uncover. A travelling cloak, forming a bundle. It wrapped the reminders of her husband's death.

Death. Even the word is colossal. She remembered the final clods of soil, strewn on an echoing coffin, a narrow bed between steep walls.

She found a place on the floor to open the bundle. Her hands picked over the reminders of his death, even as her heart remembered the function of him, living. A heraldic gonfalon, scorched with powder, the shards of a rapier, too delicate for that battlefield. Notes of his orders, a sketch of some fortifications; her husband had used a draughtsman's abilities to raise many a siege. A small pistol that she had given him, back when her days were young. Now, her nightly incubus was the pitiless steel that pierced him. His men, those ranks of pestilent, jocular soldiers, all dead, strewn in random hurried graves on the weary fields of Flanders. More remnants, these few unworthy objects; a button, a blade, the cuff of a uniform. On her husband's clothes she had discovered the rusty stains of blood. Under her nail, the tiny scarp of blood glowed red. It had flowed from him, an unguent of oblivion.

The battle report – borne a year to the day after her husband's death by a small aide-de-camp, his face burning with shame for her, his uncertain hands holding the stiff rolls of parchment – said that her husband had received his wound and then, knowing it to be fatal, retired from the fighting. He had tried to write her a last letter – here it is, burned, for some reason, bloodied, stained with mud. So death had sampled him and found him a mere man, his Christian cross unhindering, as it had emptied his veins and scorched him through the portals of memory, from where he would never emerge. Nothing was left of him to revive the fading experiences. There had been no time for him to write, not even a brief salutation, before his life emptied. As he faded, she wondered, had his memories of her dissipated as well? Unlike her own reminders that wounded her continually, breaking into her otherwise accomplished serenity, the ugly ravens of a powerful divinity. He died resting on a bank, the report said, while his battle, almost won, thundered on.

Another scroll, tied and sealed with the insignia of the Emperor, stated the date and occasion of her husband's death, and in a rote paragraph, conveyed the honour with which the Empire held his memory. It mentioned that he had died bravely (of course), without fear (of course, he was firm), and in good conscience. How the document had managed to convey – in its paltry sentences of solicitation – an absolute sense of unconcern was an irony that did not lighten her mind. And this 'in good conscience', what does that mean? It was undoubtedly a phrase of the Emperor's. It was undoubtedly a letter from the Emperor – there was his pitiless scratch at the end of the paper. It could only be the phrase of the Emperor, who, having monopolised God, could decide whether or not her husband had a faulty conscience to his account. Her husband, as humane and able a soldier as any army could wish, in an age of bloody and useless conflicts. This Empire's pawn in a scourge of deranged struggles. 'In good conscience'? Why, the phrase was laughable. He had been a worthy gentleman, affable in the moment, firm when it was required, noble in everything, unsolicited by vices – except perhaps for work – forgiving, humble . . . She remembered his eyes, his soldier's tonsure, the unreasonable crimson of his lips. Probably he had died from putting himself in the way of death, to save another. He was a great soldier, some said the best that the age could afford. All the soldiers remember him with tears. And what was this 'good conscience' of the Empire? Only one thing might have afflicted her husband's last moments, the realisation that his was a meaningless death. But no, that is my burden, she thought, her hands holding the gauntlets of a dead man, and it would not have been his particularity. But perhaps it is a hell to which he has been consigned, for the sake of this pitiless Emperor, a carcass now and when he was alive. And the Empire, unyielding to the occasion, blunders into another epoch. Perhaps its demise, she thought. Has it not had enough of death, sending its heart out every day to the remorseless weapons of foreign powers? Our nation, she thought, a wolf in a trap, gnawing upon its paw, a maimed struggle to be free of terrible, burning iron.

She picked up the scroll again, knowing about her grief, that it would ebb, and then, according to a mysterious summons, surge back into her sensibilities, a weight of turmoil in her mind and heart. There had been so many reminders, not least the open sorrow of the servants in the house. Soldiers, recognising the crest on her carriage, had saluted her on the road. There had been letters of condolence, none of them so tardy as the Emperor's; an item which had caused a bitter reunion between the shadows of her unresolved feelings, and her black thoughts. Then there would be the inconsequential discoveries that would add to her loss. Waking up in the unknown side of her husband's bed. The robes, clothes, items mixed with hers; the bedroom and closet became a dangerous maze. There was two of everything, and she had to exorcise the number. Whom could she dine with? There was no-one else. A favourite servant? Her maid? None of them could bear to be with her, and would hurry through their duties in her company.

She shook herself. My body, she thought, is a slave to memory. What shall be done with these relics. Her agitation had stirred dust into a small delicate cloud. Be rid of them, she thought. After all, they do not honour him, and they keep me in a prison of regret, when our time together was cause for joy. She gathered the items together, wrapping them in a cloak. In her arms, the bundle felt like a dead child. Her steps grew heavier as she descended the stairs.

Some instinct guided her and she found her maid in the garden. Cara looked at her in nervous anticipation. 'Here,' she said to Cara, her face aroused by painful exultation, 'burn these.' She handed the maid a bundle and was gone.

In the garden, remote from the classic eyes of the mansion windows, Cara untied the contents of the cloak as she stood over the perennial flames of the gardener's leavings. She discovered the stiffly stitched soldier's doublet of the dead master, along with stockings and leather gauntlets. She shivered as some remote superstition touched her. As the flames ate the relics, she hurried back to the house, busy with death and celebration. What was her mistress doing? she wondered. Was her grief as fresh as ever? The young girl shook her head at the complexities of the woman she served. She was an odd one.

Her mistress, watching from the windows, seeing the smoke from her dead husband's reminders, had the irrational thought that she would entertain no more soldiers in her house. They were, after all, the human risk before a thousand tools of oblivion. They cast themselves like dice, they wager with their spirits, and having lost, leave everything empty, wives, houses, children, the domestic retinue. No, she thought, no more soldiers in the house. This is my bivouac against the Empire's ants. Here shall be the study of the excellent in life, and not a preoccupation with its risks. And should the Empire come and visit, it shall leave its weapons at the door.

Some months after the Emperor's death and the Duchess's pyre to memory, life had been revived by the activities of her Academy. Vacant hours relieved by a rotation of poets, fresh with verse, ardent with her famous beauty. Their squabbles within the Academy were like a light rain compared to the troubled tempests she encountered within herself.

Also there were other visitors. Courtiers and officials of the court, bitten by gossip and speculation as the Empire strained between one era and the next. If she could remain calm, she knew, above the petty loitering of their minds, they would go away, and eventually leave her in a peace that she had cultivated, wherein she could dwell, and eventually, if fate allowed, she could heal.

But fate, as ever, played another hand.

The Marquis of Denia

The occupant of a carriage and a bold decision.

*T*he carriage that had so nearly made an end of our shopkeeper and had swerved, obedient to higher will, away from the old man, was carrying one passenger. He was the soon-to-be Duke of Lerma, and he was en route to the mansion as a respite from his journey, where he would deliver the gossip and news of the court, and then travel on to the nation's capital, Valladolid. As both the passenger and his news are interesting in content, we shall take a moment to describe them, and then resume the plot, which if somewhat perilous, as the roads of that time, will concede a resolution.

The present title of the passenger was the Marquis of Denia. He was a power on the rise, poised for the era of a new Emperor and the spoils of political appointment. Denia's mind perambulated as his carriage jittered along the roads of an anonymous Empire. He was gathering the strands of recent history together, and sensing many possibilities, planning the flourish of his ambitions. He knew that the court was agog, full of anticipation. It has, he reflected, buried disillusionment and crowned hope, the youthful Emperor. My Emperor, he thought, the young Philip III, who on my advice is even now consolidating his position on the throne with a broadside of appointments. Denia sighed in satisfaction as the fields and roads lurched outside the window. After all, the deceased Emperor – that autocratic, suspicious, overly severe father – was now dust. How shall we eulogise him? Let's see. That great Emperor of Disappointment, whose sole achievement was the wrecked exploits of the Armadas, and who is now incarcerated in funereal gloom, a joyless splendour.

'In a tomb,' Denia said aloud, 'that is as large and as empty as were his plans.' And so many plans. For this autocrat had tried, along with so many other monarchs and rulers, to rule the world from the single eye of his throne. Denia's influence over the dead Emperor, like others of his rank and station, had been negligible. After all, how do you make friends with a friendless man? For an army of peasants cannot fight the war of a king. If his advisers had been allowed to help with policy, thought Denia, if he had been their chief, it would have made the difference between an Empire that knows itself, and one that does not. But the dead Emperor had never permitted so much as a whisper of advice past the cold folds of his ruff. For Denia, the Emperor's death had felt like the rescinding of an ancient curse. I think of him every day, observed Denia, the respect one pays to a vanquished enemy. It was his inclination, continued Denia – picturing the dead Emperor's tiny study within the vast stones of his palace – to make everything his by occupation, by appointment, by fealty, by legacy, by loyalty, by terror. And, thought Denia, snuffing aloud in derision, he tried to rule the world through paper. In his long and stifling reign, he generated a vast supply of papers, reports, and documents. And no-one receives an official paper without a jolt of culpability. To have an Empire terrified of paper is a miserable result. But now that this style of written authority is in, and the old Emperor out, then how shall paper be made an advantage?

Denia already had an answer: let the profusion of paper continue. Merely change the contents. My Empire, thought Denia, knowing the phrase to be treasonable and enjoying it, shall be ruled through poetry, dramas, histories, fictions, satires, treatises, commentaries. And yes, let us not forget comedies. Denia's mind flashed to the name of an author, recently famous for a comic piece. He put the name aside. It shall be thought of later. But the Empire, thought Denia, shall be ruled through poets and writers.

'And I shall rule them,' said Denia, repeating what he had often said to the jouncing interior of his carriage.

And the dead Emperor? His grave shall be my dance-floor, thought Denia. His epitaph shall be my song. For who could remember with any affection this strange, compulsive, moon-faced Emperor? And there was the mysterious entity of his missing eyebrows, as though the realisation of his power had robbed him of sleep and stamped him with cold, handsome surprise. Insomnia is the birthright of all princes, Denia thought, whose fits of restlessness were well known in his circle, but how shall a sleepless man enjoy these granted hours? It shall not be in studying a God frozen in theology. The Marquis, who had the Mediterranean in his blood, shivered in the quilted interior of his carriage. Let the expired Emperor haunt his palace of death, and administer the rotting portals of his decaying ascendants. Let him scribe their names and titles on bones and remnants, and keep his insomnia in the service of his 'terrible God' for an eternity. I'd rather serve a warmer master, thought Denia. This is the new age. Revels, celebrations, songs, titles, fiestas, these shall be the theme.

And comedies, came the thought again.

Denia's mind would often prompt him in this way, a facility that he used in the elaborate chess game of politics with his rivals at court. Yes, thought Denia, it was a few days ago that the new Emperor – my Emperor – had been roused from his usual bovine vacancy by someone recounting the plot and theme of a new comedy. And then, to bring the point home, some days later, the Emperor had seen a student walking with a book in his hand, slapping his own brow with merriment; it was the same comedy.

Now what was the name of the author?

But the previous subject remained compulsive, and Denia returned to it. There is reason for my optimism. Spain has moulded the heel of its Empire with the territories of the New World. As it had been the dead Emperor's mission to destroy the anti-Catholic conspiracy festering in other kingdoms of Europe, Spanish armies were everywhere. But it was an Empire ignorant of its power. For how can you force the contents of a vast demanding territory, filled mainly by peasants and farmers, with the single zeal of a monarch whose name many villages had not known?

Having surmised that the Spanish people neither believed in nor cared for the Empire, Denia had formulated the following policy; to plunder the wealth of the new territories, leave the peasants and farmers to the ways they had practised for generations, and give way to no-one. Corruption, you might expostulate. Denia will look at you with predatory wisdom, and say, I offer you an alternative many times more just. What would you have? Remember that the dead Emperor taxed his people on everything, taking even the harvest of their famine years as supplies for his ridiculous armies. Even dead, he haunts them. Now his palace, his memorial, his tomb weighs in his place; the Escorial – a gigantic model of the griddle on which St Anthony was roasted – which, with deadly mortification, brands his subjects, unwillingly, as the devout, the defendants of the true faith, the architects of the true Church. And so on, and so on. And look what had happened to the Golden Age literati who, infected with some grotesque zeal, had signed up for the wars and set sail to conquer. But their frail trick of individuality foundered on foreign shores. Just as their pleas for recognition received nothing from the Emperor, thought Denia with knowing sarcasm. He had about as much room for them as does the inside of a courtesan's bodice.

So now we have a bovine for an Emperor. Is that not better than an Emperor who, should a man show signs of some individuality, would erase him altogether? Remember, this was an Emperor who starved his eldest son to death. Granted, the boy was a mad, murderous parasite, and it would be hard put for any man to love such a son. The Emperor could not forgive the ugliness of the boy, or his vicious nature, or that he, the world's greatest Christian monarch, should have produced a grotesque as his heir apparent. Beware then, if a man were ugly or non-Christian, or otherwise met with some aesthetic disapproval. He was manure for fields.

Unconscious of the cue, Denia paused in his thinking and looked outside. Hazy fields, ancient walls made of heartless stones, the beaten postures of olive trees. He enjoyed olive trees. They were like tough peasants, silent yet filled with the mysterious soul of nature. Their small, insignificant fruit dedicated to producing an ointment of gold. In my new palace, thought Denia, we shall have an orchard of them, the finest, the ones with the most character.

Suddenly, it flashed into Denia's mind that the carriage had almost run over an old man some minutes earlier. Absorbed in his plotting intricacies, the Marquis had been unmindful of it. But now the appearance of the old man was coming back to him. White hair, cheerful countenance, marching like a soldier, singing. No hat. Careless in the road, so that the carriage had to swerve in a blink, which it did, without anyone knowing how it was done. The old man had waved. How had he seen all this, he thought, and not really seen it? This was too deep a question for the moment, and his mind passed to another. Unusual, this old man. None of the appearance of simple beggary, no disfigurement, no disease. None of the cowed lurking of road vagrants. Upright, like a javelin. Must be mad, thought Denia. But marching, singing songs. Must be a soldier. Who? Denia shrugged it off.

For the Marquis, in his black silk interior, was feeding on several items of personal gratification. The first was that he had news of an appointment – that of Court Poet, part of the Emperor's personal retinue – with which he knew he could stir the jealous hive of writers and poets throughout the land. The second was that it was he that had arranged for the court to move from Madrid to Valladolid, a political move so audacious that even he had lost sleep over it. And now that he had succeeded, with the great houses packing, the whirl and scurry of minor courtiers seeking to retain the positions that might disappear in the dusty miles between Madrid and Valladolid, the Marquis was selling his influence, and increasing the power of his position with the news, told in whatever way was advantageous.

The Marquis was also feeling the spice on his tongue of an approaching encounter with one of the most beautiful women of his acquaintance, the Duchess. There was good reason for the Marquis to target her; his mind played with it. The Duchess maintained an influential Academy, writers and poets, who might be eager for position and influence at court. They would all, no doubt, have altered their maps of influence to include the old and the new capitals, and the residual peace of the Duchess's mansion. It was the intention of the Marquis to consolidate his influence over the young Emperor with a slew of high-flown and artful praises – popular history, he thought, written to flatter the Emperor into an improvement, and anything will do, for God knows the boy is as blank as a statue. And whilst this glossing of lineage and burnishing of blood played across the pages, it would be fitting to paint himself in the same peacock-coloured virtues. He was after all, *validos*, the royal favourite. The Marquis had already hired a number of writers with a series of commissions designed to achieve political ends. He would have it that if you turned the Emperor's head on a coin, the bold, plundering countenance of Denia would be stamped on the other side.

Thus the Duchess was among those whose influence might be felt at court, although the Marquis already knew instinctively that she had no designs on power. That is the trough I feed at, he thought, and it is my nature, for my wet-nurse could not keep me from her nipples, and I have always taken things with both my hands.

The Duchess has reserved her true self. But for what? 'Good people,' he said to the carriage interior, instinctively ascribing a hypocrisy to the term, 'admire her.' She is beloved, by her servants, her family, her friends. Why do we never see her at court? And why has she remained a widow? It must be some years since her husband was killed. That is too long, unless one mortifies the flesh. And by all accounts, she is as beautiful as ever. And no recluse. Her Academy is famous. And she writes herself, and keeps the best gardens that one could hope to see.

Therefore, she will not be received at court. She will not be received by the Emperor. And for many years, she had not been received by the dead Emperor. Small wonder – he may have considered her as a consort, but given a distaste for women other than to breed heirs, and also the unlucky effect he had on his wives, she may have decided, sensibly, to escape the fate. But perhaps there was another reason. The new Emperor had already been eased into a devout marriage. If there is a reason, I shall discover it, Denia decided.

It is to be relished, he thought, my new capital, howling with the discordant suits and conciliatory pleas of poets. 'Take me,' pleads one, 'to write you an epigram of praise.' 'Take me,' says another, 'to write an epic on your prowess.' 'Take me,' says another, 'to write your epitaph when you are gone, aye, and eulogies for all your family too.' I could have a poet for every one of my limbs, and my senses too, thought the Marquis, and they would none of them lack words or phrases for the occasion. He laughed aloud in the carriage.

Then the name came to him.

One Miguel de Cervantes Saavedra. A veteran of the wars against the Turk. Had birthed a comedy, the like of which the world had never seen, and already has most of the world laughing. The comedy was in the ears of everyone, for it had travelled the Empire by inn and tavern, village and town. How better to entertain the new court than with such a genial spirit? I will suggest it to the Emperor, thought Denia, who loved to be entertained, and perhaps lighten his brains a little, even if the court found it vulgar. Perhaps we can also find him a patron, and concede him a place among the proud poets and ambitious scholars.

But then Denia frowned. Perhaps there was something inappropriate about a veteran soldier, clanking through the Emperor's apartments, ready to recite the latest episode in a comedy. Is there any philosophy in it? Perhaps it has some verses, disguising the popular theme. Not that I mind a popular theme, thought Denia, more than all these meditations, chants, discourses, verses, hymns, and so on, these numerous assays to my spiritual purity. None has altered my nature. I prefer a good story for my leisure. After a large meal and wine, seated in my salon, what else is more appropriate? But that would be my wish. For the court, perhaps it would not be successful. A new Emperor without brains at all, an anxious string of smiling sycophants, and a parade of poets and writers, all jealous for position. Our comedian would soon have many enemies. It would quench the laughter right out of him.

And then an inspirational thought struck Denia; I could spread the rumour that this Cervantes was the likely choice for the Emperor's new poet. The news would cause an unwholesome scrabbling for the position, thought Denia, and of course, raise its purchasing price – from me. And then, we will find a pocket of gold for Cervantes, without causing the dust to whirl with his presence at court. I shall try this as an item of information in my meeting with the Duchess and any attendant poets. And if the poets jump, as though touched by death, it shall be worth a whole page of obscene epigrams. These are my intended aims, he concluded, listing them on ready fingers. Divining the Duchess. Purloining her writers. Scalding poets.

The carriage was some twenty minutes from the Duchess's mansion. But the Marquis was already at supper.

A Slim Volume

Bribing an Empire.

*T*he Duchess, as the carriage careered, was walking in the comfortable shade of a corridor. She held an abundance of long-stemmed flowers for an arrangement at the top of the stairs, and she was thinking about the impending visit of the Marquis. His messenger had requested that the 'arduous pains of travel be lightened with an all too brief stay at her mansion'. She did not like the Marquis, something that he did not know she felt, but would not have cared if he had known. It was rare that he was liked. He used people, for pleasure or with pleasure, sometimes both. But that he did not know her dislike for his usurping manners, his reptilian lashless eyes, the oil in his voice, and his stolen money, this was a mark of her control; she did not waver from her manners, and she did not condemn. She entertained, drew people out in conversation, found them out because, like Diogenes and his lantern, she was looking for someone of honour.

As she walked with the glowing buds and stems in her arms, she heard someone giggling, muffled by an intervening door. She knew who it was, even by the tone of the mirth. She had arranged that her maid meet her to help with the flower arrangement. This was a task that few in the mansion looked forward to; not that the work was unpleasant, but because

60

the Duchess would remain so resolutely silent, and so sternly beautiful during the process. A figure like Aphrodite, the eyes of Athena.

She stopped by the small door of a laundry closet.

'Cara?' she said. 'Is that you?'

The door opened abruptly, and the maid appeared. She was pink from giggling, and wide-eyed with fear at what might happen. She was trying to hide something behind her back.

The Duchess was surprised at Cara, usually so reliable. She held out her hand for the hidden object, and said in her gravely measured voice, 'Did you forget our appointment, Cara?'

'Yes, my Lady,' said the maid, abject. The object passed between them, almost like a covert handshake.

'Bring another vase,' said the Duchess, 'the one on the table is too small. Bring the maiolica.'

The maid clattered downstairs. The Duchess suppressed a sigh, and then looked at the object she had taken from her maid.

It was a pamphlet. Another surprise, Cara could read? For some reason, as she held the contraband, the maid's footsteps still clattering down into the basement of the house, her heart-beat increased. Why? She read the title: 'Being an Episode in the Further Great Adventures of One Don Quixote De La Mancha'. Ah, yes. She recalled hearing that most of the students in the universities were neglecting their studies for the latest episode of this comic romance. It would not make *her* laugh. Few things did. But why did her heart jump so? It was that something literate could make the life of a maid light. And yes, that was what her heart had so quickly told her, in the smallest spasm of a moment, how something so crafted could also be so carefree. But a pamphlet? She looked at the papers in her hand, at the cheap but efficient block print. This was too paltry. It would have to be confiscated. Cara can be commended on learning to read, but not on bringing such things into the house.

So continued the denial that would further barricade her

heart from her soul. But the moment for reconciling opposites passed. The sound of carriage wheels and the heave of horses could be heard. The Marquis was here and the flowers were still to be arranged. Cara's pinked face appeared at the bottom of the stairs.

From Cara's viewpoint, she was looking at a marvellously pretty woman, standing on high with her arms full of flowers. The eyes, when they levelled with her own, did not diminish the impression of something faultless, a mixture of sadness and control, kindness and intelligence. At the same time, the light ushering through the cupola gave her figure a nimbus of late afternoon light. Then the goddess said to her, 'The Marquis has arrived. Make sure his room is ready. Here,' she said, offering the flowers, 'we will find time for these later.' Cara ran obediently up the stairs to take them. As she looked again at her mistress, the face was hidden, obscured by the too-much light behind her; it was shadowed, incomprehensible, another face of the goddess. She turned with the flowers to run back downstairs. 'Cara,' said her mistress, 'we shall talk of the other matter later. Come to my room after evening prayers.' Cara turned an uncomfortable rouge. 'Yes, my lady,' she said, and then a meaningless, 'Thank you.'

As Cara left, the Duchess turned to view the drive from a small window-seat. She expected to see the sprawl of luggage and scrabbling of exhausted servants; having ridden all the way clutching the roving roof of the carriage, or sitting postilion, hunched in grinding dirt or whirling mud, they would sometimes do unconscionable things to the bags, especially if they thought they were unobserved.

But looking through the window, she saw nothing of such turmoil. Then she remembered; the Marquis rarely travelled with an entourage. As a means to achieving political ends, he liked to travel swiftly and without baggage. Sometimes, even with all his riches, he would borrow a coat to keep moving. She sighed a little. This meant that he would already be seeking her out. Something in her clouded; he was an uncomfortable person, and required expertise. He would scrupulously search the mansion for her, perhaps relenting at the door to her room. Perhaps not. She remembered that he was an insomniac. So rest, seclusion, peace, all so essential to the nourishment of her spirit, all these were illusions to him. She was interested in the comparison.

Then the urgency of the Marquis's proximity flashed in on her. God curse all men, she thought, for their violence, for their loud voices and immaturity, for their foibled tongues and their incredible lust.

At the word lust, she knew her mind had turned against her. She moved down the corridor rapidly; meeting Denia in a neutral place was now her immediate aim. The salon, brilliant with the morning light, would help her in meeting one of the most predatory gentlemen of the Empire. She would be reading a book, and her silence and composure would at least give the illusion of serenity, even as her inner world ebbed at the thought of fencing the wiles of the Marquis.

But her planned respite was not to be. A servant had just opened the room to her, and she had taken a moment to watch the light glowing on the ordered shelves and statuettes. Then, as her breath settled, there was the sound of the Marquis's powerful heels. The door clicked open behind her, and as she turned with perhaps one of the most beautiful smiles in the Empire, the Marquis's swarthy physicality had already entered. He was already lighting on her hand, had used the delicate fingers with unscrupulous lips, had bowed as was appropriate and had, in some intricate manner, kept his eyes upon her at all times.

'You are always beautiful,' he murmured, and patted her hand roughly. The unsensual touch felt odd to her. She smiled and withdrew her fingers.

'Your Grace is welcome,' she began, moving to one of the couches, 'a room has been made ready for you. Perhaps—'

'State business has made my visit necessary,' he interrupted.

'You must pardon me if my manners are sacrificed to expediency.'

Having delivered himself from the necessity for consideration, he settled himself on a couch and regarded the Duchess with smiling affability.

The Duchess, still standing, could only wonder at his manners. Then she sat gracefully opposite and joined him in a silence that at first was polite, and then became a contest of character. Not once did the affable gaze of the Marquis leave her face. With every second, his expression became more the leer of conquest than the attempt at compatibility. The Duchess, however, surrounded by the best minds of all ages, bound in treasured books, and the statues and figurines of antiquity, could meet his look with calm, solicitous of his every need; that is, if the needs were that of a gentleman.

The Marquis, having established that his silence was a mockery of civility, clicked his tongue, startling in the refined air.

The Duchess asked, 'Do you require anything, some refreshment from your journey—'

Again he interrupted. 'Your gardens are perhaps the best in all Spain.' He pronounced the word 'perhaps' with the real sense of weighing considerations. 'I will use them as a model for my own palace.' She knew that he had deliberately mentioned 'palace' to indicate his rising status.

He rose suddenly and began to measure the room with his strides. She realised, without humour, that his prominent girth was a pivot for his lunging legs. 'And this room . . .' he clicked his tongue again, 'has the innocence of a high mind.' He stared at her with his eyes obsidian, cunning. The Duchess, herself proud of the instincts that had made the room so delightful, looked around and, as a measure to gather strength, smiled at the depth of light, and the noble company of the statuary. 'My husband,' she said, her voice steadier than she had hoped, 'collected much of the art.'

'Your husband,' said the Marquis and paused. He was staring

at the figurine of a young Dionysius. She realised that the Marquis was playing with the formalities of conversation. Peremptory acknowledgement, abrupt pauses. Perhaps he was deciding on the words, she thought, that would cause the most harm or make the best flattery. His amorality made him capable of both, she knew.

He looked at her suddenly, as though he had sensed that her deference hid her thoughts. 'Your husband,' he said, 'did much for the Empire.' He sat down again suddenly. 'These spoils are little recompense for his service.'

Startled by the assumption, the Duchess said quickly, 'He had no hand in looting. This much was forbidden by the Emperor. Everything you see, my husband owned.'

The Marquis smiled, as though tolerantly glossing over a vice. 'He was an honourable man,' he said, as if this mention of character would absolve his dubious method of collecting art. 'Why destiny had pricked him for an early grave . . .' He looked at her again. 'When was his demise?' he said, grinding at her wound.

She flinched. 'Why do you ask?'

The Marquis did not respond and gazed at the statuary.

'The Empire,' and her teeth entered the word, 'has already forgotten him.'

The Marquis smiled without charm. 'An Empire has no respect for its servants.' His mordant gaze transfixed her. 'Heroes, diplomats, the rich, the cunning, the lascivious, these, an Empire will honour.' He once again made the clicking sound. 'But how can an Empire confess? It may have the policy to brag, but the sensibility to feel? How can that be?' He turned his head, as though dismissing her feelings as errant in a new pupil. 'An Empire has lands, titles, coffers, conquests, armies, government. But a heart, conscience, compassion; surely not.' His eyes back on her, teasing, remorseless, corrupt. 'It is to be hoped that your husband died according to his code of honour. And for that, he can be remembered.'

'That is not enough!' she said and immediately regretted the outburst.

'No?' and his question chided her. 'Not for him? Or not for you?' His eyes slid to the shelves of precious books. 'Surely, you have found your ease in this library of greatness?' He yawned. 'As for myself, I have never been moved by devotion to another's death. Be they ever so much of a wonder,' and there was definite sarcasm in his tone, 'whilst they lived, they cannot mean so much to the living at their demise.' She was looking at him with repulsion. He had unearthed her feelings so quickly. 'What does the demise of another mean? That we are left alone, without comfort, or someone to confess our weaknesses to on days when the moon is full.' He stretched, lounged, looked at her indolently. 'I shall be forgotten the moment I perish. And by this knowledge, I live my life. My aim is the attainment of material things, for the spiritual is in a domain of which we have little or no knowledge. I therefore shirk manners that keep most of us in abject stupidity.' He gazed ahead. 'The new Emperor, if anything, is just a little less than stupid.' And then he looked at her without pretence. 'And that has proved to his advantage, for he suffers from few illusions.'

Having divined the secret anger of her heart, the Marquis settled back on the cushions and looked idly at the intricate motifs on the ceiling.

However there was another character, en route to see the Duchess, who shared a like ruthlessness with the Marquis, but in an altogether different realm. This man, driving in a carriage that he could not afford, the luxury of a mistress still fresh in his senses, was one of the cultural satellites of the court, in an age where the patron ruled the purse of the artist. He was a poet, and considered one of the literary hopefuls of his day. He was a friend of the Duchess, an unqualified acquaintance of the oily Marquis and, for developing reasons, soon to be Cervantes' relentless enemy.

Wiles, Plots and Other Subterfuges

The character of an evil magician.

*P*erhaps it is best for your understanding of the poet that you meet him, already advancing his best ploys, as he concludes a business arrangement with Robles – the printing of a small book of verses – while advancing a hidden plan to seduce Robles' wife.

Robles, if you remember, had been left in a state of unhealthy introspection after Pedro's unfortunate remark on the pliable influence that a new pair of boots would have on his wife. The door clicked behind the exit of friend Pedro, whilst Robles stood in gloom, thinking of the various undesired attentions of poets on his wife. And these were his thoughts, which like baby vipers were ready to hatch and destroy the shell: why, oh why, is it poets that write poetry, for not a one can be found but that has to be kept at arm's length from your wife's bed-chamber? Why has God elected a set of vainglorious, libidinous fools to write the majestic verses of the Golden Age? Why cannot the women write the poetry, and thereby take away the suspect wooing rights of a dozen rhyming boys? And why is it that women should fall for this elegant excuse to avoid real labour? My trade, he continued, has more honour in it than a dozen parchments and their mystifying scratches of ink. But no, not only am I foolhardy enough to desire the company of a beautiful woman, but have the fate to follow a trade that has no glamour, and the luck to have looks that could not even inspire the ardour of a turtle! He paused. His tirade was caused by a very real anxiety. There was one poet who seemed determined to catch his wife's attention. Robles' lean sinews tremored. 'Poet?' he said out loud. Robles' mind tossed the title sarcastically. I shall print this interloper a calling card, he thought, and it shall bear the title 'Seducer', followed by the description that my friend Cervantes has made of the talents of his many antagonists in the literary world, an 'entertainer of maidens'.

But his bitter thoughts were interrupted. The door of the shop creaked open. And entering, summoned by Robles' fears, came his wife, her blonde skin and extraordinary eyes glowing in the shop's interior, while her smile, as he noted, was directed at anywhere but himself. Her hand, lightly, pleasantly – and falsely, perhaps – rested on the arm of a young man, restlessly handsome and elegantly dressed. The poet Ongora.

His wife disengaged herself, struck an affectionate pose for her husband, and then left them both – unacknowledged but already irreconcilable enemies – while she entered the house through the back of the shop.

Ongora, affecting boredom in the presence of this uninteresting tradesman, decided to make his opening remark a model of sexual innuendo. 'Your wife's company is a welcome release from standing attendant to a tardy muse. The beauty of a woman, one would like to think, is a necessary unction to the progress of a man's toil.' He jingled coins in his purse and smiled. 'Are my verses ready as promised?'

'Her company is a duty that she owes to her husband,' Robles said immediately. His tone carried no rancour, for despising the poet, he could be even with him. Born in Toledo, Robles had something in him of proud steel, the zenith of that city's activities. He lifted a package of two books, wrapped for carrying.

'I see that the manners of society in our new capital are not too cosmopolitan,' Ongora said.

'You forget,' said Robles, a hawk with truth, 'that many are lately moved from the old capital. And in that city also, the manners of flatterers and seducers were the same as anywhere.'

'You have already formed an opinion of me,' Ongora said with a smile of conceded pain, 'which will not serve you well. Jealousy is inelegant, don't you think, especially in a senior? Whether I promenade your wife or no, I am in a position to do your business good.'

Robles actually snorted. 'This I have heard, and many other such vague promises, that will end, no doubt, in my staring in the face of your creditors. As you have undertaken to print a book of your verse, then this has been done, and will be delivered on receipt of funds from you. Your speculative interest in my wife shall be curtailed immediately. Though she may be on display, she is not for sale.'

Ongora smiled briefly. 'My verses can be printed elsewhere.'

Robles, in the dark of the shop interior, saw Ongora lean forward with subtle menace. He nodded inwardly. This much, he had divined; by scratching the poet, galling him with candour, he found not only a superficially unpleasant vanity, but a deeper, more complex nastiness. 'This would be no loss to me,' he said.

Ongora leaned forward again. 'I could destroy you,' he said softly.

Robles was startled by such a quick descent into hostility, and at the same time, responded immediately. 'You? I do not think so,' and knew this to be true. 'Come, let us not quarrel,' Robles said, for something in Ongora's handsome face reminded him of his wife's beauty, and he thought of them as the same kind of creature. Damned to vacuity. It cannot be helped, he thought, that they are both beautiful. He felt relief from his accusatory mind. If anything it is unfortunate, for they both outwardly display the ideal of beauty, without an anchor of the same in their innermost parts.

Robles extended his hand in conciliation. Without a word,

Ongora delivered the bag of coins and took the books. Then he turned his back on Robles, made a show of easing on his gloves, and with his package of books, quit the shop.

As he stepped through that doorway into an attendant carriage, we shall, with the grace of our art and the purpose of this story, step through another portal into his interior, the private den, if you like, of his character. For all good stories, it is said, pursue the life of the character, and with this individual, if no less is true, then we must pursue the same, although the catch in this respect may well be paltry.

The shell of this particular gentleman was, as has already been mentioned, a handsome one; slim, elegant, wide-shouldered. His features might have been thought too effeminate but for the vigour in his walk, the precision of his muscular grace, the confidence with which he held himself, both as a man who could protect himself against all danger and as an accomplished artist.

This brings us to the true centre of a description of Ongora. For, as all poets, he was a creature of the muse and had experienced the dregs of the banquet at which the gods feast. But there are some that the muse chooses to impoverish, for as it has been noted in the Greek apocrypha, where Love was the child of the parents Resource and Poverty, then Poetry was the child of Silence and Humility. A brief experience of the muse had left Ongora with the beginnings of a career, a craving for distinction, and a few small poems. The muse abandoned him with a few possibilities that his possessive grasp could only tarnish further. A single night with the love of his existence. But in an age when poets were the new voice of a Golden Age, it would have been hard to refute the abundant though undeserved praises of all, inexplicable to refuse an early fame even before accomplishing anything, and foolish to renounce access to any society, whether for influence or plunder. Thus Ongora, let loose from the one encounter that could have proved his merit, had already begun to realise that as his reputation grew, his inspiration dwindled. And it became the chafe to this realisation that writing for the Emperor, dukes, and princes should be his acknowledged right, as well as gold and fame. And it became his fear – half-recognised, half-denied – that the muse ruled rather than served, and had dismissed him as inopportune, the child of toys rather than an adult with gifts.

The two books that he carried so insolently from Robles' shop (he intentionally left too small a fee), were both copies of his newest collection of verses. A sporadic undertaking that he had been working on for some months. He had little relished encountering his blank mind and heart, required for producing the first quatrain of a sonnet. The page, in his experience, still remained void. The sonnets, he knew, were the right subject, the right tone, dextrous, technically able, charming. And hopelessly lost.

He thought of his mistress, an actress named Micaela, and the paste jewels that she wore for the stage. They glittered with artifice, not quality. The heat of her body in performance added to the lustre of her false diamonds. He relied, he knew, on a similar agent, someone's hot influence, to carry the poems to success. The two books were for presentation. One for the new Emperor, the other for the Duchess, with whom his friendship was new. The book for the Emperor would be carried, with an appropriately deferential note, by courier. He was presently on his way to visit the Duchess where he would present her with the book as a gift. After all, the book had been written for her. This much he had hinted at, for it was part of his policy to have his poems prove his influence.

Presenting her with the verses would be difficult; she did not accept flattery. But he knew that it would stimulate the vaporous minds at court to suspect that if the poems were for her – the most beautiful widow in the Empire – then they were lovers. He could go far on this alone. The hint could bring many objectives closer. And if he could not have her in person, he could enjoy her in speculative gossip. The book, he knew, would woo any other woman, if they but received it. That she should remain inviolate would be her loss. For him, their brief friendship had ended the moment she had made it clear, without her awareness, that she would never be his lover; some resolve in her character, something in her tone, her indifference to all forms of flattery, these were unmistakable signals. He had on occasion cursed himself for not realising sooner that this was a desire he could not satisfy. Their friendship remained dead to him, although alive for her. It was a deceit that he relished. She valued him, and raised him as an example of a youthful, ascendant talent. The book, their friendship, his approaching visit, all these were ploys. His behaviour with Robles, the sudden, murderous tone, this was characteristic. Ongora had not been crossed that often, for his fallacious charm and quick mind had often made his path easy. But to be uncovered so quickly! And by a tradesman! This could not be countenanced. And whilst in the pursuit of his desires, too! For Robles' wife was attainable, he was sure of that. Why, he would provide a service that the old fool could probably not perform himself. She would be for the afternoons, when her serene stupidity would suit the languorous hours. Micaela, his tempestuous mistress, for night adventures. And the Duchess? Time, he thought with optimism of their anticipated meeting, may well unmake her.

And the muse? It had left him, like some winds leave the terrain, robbed of loam, scorched into a wasteland. He could taste the loss in his mouth. He had a frequent nightmare, in which the playwrights and poets of the court were contemptuously reading out his verse, laughing aloud at the predictable rhymes, sneering at the romantic conceits, sarcastically tripping over the delicate – too delicate – metre. In the nightmare, he was a man who visibly shrank when anyone laughed, dwindling into a petulant child. Then the finale of this grotesque, the Emperor, who would repeat often that he was Spain's most insignificant poet, strip his pantaloons, and say to the assembled court that his genitals were so tiny, it would be a small event to remove them altogether. The assembly would move forward, as though to immediately act upon this suggestion, and he would wake, clammy with panic, writhing in anticipated agony.

It was invariable, and unknown to him, that after such a nightmare, he would pick a quarrel with someone, usually a servant, and find some means of hurting them. On some occasions, he had fought in duels. And in this, when he knew he would be the victor, he was very dangerous.

This ferret-like rage, at this moment, was far from apparent. The brief foray with Robles had left him puffed with pleasure. He had the book, had cheated the printer, and was on his way to make his reputation sound with a gift to the Duchess. He would stop a moment on his journey and write a dedication. If the book fared well with the Emperor, although it must be acknowledged that dozens of such creations would be offered every month at the new court, then perhaps a new appointment would follow the grinding out of these small verses. Ah, merely to write them had cost blood. But a year or two in some royally bestowed appointment would vivify where absence still bled. But now, on to the Duchess. Where, if I cannot penetrate her petticoats, he thought, then I will seduce her vanity.

Later in the journey, Ongora put his neatly devised head out of the window and, as his carriage rounded into the driveway of the Duchess's mansion, he had full view of Denia's carriage with the ancient crest, dusty from the hot roads.

This is fortunate, thought Ongora, stepping with a studied delicacy from his carriage; although a dangerous man, the Marquis is a shopkeeper of influence. If he could ally himself to the reputation of the Duchess, perhaps the Marquis may reveal an open opportunity for a position at court. Or even create one.

Ongora inspected the Marquis's carriage. This was circum-spect, for he was spying for anything that might aid his opportunity. Nothing remained inside but the spiced odour of the Marquis's perfume, and the substance of the Marquis's machinations, a trace of some thick electricity.

His pageboys – who resembled Caravaggio boys – were standing attendant in the porch of the mansion. Ongora shooed them impatiently.

What was the Marquis doing here, thought Ongora, other than to visit the Duchess, who everyone knew was the most beautiful woman in the Empire, and who every man who had tried to win her knew was as inviolate as the blue of the sky. But perhaps the Marquis had not realised this. And, Ongora further cogitated, it would not matter to the Marquis, who carried his lust before him like the prow of a sea-clipper, ready for any port and any merchandise. Ongora's imagination leapt to the image of himself duelling with the Marquis, the quivering steel of their rapiers, while the Duchess exhorted them amongst her broken fragments. But, he further realised, the Marquis never travelled without some political purpose. He was here then to increase his influence and power at court. He would know, raced Ongora in his mind, that the Duchess would be obliged to keep her Academy at the service of wherever the court resided. And so this meant that the Marquis had some information for those gravitating to the sphere of the new Emperor, who, like hungry carp in a fountain, would feed on any opportunity. This means, thought Ongora, and he bit his lip, that there was already a new position at court. This was further proof of his good luck that day.

And then his ambition lurched, for the well-husbanded doors of the mansion opened and he was ushered in.

The Marquis's visit, thought Ongora as he waited to be announced, not only meant that he had news of the court and of a new position. There was another purpose. The Marquis knew that he, Ongora, would be a likely visitor. And if he did not figure in the Marquis's game of chess, then this was underestimating the Marquis's abilities. Was he rook or pawn? This had to be discovered.

The doors of the salon opened. He was announced. The room flowed out towards him, for the Duchess tended to beauty in everything. He entered, fluid and mannered, piracy in his heart.

The Scalding of a Poet

A position at court for a poet and personal attendant to
the new Emperor.

'Ah. I see that one of your dependants has arrived,'
said the Marquis, and rose slightly – a breath
above the cushions – from his seat. Ongora
bowed deeply, resolved to hold fast to the
game he knew he had entered. The Marquis would find every
means to slight and patronise him. He must remain composed
through the Marquis's smoothly deployed insults, for to serve
an Emperor one must wear an inferior cloak. His face, as he
rose, then assumed an expression of gentle politeness. Ongora
was certain, as he looked into the intelligent and corrupt folds
of the Marquis's face, that this man had also forced civility onto
himself like a nasty medicine, the better to cure the penury of his
ancient house, and fortify his faded blood with the lands and
houses of privilege. Denia had probably bowed in submission
a thousand times before the advent of his new influence; I must,
thought Ongora, bow as many times and even more. Humility,
he thought, will hide my steel. And he counted another few
seconds of polite deference to the Marquis's immediate person,
and then turned to greet the Duchess.

Ongora saw at once that the Duchess was angry. As his lips
deceived her hand with their solicitous touch, his mind divined
the reasons for her dark brow. He wondered if any rumour of
his profligacy had reached her, then knew this to be unlikely.

It was a principle of the Duchess to ignore and even chastise the slightest instance of gossip and rumour. In fact, Ongora remembered as he leaned up from her hand, the Duchess had on one occasion reprimanded a guest for slighting another. No, he thought as he retired to the polite occupation of a chair, something else has irked her. He looked at the Marquis, who was watching, as ever, and smiling, his head dipping in small nods; a habit. What had the Marquis said, he speculated, for the Duchess, if anyone, could dismiss any crass advance, or roundly reject the opportunism of charm. No, he continued in his mind, there was something else.

'The Marquis,' said the Duchess, her voice edged with control, 'is travelling to Valladolid. He has some report of the health of our new Emperor and of developments at court.'

The Marquis smiled, as though somewhere, out of sight and hearing of the others in the room, a grateful assembly were applauding him.

Ongora had the lightning realisation that the Marquis had discovered something about the Duchess, and had threatened her, with perhaps a pawn of information, into her present dissatisfied mood. He looked at her curiously. 'May fortune smile upon the Lord Marquis like the sun,' he said, with the rote of protocol. 'All who attend her Ladyship's academy shall be pleased to hear more of the advances at court.'

The Marquis almost leered at this platitude, and then moved with alacrity, considering the mass of his sensual bulk, closer to both Ongora and the Duchess. Almost startled by this odd proximity, Ongora continued to abstract the reason for the Duchess's mood. 'The rumours are of some fresh appointments,' he said, almost recklessly. 'Have you benefited from any renovation?'

'Nothing occurs at court,' said the Marquis, looking from one to the other, 'without my approval.' The Marquis's eyes closed briefly; savouring a moment of megalomania.

Ongora observed that the Duchess's disgust at this was almost manifest. His summation was brief and exemplary;

the Marquis had developed an unwholesome relish in his own power and influence, without losing anything of intelligence and will. Therefore, as his startling manners seemed to indicate, the Marquis had deeply undermined the sensibilities of their hostess. But, he continued in his mind, he cannot have discovered anything of fault in the Duchess. It must be, he thought, as his head dipped deferentially like a marionette to the Marquis's comment, that the Duchess had some secret thought or feeling, thus far unrevealed to him. The Marquis then had pried, tricked, or startled this out of her, and she, assuming that the Marquis could not have so succumbed to his love of influence, had found her composure scattered by his new arrogance.

'It is to your credit and for all at court,' Ongora said, knowing that his insincerity made the statement sound false as soon as it was uttered.

But, he thought, what was the information? And why was the Marquis involved? And what did the Marquis gain from the discomfort of the Duchess?

Ongora, his subtle mind having construed this far, was never to find the answer to his question. If he had, he might have reconsidered his own plots. But the moment pressed on, and the Marquis, who had aimed to sweep the games of all before him, now turned his resolve to hooking the poet. A deep barb in the mouth would conquer him, he knew, and all poets were creatures of imagination. To hook him with a dream would be simple enough.

'I have been telling our beautiful hostess,' he said very loudly, as though an audience were perched in the rafters, 'that there is a new position at court. One attendant to the Emperor. Part of his personal retinue. To live within the royal apartments. A monthly allowance from the exchequer. Duties to be determined.' He yawned, as though the list were a tedious musical ensemble. 'Breakfast everyday with the Emperor,' he continued, and nodded at the Duchess and Ongora, as though this were very good news for anyone below the age of six.

'A great honour.' He then turned his head, and gazed out into the grounds. He had been satisfied to see the glimmer of perspiration on Ongora, as though his ambitions were trying to exit all of his pores, all at once. He manufactured a smile of serenity at the view before him, and sighed deeply.

Ongora, stunned into waiting, could not help but look at the Duchess. Aware of but not acknowledging his look, she said to Denia, 'This opportunity has no doubt arisen from your cunning, Marquis.'

He deliberately turned his head with a look of gentle surprise and said, 'Cunning?'

The Duchess laughed and said, 'It is well known, Marquis, that although you manufacture the manner of one unknown to the arts, you are, in fact, one of its most ardent proponents.'

'Then the word is "effacement",' said Denia heavily, and turned back to the window.

'And what is the function of this new position?' Ongora asked quickly.

'I have not mentioned it?' said Denia, as though this was the first time his memory should fault him.

'I mean, what is the title?' said Ongora.

Denia smiled at Ongora. This oppressive leer on Denia's face lasted so long that Ongora's mouth tasted the brine of acute discomfort. 'It is, I believe, Court Poet.'

'Court Poet?' said Ongora, and he rounded the words with their capitals. Glittering with excitement, Ongora moved delicately to the couch, saying in clear and precise words, 'Perhaps the Emperor has indicated to you, being so close in his observance, the kind of gentleman' – the word was carefully chosen – 'that would suit the honoured function of Court Poet.'

Denia, who knew ambition when he saw it, did not hesitate to flush it from cover. 'Your meaning is unclear,' he said. 'Perhaps you are being too polite.'

Ongora, who could only manifest as far as the good character that he had established with the Duchess allowed, swallowed bile, smiled charmingly, and said, 'The Emperor could only welcome true breeding and education as a servant to the court. Has he mentioned any qualifications of this kind?'

'As we are busy with the optimism of a new reign,' said the Marquis, 'then the Emperor has relied more on inspiration to make his appointments than the previously accepted list of avowals and letters of submission. These have been passed over. This, as you know, had been the method of the Emperor's father who, although for a worthy aim, made more of paper than of people.'

'And you have profited by this current wind at court,' said the Duchess.

'I have,' said Denia with a smile of vanity, 'and I will not try to hide that I am the Emperor's creature. But the duties of my position are many, and rewards are not bestowed for wearing jewels, more for the results of my work. This should be understood by anyone,' and he looked deliberately at Ongora, 'who seeks a position at court.'

Ongora parried this in his mind; his head nodded and he smiled disarmingly. He probed again. 'Then this coming appointment, has it already been filled? Perhaps someone close in blood to the Emperor?'

The Duchess glanced quickly at Ongora's handsome face. 'Your Grace must realise that we are hungry for all the developments at court,' she said, excusing Ongora's eagerness. 'After all, it is the lifeblood that supports us.'

The Marquis frowned. 'Well, I cannot tell you everything,' he said grumpily, 'there would not be enough time.'

Ongora could only stand frozen at this display of the Marquis's whimsical politics. The Duchess rescued the moment. 'We can resume this as a topic of conversation for dinner.'

'I have not the time,' the Marquis said in a tone of pedantic anger. 'Tell me, what does he want to know? It is unclear.' He looked directly at the Duchess and closed off the presence of Ongora.

Ongora moved around the couch and settled himself on the corner opposite the Marquis. This proved difficult to do with any impression of ease and grace, for he was trembling with anger and humiliation. 'I mean,' said Ongora, slowly, but without a hint of anger, 'that your Grace has indicated a new position at court for a poet. As a patriot and lover of my country's great culture, my interest, of course, is strong.'

'What does he mean?' the Marquis said to the Duchess, delegating her as the only possible interpreter. 'It is unclear.'

'Our friend, knowing your love for the arts and your patronage of those who are employed as servants of the muses,' said the Duchess, very smoothly, 'wishes to discover whether you have found a suitable person for the new appointment.'

The Marquis, in the recess of his mind where he was not counterfeiting, smiled internally at her adroit delivery. 'Why, that has already been mentioned,' he said. 'It need not be reiterated.'

Ongora almost jerked in response to the Marquis's conciliation. 'And who might apply?'

'Who?' said the Marquis, looking puzzled at the Duchess.

'The position is still open?' demanded Ongora.

'Oof!' said the Marquis, and lay back on the cushions, smiling at the Duchess, 'the line is long. There is not a glimmer of space in the Emperor's apartments.'

The Duchess and Ongora laughed.

'I will, of course, be making the selection. And that cannot be too delayed.' He looked at the Duchess, affable, genial, cruel. 'Perhaps it should be mentioned to the Emperor,' he continued, 'that our young friend is interested.' He frowned. 'But by whom?'

Startled, Ongora flushed quickly. He was forced to say, 'But I am not asking on my own account.'

The Marquis ignored this. 'How should this be mentioned to the Emperor?' he enquired of the Duchess.

She raised her beautiful brows; it was an invitation.

The Marquis frowned as Ongora held his breath.

'It cannot be done,' he said at last to the Duchess, as though Ongora were not in the room. 'I would risk too much. He must shift for himself.'

Ongora felt the disappointment so keenly, it was like a murderer's knife.

The Marquis turned back from his conference with the Duchess and sighed, as though great business had just been accomplished. His eye fell on Ongora, and he nodded approving, as though all poets should be as handsome, and carry themselves as well. 'I am at present looking for a likely author for a commission.' The Marquis looked at the tended ovals of his nails. 'Something that will please all, I am certain.' His gaze, as he looked up at Ongora, was suddenly disdainful, as though he had to play cards on a rainy day with someone he disliked. 'A history of the Emperor.' The cunning that flowed out of him was almost rank, the acid of a fox. 'The new Emperor.' The Marquis used the tiny second of silence as though it indicated an unsaid but definite refusal on Ongora's part. 'Well, you are a poet. It is not likely to please you.'

Ongora, with another opportunity spoiled the moment it was born, smiled politely, and scalded with rage.

'But now it comes to mind that there is already one who seems likely to be chosen for the new position,' continued Denia, matter-of-factly, looking at the Duchess. 'His name you will already have heard, I'm sure. One Miguel Cervantes. He has written a comedy that is fresh in many mouths across the land. He will lighten the temper of those at court. He is also distinguished by being a veteran in the wars against the Turk. Need any more be said?' Denia went on remorselessly. 'A mature gentleman, without the vanity and strident ambitions that characterise some of our younger poets. A genial spirit who, it is said, can reach the hearts of all, high-born and low. And a soldier, a hero of our justifiable conflicts against the infidel!' Denia spread his hands. 'The Emperor will be delighted!'

Ongora's mind could only reel at Denia's manipulations.

'Did you meet him?' asked the Duchess lightly to Denia.

Denia dismissed this. 'I do not need to meet him.'

The Duchess pressed again. 'His name raises only a faint recollection. Is he also a poet? Perhaps he is more famous in his region.'

'He presently resides in Valladolid. Which again is something to recommend him, as he is doubtless following in the footsteps of our Emperor,' Denia said cruelly.

'We at the Academy could read him, sir,' said Ongora, almost breathlessly, 'and present our considered opinion to yourself.'

'Yes, read him,' said Denia, 'it might do some good.' This time, as he looked at Ongora, Denia revealed his contempt. 'He has the nation to recommend him. What else could be better?'

Denia, having razed, pillaged, and plundered at will, rose from the couch, and stretched himself into a straight-backed bow before the Duchess. 'I leave you,' he murmured to her elegant fingers, 'with honest regret but for a previous duty.' He straightened and looked at her benignly. 'An Empire must be re-made.' Ignoring Ongora, Denia bowed again and surged from the room, and as his rampant heels tattooed the hallway, his voice rose in a military ballad, an old song of the patriot, mourning his colleagues lost in battle.

'This news must satisfy you,' said the Duchess. 'You are ably qualified for the position.'

Ongora, preoccupied, agreed. 'You have heard of this Cervantes?' he asked.

She nodded. 'He has written some comic episodes. They are popular. Even my maid knows them.'

'Comedy is hardly an elevated subject,' said Ongora, 'and such an author could not be chosen as the Emperor's designated poet.'

'Perhaps the new court is more genial,' said the Duchess.

'Poetry is not a shallow pursuit,' said Ongora correctly.

The Duchess could only agree with this, and nodded. 'Then you are concerned about the ambitions of this Cervantes?'

Ongora realised that his mulishness was affecting the Duchess. She could so easily read him. 'It is nothing,' he said casually, and sat by her on the couch. 'I have something for you.' Her interest was polite. Receiving gifts was never easy for her. 'It is my latest collection of verses. You are the first to see them. After, of course, the Emperor.' They both smiled, he in deceit, she amused by his flattery. One of the liveried boys brought forward the book. Ongora took it, a fine, handsomely bound piece, and gave it to the Duchess. She smiled, bowed her head slightly, and read the inscription inside the cover. 'I shall read this tonight.' She held the book on her lap. He was stung that it was already forgotten. There was a pause. 'I have just remembered,' she said, 'why the name of Cervantes is familiar. He wrote a poem for the late Emperor's funeral.'

'Ah, yes, I think you are right,' he said. Bile had already entered his throat. Ongora then knew that this Cervantes – this old soldier and faltering poet – was his enemy. In the ebb of this realisation, faster than venom, a plot took shape in his mind. As it took form, he relaxed. He leaned back on the couch, and politely yawned. 'Perhaps,' he said, 'you might consider the position yourself.'

She smiled without amusement. 'I do not think it is in me to write for Emperors.' The irony was acute. 'I am not a creature of ceremonials. This house, myself as hostess, is how I have chosen to serve the Empire.'

He looked at her, touched by amazement; she thought of the position as its announced function, rather than a stepping stone for ambition.

'True,' he said, as though this were the end of the matter. He let the silence work. 'Nevertheless,' Ongora said, 'you have the best mind of any woman that I have met.'

Sardonic, the Duchess said, 'This makes me fit for an Empress, perhaps.'

'It was not my intention to slight you,' he said, and smiled charmingly. 'But there is no doubt in my mind that you would have an excellent chance at the position should you aspire to it.'

'But I do not aspire to it,' she said firmly.

'It would be a shame that someone as ill-connected as a Miguel Cervantes should become the Emperor's poet,' said Ongora.

'You are envious of him,' she said, in that lightning appreciation of truth that he knew could swiftly unseat him. Mercifully, he was prepared. He pretended to consider this as a real possibility, and then deliberately shook his head slowly. 'It is true that envy is one of my faults. But not in this case. It struck me that any truly gifted individual might never have the chance to gain the Emperor's favour because of an impostor, a favourite with commoners who have no education, and students intent on rejecting theirs.'

'It is not an election,' said the Duchess, to end the matter. '*You* have the gift. You cannot tell me that you do not have the ambition to further yourself in the eyes of the Emperor.'

Ongora feigned surprise. 'For once,' he said, 'I was not thinking of myself. No, I was thinking of you.'

She smiled. 'You are playing a game,' she said. 'What is your purpose?'

They laughed together. 'Would you be prepared to accept a challenge, a small wager,' he said lightly, 'that you could become as popular as this Cervantes within a few short weeks?'

The Duchess was taken aback. Surprise made her more beautiful. 'What are you proposing?' she said.

Ongora knew then that he had snared her. 'I myself have read an episode of this Cervantes.' He laughed, a pretence at his own folly. 'As you see, I cannot excuse a sharp interest in a writer who has become the fashion of the moment. I confiscated the text from one of my pageboys.' He turned slightly on the couch and looked directly at the Duchess, the better to make his false sincerity effective. 'It was a dreary piece of paper. The theme popularises a mad old man's deluded taste for chivalry. Such clowning, and such an ignoble theme, is the only reason that this pen-spluttering has proved popular. The scribblings of a tavern poet have nothing to do with a true gift, nor should such a person ever be considered for the position of the Emperor's poet.' Ongora looked out of the window, pretending to reflect further on the vanity of others. 'It is an abuse of the classics that we have inherited, and that the best of us emulate.'

'Yes, and to which we return for guidance. As you know, it is the charter of this Academy to cultivate the classical ideal. It is right for you defend it.' She paused, looking at him. 'But you are a little vehement,' she said. 'Has this Cervantes stolen something from you?' She looked at him with tolerant affection. 'Or has he failed to praise you in some fashion?'

'Ah, my Lady,' he said, and touched her lightly and quickly on the hand, 'you must never cease to remind me of my faults.' He gazed at her and tried to make his eyes moisten. 'Envy. My vanity.' He shook his head at the enormity of his foibles. 'But the truth is, the form of his text does not follow accepted – and I might add – classical rules that we all accept.' He pressed his hand to his chest. 'It is not merely this that burdens my heart, for that would be small in itself. Now, be aware my Lady, that if I speak my true passion, then I must be vehement.'

She nodded for him to continue. 'You will not alarm me. I have also had cause for much indignation.'

He registered with annoyance that she had used the word 'indignation', thus reducing his articulate vehemence to complaint. She was tolerating him, not accepting him. He had admitted too much to weaknesses. He must redress the balance, and yet not create an indignity for her.

'I am not complaining,' he said clearly, 'that too would be a fault. I cannot,' he continued laughing, 'admit to so many in one day. But one of the tenets of my art, with which perhaps you are unfamiliar, is an unqualified faithfulness to the classic roots that presently feed the accomplishments of our age.' He looked at her again, confident that he had regained ground, which he had. 'The writings of this man Cervantes are a subversion. He mocks our history, he undermines the gold of our nation's poets. If I had to guess, my summation of this man's character would be that he is a lonely, embittered veteran of the wars, who has never had an education, never made connections, and never had any success. Envy,' continued Ongora in the same breath, 'is not the issue. I am merely trying to preserve our nation's culture. Should that mean encouraging you to exercise your gifts, then it is a duty that I will not shirk.'

'You need not say more. You have made eloquence a proof of sincerity,' said the Duchess smiling, for the sentiments, false on Ongora's tongue, had excited her immeasurably. And in the moment when she could have asked herself the reason, she did not. There was a pause, lit by her smile, and his responding expression, a lowering of his eyes, a token to modesty. 'What is your proposal,' she continued, 'and what is this wager?'

Ongora, who had wagered many times before, for money, influence, flesh, had never before experienced the sweet excitement of this victory, secret though it was, and for the moment, not to be savoured.

'My proposal is a small matter,' he said, 'and you could accomplish it in little time.' He paused; she was attentive. 'Take for example, the so-called heroine of this –' he paused for a definition, scrupulous in finding a word that would describe and condemn in one '– farce, this Don Quixote's declared love, and write a satiric piece, in her words, of his unwarranted attentions.' He looked at her. She must join him in his thought, showing that she was fired by the plan. He was gratified by her quick nod and even more when she said, 'And she has no intention of carrying favours for a by-gone age, but intends to marry a baker from a neighbouring town.'

He laughed approvingly; she had already found the vein.

The Duchess had a quick compulsive thought. 'It must not be known,' she said, 'that I am the author.'

'Indeed,' Ongora said quickly. 'The author can be no other than this country-beloved, who, having decided to set pen to paper and realising that she cannot write, has hired a scribe to put down the words of her indignation and scorn.' He rose from the couch and looked down at her. 'My departure will hasten your beginning,' he said, and kissed her hand. The doors of the salon were already drifting open. He had a remaining thought, the last scaffold to his plot. 'When it is finished, I would respectfully ask that you send the manuscript to me. I will read it, no doubt with pleasure, but to make an added touch if it should prove necessary, which I am sure it will not. Then I will have it set, printed, and circulated.' He shrugged away the costs, for nobility would assume it all. 'This will be simple.' Her silence was agreement.

He bowed gently and turned to leave.

'And the wager?' she said after him.

'That you will be famous in a week after its publication. That shall be to my satisfaction,' he said, citing generosity where he intended revenge. 'And should this fail, then you can name what price you choose.' He readjusted his coat. 'But I shall win my wager.' He bowed again, and left.

Walking to his carriage, already glowing with the apprehension of his success, Ongora had the rarest of feelings. Perhaps the pursuit of his plot was too much, and that embroiling the integrity of the Duchess in his unpleasant plans would reap more harm than satisfaction. But a coil of callousness summoned this thought in him; there was very little that could affect his position that bribery, connections and his own resources could not remedy. And if it came to that, there was also fame in notoriety. And then, he thought, stepping into the carriage, and settling into the seat, should the Duchess discover his stratagem, or find that the reason for his plot was an infantile revenge, it would not affect him. His feelings for her had long since deteriorated into tolerance. Had she become his mistress, then he would not have had to subvert her. How much simpler for her, he thought and he clicked his tongue, had she allowed him to have her sex.

The Marquis Meets with Madness

Nocturnal friends and the knighting of the old man.

S avouring his own victories from the salon, Denia sped onwards on the road. His drivers and attendants knew him to be heartily pleased, for as the carriage veered, he could be heard singing in a coarse baritone, banging the floor in time with his stick.

It so happened that the carriage had to retrace its route to find the road going north to the capital. Denia was now singing rousing songs, his head out of the window, as though his fit of joviality could alleviate the stinging debris of the road. And such are the tricks of destiny that he had a clear view of the old man, standing once again in the way of danger, in contemplation of a small stable, which I can reveal for the purposes of this story as the property of an old cart-driver. Denia had a sudden impulse, and banged on the roof of the carriage to make it stop. The carriage drew alongside the old man and Denia leaned out to interrogate him. But before he had time to formulate the question, the old man had turned, appraised him briefly, and with some agility, opened the carriage door and climbed in. Denia was amused at the presumption, but also a little on his guard; the old man might be the assassin of a political enemy. However, this thought was banished as he looked into the calming beneficence of the old man's face.

'You are lost,' said the old man. 'I saw you not two hours ago going in the opposite direction.'

'A brief visit on state business,' said Denia. 'I am now returning, and stopped to make your acquaintance.'

'And what were the peculiar circumstances that led you to a life in a portable prison?' enquired the old man.

Denia blinked, and then laughed. 'You are not used to the latest mode of transport? Why, carriages are plenty, especially in the great cities. I am especially fond of the motif with my coat-of-arms.' Denia pointed at the cushioned panels covering the inside of the carriage.

The old man nodded kindly. 'And for what kind of thievery were you incarcerated?'

Denia's political senses rallied him. Exulting in the routing of Ongora, his whimsical friendlines to the old man had proved mistaken. 'You have been too long in the sun, old man.'

'I have been too long out of it,' said the old man. 'You are in a position to render me a service,' the old man continued, having already settled himself opposite Denia, 'which is to allow me to experiment on you with a certain power.'

Denia laughed and showed all his teeth. 'If you touch me, my men shall hang you from the nearest tree,' he said with sudden violence.

The old man said nothing. Denia realised that his smiling affability was not idiotic, that he had heard the threat. His innocence has robust power, Denia pondered, which explains my attraction to him, as long ago I undertook to expunge all purity of heart, and summarily executed kindness in my political youth. Maybe this old man is the shadow of my humanity, come back to look into the face of its persecutor. 'You must be careful,' Denia said as gently as he could. 'I am an important man. Many will pay to have audience with me. And so, what would be my return for rendering you this service?'

'See, I had perceived that you have the face of a usurer,' said the old man. 'But I wish to prove that my hands are better than my eyes. I shall be able to detect the kind of animal you are disguised beneath your skin with a simple touch.' The old man reached out his hand. Denia jerked back. 'No!' he shouted. As he had already shown in his threat, he hated to be touched; rather, it was he that should touch others. He banged the roof urgently with his stick. But there came no reply, as the driver and attendants had climbed down, and were relieving themselves some way off down the road. 'You are presumptuous, old man. I am the Emperor's favourite.'

'Well, he was never one for making good choices,' said the old man, referring to the now dead Emperor Philip II. 'In my case, to be his favourite was never my ambition, and the luxury of it in part made me mad.'

'What do you mean?' asked Denia, now curious yet keeping himself well back.

'As you are a traveller in this particular region, I must warn you, although you are undoubtedly a usurious politician of some sort, that there are many demons and much evil that afflicts this place.' The old man climbed quickly out. 'I am at present in search of arms and a good horse. I have reason to believe that the mansion yonder is the stable of that most wondrous of steeds, the great Bucephalus.' The old man turned as though at drill and marched through the gates of the stable courtyard.

Denia watched him with a slowly savoured interest. True, the old man had a little disturbed him. But as the assumptions of usury, well, that was only half of it. He had resolved to steal an Empire, right from under the nose of its people. And if anyone had challenged him, he would take some pleasure in acknowledging it. For Denia had his own particular philosophy of the best way in which to live, and it had nothing to do with the kind of puling and obnoxious virtues that men die for and women so admire. But that the old man had controlled their encounter, this was the subject of interest. He watched as the old man turned the corner out of sight, and heard with amusement as a variety of farmyard animals began an outcry. And then immediately, bursting into view, came the protesting animals, ducks, chickens, geese and two excited dogs. Eventually outstripping them but for the dogs came the old man, leading a very sorry looking dirty white mare who, and Denia could not but help question his perception, appeared to be gleefully smiling.

Once outside the gates, as the dogs circled and barked, the old man stroked the nose of the mare and looked tenderly into its eyes. He then gently shushed the dogs, who stopped their protests and fell over on their sides in the dust. The old man walked the mare over to the carriage. 'As was my intuition,' he said to Denia, who was leaning with mordant affability from the carriage window, 'here is the steed of all steeds, faster than the wind, lighter than air, and with more spirit than a dozen Arabians.' The mare stamped its foot and whinnied, knowing that it was being well spoken of. 'Do you not recognise him?' asked the old man.

'I am an expert in horse-flesh,' said Denia, 'but this particular breed has escaped me.'

'This is Bucephalus, the best of all horses,' said the old man. 'He and I shall share our quest together, drink from the same basin, eat from the same dish, and warm each other on freezing nights.' The old man then startled Denia considerably by mounting backwards and sitting facing the mare's hind-quarters. The dogs were equally surprised, their heads twisted in perplexity. 'Well, I must say farewell to you,' said the old man. 'My quest continues, and once regaining my sword and armour, I shall attempt the Grail.'

'Good luck,' said Denia, with sarcasm.

'I salute you,' said the old man, 'for although you are involved in thievery, we share a common origin in royal blood.' He bowed on the back of the mare. 'My crest is similar to yours, but with a crowned swan.'

'Why are you mounted backwards?' asked Denia, as the mare began to amble away.

'It is not a mystery. Bucephalus knows very well where we are going, and I want to know where we have been.' And with that, the strange duo ambled away.

Denia watched until trees hid them on the road and then sat back inside the coach. The driver and attendants returned. When the driver asked him if he wanted to continue, he didn't notice, absorbed in analysing his encounter with the old man. So, the old man was an aristocrat, a one-time favourite of the Emperor (he guessed that it must be the now dead and decaying Philip, rather than the live and somnolent one), and mad to boot. And what had the old man said about his crest? And it seems he must be a soldier, given his salute and military bearing.

Denia wondered what this strange destined encounter meant. And of course, whether there was something in it to his advantage.

As the mare Bucephalus ambled – entirely besotted with the light weight and charming manners of the new master that she carried on her misaligned back, his flattering words spinning in her with the sharp savour of green apples – and as Denia ruminated among the effulgent crowns of his carriage, Pedro and his friend the poacher were tying pheasants and putting them into sacks.

Pedro had gone to the poacher on this particular day to talk of his enterprise with Cervantes, and to help take in the haul from the poacher's activities. Given that a lot of the poacher's haul was a large percentage of Pedro's stock, Pedro had arranged that he help in this as part of his fee to the poacher. The pheasants had been trapped in the early hours in their nocturnal browsing for food. The poacher had laid little cakes of grain laced with opium which the birds had gobbled and then, teetering on dizzy legs, laid down unconscious in the undergrowth. Smaller birds, thrushes and pigeons were also part of the catch, but the pheasants were the main meat.

The poacher was a lean wiry man of indeterminate age, habitually in black, with smudged laconic eyes and, best of all, a dry voice that tingled with insurgent humour. 'Tie them by the legs, friend Pedro,' he was saying as Pedro struggled with the feet of a large bird, 'for it disturbs the general populace to see a walking sack.'

'This one will not be tied,' said Pedro, 'and I think it wants to kick me.'

'So it is in our case,' the poacher said, 'to be prisoners, poisoned by sleep, and kicking out against our captors. But it will not have failed to escape your amusement, friend Pedro, that the captive captured captures the captor.'

'I am willing to be amused,' stated Pedro, 'but such mental jiggery makes me mournful, as it reminds me of exams.'

'I mean that this ignorant bird, now our prisoner, and although objecting to his condition, cannot see that our responsibility for his fate forms as much of a bind as the one that ties its legs.'

'Small comfort for it and for us,' said Pedro, still struggling.

'You must have observed,' said the poacher, taking over from him, 'that such miserable thoughts as these I find stimulating and delightful, and any such observations and conclusions that bring less than hope.'

'Indeed, and you have proved many a nightmare on me,' said Pedro, who did not like menial tasks, but was always ashamed when someone finished one for him, 'as for example, whether one can observe the end of the world more closely through a telescope. It did not lighten my house to be screaming in the night for a week afterwards.'

'My small revenge against that harridan, my relative, and all your useless daughters,' said the poacher smiling.

'And they in turn exact a revenge on me,' said Pedro.

'Which leads you to spending more time in my company,' said the poacher, 'as talking of various esoteric subjects with me serves to alleviate your miseries.'

Pedro sighed, for this was true.

The last sack filled, Pedro and the poacher now sat together, sharing a bottle.

It serves the purpose of the story to tell you a little of where they were located, for what happened next depended on this. The poacher's activities, clandestine and nocturnal, meant that his catch had to be accounted and handed over to Pedro in a secret place. He had chosen a small hut, ironically once a keeper's cottage for an estate that bordered on the outskirts of the city, which had long since fallen into disuse. Wars and the reversals of the court between Madrid and Valladolid had divorced many landlords from their estates. The hut was hidden as well, protected from the road by briars with a long meandering path leading to it from the country. Inside the hut were the tools of the poacher's profession; nets, loops and hooks for prising drugged birds from tree branches, leggings for wading in water, some adapted weapons, like a flintlock with a lantern attached to it for hunting at night, some bedding, a change of clothing, bottles of liquor and some pamphlets. It still being day, the poacher and Pedro were sitting outside the hut, listening to the approach of dusk as the sun went down. Pedro's cart was stowed in among the briars. When the dark was absolute, they were going to load the cart with the staggering birds in their sacks and Pedro would then drive back through the country – a journey that he disliked immensely – and then quietly trot out in a bend of the road closer to the city.

Their pleasant silence was then interrupted.

'Hello there,' cried the old man and ambled into the clearing on the mare, who seemed to be smiling. The reactions of Pedro and the poacher to the sudden appearance of the old man were characteristic. Pedro buried his head in his hands and mourned. The poacher, thinking that one of the inept constables of the city had gone mad and was attempting to arrest him, immediately disappeared.

'What are you doing here?' asked Pedro in depression.

'God is good, and put it into my mind to find your voices and put bodies to them,' said the old man.

'Holy Christ,' said Pedro. The liquor made him despondent.

'You have surely recognised that I am riding the wondrous steed of legend, the incomparable Bucephalus.'

'We are so familiar,' said Pedro, 'that we had supper together yesterday night.'

'Your friend who is hiding behind that tree must be one of the race of shy human beings,' said the old man. 'He wants to be invisible.'

'You cannot see me,' said the poacher from behind the tree, 'because I am not here.'

The old man nodded agreeably. 'Then let us continue talking,' he said, 'but pretend that this conversation is not taking place.'

'What are you doing here?' said Pedro, exasperated. 'The business with my friend is very delicate and confidential.'

'Then I can only do some good by my presence,' said the old man firmly, and dismounted from the mare. Disappointed at having been left by the old man, the mare thrust her head into the briars and stared at the roots. 'I heard your voices from the road,' said the old man, 'and Bucephalus thought it was a good idea to make your acquaintance.'

'Good ideas are indeed hard to come by,' Pedro said acidly.

'You are being eaten by one of the lower demons,' said the old man, 'if you say something nice it will go away.'

'You go away!' said the poacher from behind the tree.

'Our invisible friend has a very loud mind,' said the old man, 'and speaks it readily. Unless of course, as we should gratify his wishes, he is not here at all and we are imagining it.' He winked at Pedro and nudged him in the ribs. True to the mishaps that plagued Pedro whenever he was with the old man, the elbow caught him just as he was drinking from the bottle. The stopper, which he had settled in his teeth on one side in peasant fashion as he drank, slipped down his throat. Pedro threw himself to his knees, choking desperately, and flailed his arms. The old man, oblivious to his discomfort, had moved forward to the hut, which he examined with great intensity. 'You had not told me that you were the protectors of this sacred hermitage,' he said wonderingly. The poacher, hearing Pedro's distress, charged from behind the tree, thinking that some mischief was being performed on his friend. Seeing Pedro choking, he seized a board and whacked Pedro hard between the shoulder blades. The stopper flew out, and Pedro collapsed and lay groaning feebly.

The old man had meanwhile entered the hut that he had called a hermitage and was examining the interior. Pedro and the poacher could hear soft cries of delight coming from inside. The old man emerged, a mystic charge of revelation on his face, and smiled at the uncertain pair.

'Again, God has proved his beneficence and guided me to this holy place wherein I might find rest and spiritual ease before commencing on my quest,' said the old man.

'Do you know this person?' the poacher asked Pedro, who was still lying on the ground and gratefully feeling the breath in his lungs.

'My ribs know him,' said Pedro faintly, 'as do the bruises about my head.'

'We must raise him,' said the old man to the poacher, 'for he is my squire and there are many adventures yet to befall him.'

A profound gloom descended on Pedro when he heard this pronouncement.

'I think that he might find his business partnership with me more gentle than the certainly penurious condition of being your squire,' said the poacher as they pulled Pedro to his feet.

'The salary and compensation for that position,' said Pedro hoarsely, 'was the choking and the whacking that you have just witnessed.'

'It was I that whacked you,' said the poacher, 'but that was to save your life.'

'It matters not,' said Pedro, 'for to preserve my new status, and to rather not have a corpse in service, this –' and he searched for a phrase bitterly '– guardian angel here would have whacked me as well.'

'Now that all things are well,' said the old man, 'I shall now pronounce my revelation to you.' Pedro, still purple about the mouth from the spilled liquor, and breathing harshly, glared at him. 'The celestial guardian of this place has invited me to stay whilst preparing for my quest ahead. But before I can take up residence, I must of course become a knight. Therefore, after a long and extensive vigil, this dark acolyte here –' indicating the poacher '– shall knight me according to chivalric code.'

The unusual nature of this proposal pleased the poacher immensely. 'Well, it is illegal, scandalous and irreligious. I shall do it.'

'If you do this, you shall no longer call me friend,' said Pedro hotly.

'Why, I saved your life not five minutes ago!' said the poacher. 'I shall do as I please and still be called your friend. If you do not defer to this, then it is I that shall not be calling you friend.'

While they were in discussion, the old man had knelt between them, hands held in prayer, eyes closed. 'It is important for the initiate,' he whispered forcefully, 'that utter calm and tranquillity should be exercised during his spiritual exercises. Therefore, if your disagreements become too loud and ungovernable, you must beat yourselves and pray abjectly.'

'I have no intention of beating myself, unless you have the power to turn my own hand against me,' said Pedro. 'Otherwise, I consider the hurts that I have already received so far in your company as more than enough for one improvised vigil.'

'Your wilfulness,' said the old man, his eyes closed and still kneeling, 'is more than enough evidence that demons are abundant in this region. I can also surmise that if my squire has been so readily and easily snatched by malevolent spirits, the vigil must be seriously undertaken to prepare me for the trials ahead. I shall therefore, if it is required, instruct this trusted acolyte to beat my squire if the demon grows too large.'

'Give the command,' said the poacher, hugely delighted, 'and it shall be done at once.'

Infuriated, Pedro leaned over the old man. 'I am a merchant, this is a poacher, that hut is an old hut, and YOU are a VERY FOOLISH OLD MAN!'

'The material world has quite absorbed your senses,' said the old man. 'Let my squire be beaten!'

And to the utter amazement of both friends, the mare, having been roused from her misery by the tones of the old man, and hearing the threat in Pedro's tones, lashed out with her hooves, catching the unfortunate Pedro squarely between the shoulders and sending him nose first onto the ground.

The poacher, considerably startled, turned to find the mare staring fiercely at him.

'I detect that my command was swiftly performed,' said the old man. He sighed. 'And how is my unfortunate squire?'

'It must be that God does not like me,' said Pedro, prone once more.

'God has assumed a strange shape in which to express his displeasure at you,' said the poacher, although he was careful with his tone, for the mare was eyeing him very aggressively.

'Whatever his shape, I submit,' said Pedro faintly.

'That is good,' said the old man kindly, 'and now that we have passed through this ordeal, I must be knighted.'

Pedro stood and shook himself. 'Well,' he said with bright and entirely false cheeriness, 'let us knight your honour and quickly too before there is nothing left of me to knight you with.'

'A sound idea,' said the old man, 'although your cheerfulness does not merit the occasion. Master acolyte, please you to enter the hermitage and bring here the sword that hangs on the centre wall.'

The poacher thought for a moment, knowing the hut intimately well, and said, 'are you referring to the switch that is used for beating barley?'

'It was thought advisable by God to render such an arcane weapon in the form of a domestic utensil, the better to protect it from acquisitive spirits. Yes, indeed, please to fetch it here,' said the old man.

The poacher disappeared inside the hut and returned with the switch.

'Squire,' said the old man imperiously, 'please it you to assist me to my feet, for my night-long vigil and fasting has left me weakened in body.'

Pedro did not question this peremptory blurring of time and helped the old man to his feet, keeping a careful eye on the mare.

'Now,' said the old man, 'I shall open my eyes. And then the acolyte shall knight me appropriately, including a useful speech on the duties of my calling.'

'How comes it,' said the poacher, flexing the switch, 'that a king is not to knight you, and an acolyte is suitable?'

'You find it fitting,' said Pedro, mindful of the poacher's delight in his pains, 'to be knighted by a bandit?'

'These are questions only God can answer,' said the old man blandly. 'You are now to touch me on the shoulder with the sword,' he whispered to the poacher, 'call me knight and then deliver some useful homilies.'

The poacher looked with dour glee at Pedro and then made his ceremony. 'I name you,' he said touching the old man on the shoulders with the switch, 'the old Knight, and I bid you to be as good as an old Knight as any, and as useful.'

The old man sighed, shook himself, and then gently embraced Pedro and the poacher.

'Useful acolyte,' he said, 'hardy squire, so ends a significant ceremony. I must begin my quest. I shall return upon occasion to rest at this hermitage. Therefore, see to it that both yourself and this useful acolyte have cleaned this spot and removed various worldly items that I saw inside, doubtless the evidence of some roving bachelors hereabouts.' The old man now mounted the mare, who waited obediently, and sat rearwards.

'Sir Knight,' said Pedro, in mock respect, 'it must be said that you are pointing the wrong way, and that if you insist on this, then you and the horse will travel in different directions.'

'That is a perverse remark,' said the old man. 'Bucephalus knows our destination, and until the success of my first quest and as befits my humble position, I shall ride in this way.'

The mare hitched what was for her a pleasing burden, and ambled into the briars. The poacher rounded on Pedro fiercely. 'Does he insist on taking over my hut?' He glared back out to where the old man and the mare had disappeared. 'The effect on my commercial dealings will be catastrophic.'

Pedro had grown a little wiser after his recent beatings. 'That he has chosen your hut for his hermitage is of no surprise. There are strange atmospheres following this particular person, and having once met him, and his attention fixed on you, then many terrible things will befall. My advice is to remove all your personal items from the hut and try to avoid him. Otherwise, your already unusual life will become thoroughly bizarre.'

'To lose my warehouse and my living quarters in one night is strange enough,' the poacher said. 'How shall I be repaid?'

'Banish the thought from your mind,' Pedro said wisely. 'Be thankful that he has not chosen you to be his squire, or his page, or his spear-handler, or God knows whatever. We shall find another place for you. Perhaps with my friend the author.'

'I cannot abide literary men,' said the poacher. 'They are always a short fuse away from completely raving.'

This irritated Pedro as it had been a generous thought on his part. 'And when did you establish this uncharitable notion?'

'They are always interviewing me on the techniques of poaching,' the poacher said. He and Pedro were already removing the gear from the hut and putting it on the cart. 'My stack of pamphlets here are the poor results of their writings. All kinds of nonsense are conveyed in them. And furthermore, when they insist on accompanying me on my work, they insist on talking too loudly at critical moments. Their delicate nerves, they say. I correct their miserable pamphlets and send them back to the printers. None has responded.'

'A little unusual that a member of an illegal profession should be so concerned with establishing the facts on their secret skills.'

'It is a time honoured profession and, once reported, should not be misrepresented.'

As you can guess, their wrangling eased the labour of moving everything to the cart, in which, once full, they both climbed.

Although their journey began with grumbling, the somewhat bizarre poetry of the old man's ceremonious knighting and the calm indifference of the deep night through which they travelled began to soothe their irritability, even that of Pedro, who had received the worst of both injuries and indignities. So at last, and well before their journey's end, the cart was halted, another bottle unstopped, and with well-meaning carelessness they discussed the stars that glimmered so confidently above them, and reviewed that evening's proceedings. And it did not take long, as the liquor worked, for their recent experiences to be recounted and for hurts and humiliations to become suddenly hilarious.

So let us round off this evening, even as his acquaintances recount how the old man has astonished them thus far, by honouring him in the remainder of this text – and true to chivalric code – with the title of 'the old Knight'.

A Reading of Parts

The author meets with his own creation.

So fateful divinities were now in employment through the new court to fillet Cervantes' sensibilities, as he soon would discover. Meanwhile, he was hesitating on the threshold of the Lepanto tavern with episodes from his comic romance, written out as parts in a play, in scrolls under his arm. He wanted his drinking companions to try out the parts in the new episode in what he hoped would be an evening of hilarity for the locals, and for himself the veracity that he required of his characters. But he was comfortable under the night sky. Inside, it would be the extrovert banter of the locals. Here, on the threshold, the bitter heat of the day cooling, a scent permeating of some unruffled bloom, he was thinking that the silence itself was an achievement, beyond all the books, money, and fame in Christendom.

Insomnia and fever reigned in Cervantes like dissolute monarchs. He lived at night, not only for writing, but because the hours themselves seemed to resonate to a universe of subtly responsive depth. The night plunged quietly into a domain navigated by a few glistening outposts: the stars, and himself, which often caused him wonder, as though being a witness made him a divinity, albeit a temporary, unqualified one. Remembering this before the tavern entrance, he was thinking why was it that, being hand-reared by God for his purpose, he should be writing a comedy, his pen flowing with crude jokes, puns, and the colloquialisms of the farmer and the tradesman? Why did his pen scratch out the ironies observed by peasants? The answer perhaps was that God lives in all simple things. His mentor, a rough and able muse, had made his companions, his associates, and his friends far different from the sophisticated personalities of the court.

He went inside the tavern. A low ceiling, smudged by candle flames, crammed closer with soot to the heads of the locals. General blurred greeting from the occupants. All knew him. The assembly largely featured the butchering profession, for there was a slaughterhouse close by. Cervantes had dubbed them 'regulars', because, like soldiers, they always stayed together, joked loudly, and carried a faint uneasy atmosphere with them, the taboo of their trade. Cervantes handed out parts while the regulars began to imitate the characters of Quixote and his unfortunate squire.

There was a new visitor to the tavern, a smartly dressed gentleman, a merchant, sporting a new sword, yet already belligerent with wine, disappointed from a soured business deal. He smiled sardonically at Cervantes handing out the parts of his play, and then rudely rejected Cervantes' affable offer of a part. He called for more wine. The tavern-keeper brought another flask, and said jokingly to the merchant that 'You might as well take a part, because it is better to have a part in a tedious play, rather than watch one.'

This brought a roar of affectionate amusement for Cervantes, but the merchant took this as a jibe against Cervantes and remarked that, 'it should be the practice to incarcerate the mentally unhinged rather than entertain them.'

The atmosphere in the tavern suddenly changed. The tavern-keeper said, 'You must amend your manner, for the author is honoured as a veteran of the wars against the Turk, and has many friends.'

'Does this mean,' said the merchant, determined for trouble, 'that he never pays his bills, that he had a succession of fevers in the Emperor's campaigns, and that his creditors number more than his friends?'

'Come,' said Cervantes, 'you seem determined to be in a bad mood. This part is right for you. Look, it is the character of a Choleric Spleen.'

The jovial atmosphere was once again restored. But again, the merchant misread the intention, and took this as an insult against himself. He tore the paper that Cervantes had given him, and said, 'It is not my spleen that is the problem, rather the company that I have, the tavern that I am in, and this dust-pile of a city.'

'Then feel free to leave,' said Cervantes.

The merchant misunderstood this as a challenge, and said, 'I will leave when my own senses bid me, not at the bidding of one who obviously has none.'

The atmosphere changed once again. The tavern-keeper urged the merchant to be polite, 'for Cervantes has a good temper because he keeps a rein on the bad.'

'What do I have to fear,' said the merchant, 'for he is obviously deluded and maimed. Come on then, if he is a man,' and thumped the point of the scabbard down on the floor.

'Pass me my pen,' said Cervantes to the regulars, 'and I will write a satire of this fine gentleman that will rob him of his anger. Quickly, for I am inspired, and once the heavens speak, then we must obey instantly.'

'I can see now,' said the merchant, drawing his sword, 'that you have intended all along to make a fool of me. If you will not accept my challenge, then prepare to be beaten with steel.'

Cervantes stood unarmed in front of the incensed merchant. 'Why,' he said, 'your steel shall not touch me, as neither shall your gibes or your impatience with my friends. I do not care that you insult my play, my wits, or that I owe money to honest and worthy people. But I warn you, if you insult the wound that symbolises the glory of my life, gained in a battle that preserved the glory of this Christian kingdom, then I shall be forced to set down the following on paper –' he began writing rapidly '– addressed to your loving parents, for it is they who must be informed of your behaviour, your taste for riot and your determination to travel everywhere in a bad temper. And after you have run me through, my last wish is that you sign this paper here, which now says: "I, an Ill-Tempered Man, do solemnly swear that I skewered an old veteran for writing a bad play, and that I care not for his death, neither for any in Europe. Signed this day I know not what, in great hurry for the Watch are almost upon me, yours, an obnoxious Merchant."'

By this time, the tavern was in an uproar of delight.

'Now if my friend the tavern-keeper here would fetch me that historic weapon,' said Cervantes, 'which I keep here, oiled and sharpened for occasions such as this, then we can continue our debate. Mine is an infantry sabre, lengthened by several inches more than is legal, the better for skewering two at a time rather than one, and shall, I fancy, turn your rapier into small and expensive fragments.'

The tavern erupted into laughter and cheers.

But then they were interrupted by the appearance of the old Knight.

This was the first time that Cervantes had seen him, even though he had some details of his appearance from Pedro's description. And now, as if summoned by Cervantes' need for authenticity, here he was, wearing a fire-bucket on his head and a breastplate, upside down, strapped to his torso. The regulars, quietened like children at a spectacle, had drawn back in some wariness to look at this creature. In some, there was the suspicion that Cervantes had arranged this as entertainment, hiring an actor to appear as the mad buffoon Don Quixote. But one look at Cervantes assured them that he was just as astonished as they. Can a character walk out of a story? Wasn't it dangerous that this particular character had escaped its pages?

Cervantes, finding his heart beating hard, carefully scanned the old Knight. A fine, genial countenance. Confident, upright bearing. And there was another quality, Cervantes realised, that had so far not been part of his description. Some kind of luminous certainty. Faith in the divine made the old Knight unerring, Cervantes thought, like an expert marksman. Nothing would alter his path, not even walls, ramparts. But as one of the regulars was about to ask Cervantes if Don Quixote had escaped his episodes, the old Knight spoke.

'Hold,' said the old Knight to everyone in the tavern, 'for such an occasion needs have the witness of a worthy Knight, according to the ancient and sacred laws of chivalry.'

'Here,' Cervantes whispered to the merchant, 'is one of my lost senses.'

The merchant could only look bemused at these developments.

'You, sir,' said the old Knight to the merchant, 'seem well prepared for combat, with your weapon already drawn, although you have a rather casual disregard for armour, which I would assume either denotes a fashion in this area, or a carelessness of combat that can only reflect poorly on your dignity as a knight and a gentleman. And I see that your opponent has no weapon. Think you this is an honourable form of combat?'

'What do you think, master merchant?' said Cervantes.

'Ah, so you are a merchant,' said the old Knight, 'which explains your lack of knightly accoutrements. Perhaps you bought this weapon to shake at blackbirds and small boys?'

'I bought this sword, dammit,' said the flustered merchant, 'so that I could defend myself against thieves and villains.'

'Even by being generous with you, I do not see that you are beset with them,' said the old Knight. 'Your manner shows more the temperament of a coward. A sword should only be worn to defend the honour of God and of all who have the Christian faith, not merely as a defence of property.'

'Go away,' said the merchant. 'You're mad.'

'Now, now,' said Cervantes, 'it would be a mistake indeed to pick a fight twice in one evening, and pick another fight before the first one has finished.'

'It is beneath my honour to fight you,' said the old Knight to the merchant.

'Beneath your honour?' cried the merchant, trembling and still holding out his rapier, 'Why you mad old fart, you have no choice in the matter.' And saying this, the merchant prodded the old Knight in the breastplate with his rapier.

'Step forward the next person who does not want to fight with the merchant,' announced Cervantes.

The old Knight turned to Cervantes and said, 'He has indeed put me in a difficult position, for he is undoubtedly ungodly, and he is no knight.'

'Perhaps,' said Cervantes, 'you could fight him as a monster.'

'That might have worked,' said the old Knight, 'but God has already told me that this is no monster, but an overlarge baby.'

Before Cervantes had time to reflect on this, the old Knight said to the merchant, 'Now sir, in my opinion, you are ill-equipped to fight one such as me, who have armour and a good broad sword. And rather than divesting myself of this armour, for it took a morning and a gallon of oil to fit me into this costume, my suggestion is that you are similarly equipped before combat begins.'

'Hell and contagion!' said the merchant. 'I will no longer stay to endure this charade.' He turned to go but before he could move, several regulars grabbed him.

'Come,' said Cervantes, 'for even if you have no honour, you can achieve it in combat.'

'What,' said the merchant struggling with his captors, 'by fighting a madman!'

'Presumably,' said Cervantes, 'you were hoping to gain as much by fighting a maimed and deluded veteran. And, at the very least, if you intend to fight madmen and veterans, you shall be suitably attired. A couple of our belts, I think,' he said, taking these from a regular who had already guessed his mind, 'and one of these stools, if strapped to your body, will be sufficient for armour, and you can hold this bucket as a shield. The only thing now lacking is a helmet, but if our Knight here will agree to fighting you without his, then these will be adequate terms for honourable combat.'

The merchant, struggling hard as his captors strapped various items to him, said, 'Curse you for a vagrant scoundrel and this old fool here for interfering in a quarrel that I would have settled a while ago.'

The old Knight said to Cervantes, 'By my troth, sir, you have both the temperament and manners of a true Knight, and it is fortunate that in this strange and bewitched land I should find a worthy equal. Tell me, are you one of the Grail Knights? Are you, by the Grace of God, Sir Galahad?'

'That is not a name that I commonly go by,' said Cervantes, 'and as a rule, am known by many other far less distinguished names.'

'Ah,' said the old Knight, 'that is the fate of those whose calling is of chivalry, for many a true knight must be unfailingly courteous in the face of great rudeness and incivility. But by your acts of courage and your courteous manner, and your modesty in not divulging your true name, I am certain that you are Sir Galahad.'

By now, a small stool had been strapped to the front of the merchant and a bucket tied to his wrist as a shield.

'And for this poor creature,' said the old Knight referring to the merchant, 'this one of the beasts of the earth, consumed with desires, and without a soul.'

'What does he mean, I have no soul?' said the merchant to his captors. 'Why does he say that I have no soul?' he said pitifully. 'The desires I admit to, but without a soul . . . That is terrible.'

'Clear the field,' shouted the old Knight, 'and let the trumpets sound.'

The tavern-keeper and others looked at Cervantes for instruction on trumpets. Cervantes shrugged.

'Listen as their stern and resolute tones clear the morning air,' said the old Knight. 'Come, sir,' he said to the merchant, 'it is a good day to fight, and such a one as you can earn honour by your death or by my defeat.'

'It has been a strangely bad day,' said the merchant, now very mournful, 'and tomorrow already looks bad as well.'

The others drew back, and left the old Knight and the merchant in the centre.

'I beg of you,' said the merchant, 'that if I die, that you give me a decent burial.'

'If you die,' said the old Knight, 'there shall be no need of a burial, for your carcass will evaporate and disappear in a matter of hours, as commonly occurs with creatures that have no soul.'

'There you go again,' said the merchant, completely hysterical, and whose wits had begun to turn, 'referring to my lack of soul, for that must be untrue. And I shall fight you to prove it.'

The merchant now looked like a strange porcupine, with the legs of the stool bristling out in front of him. He suddenly charged at the old Knight, who stepped aside, and as the unfortunate merchant passed by, whacked him hard on the back of the head with his bucket. By the time the merchant had crashed into the tavern wall and collapsed in a racket of wooden legs and clanging metal, he was already unconscious. The crowd groaned in disappointment.

The old Knight went over to the merchant. 'The breath of God is upon him,' he said. 'Come, place him here on this table, and I shall keep vigil until he revives. Then shall I enrol him into my service, for it is to his honour that he fought me.'

Removing the bizarre protection from the merchant's chest, they placed him full length on a table. 'Candles, friar, for a vigil must be kept,' said the old Knight to the tavern-keeper. Without questioning his new title, the tavern-keeper departed. Eventually, the merchant was arranged on the table, candles burning at his head and heels, his oblivious face turned to the ceiling, and his hands crossed on the hilt of the rapier.

The old Knight knelt briefly to pray. 'Come, Galahad,' he said rising to his feet, 'we must talk of our adventures. Blessed friar, look you to this man until I have returned for vigil tonight. And do not be concerned if he rails or appears mad, for it is the devil quitting him for a new master.'

Cervantes, unused to his new title, joined the old Knight and they left together. Once outside, the old Knight stopped, turned to Cervantes and said, 'It is put in my mind that our newest friend insulted you as maimed. I look at you –' and the old Knight drew back with his words and looked at the full person of Cervantes, '– and I do not see any affliction to your limbs.'

'He meant my hand,' said Cervantes. 'He must have noticed it by my way of handing out the parts of the play.' He showed the stiff fingers. To his utter surprise, the old Knight dropped to his knees, clasped the damaged hand, and held it to his brow. Cervantes had to control himself not to snatch it away. The old Knight then kissed his hand reverently. Astonished, Cervantes felt warm tears from the old Knight's face. 'Please,' he said inadequately. But the old Knight stood, and still clasping his hand, looked tenderly into his face and said, 'Thou best of all knights, think that thou art maimed? Nay, thou sharest in the great labour of God, and have bestowed the use of a limb for the sake of rendering heaven.'

Cervantes found himself unaccountably moved by the old Knight's emotional statements and high-flown courtesy. Further, the Knight's tears on his hand caused a tremor of such sweetness in him, a poignancy so mystifying that he found himself dazed and wordless. The old Knight turned and walked Cervantes along with him. 'We were discussing earlier that you might be the Grail Knight, Sir Galahad,' said the old Knight. He hooked his arm around Cervantes. 'I must tell you that I am, or was, or perhaps will be Sir Lancelot. Although I am far from convinced of this identity, as it is clear to me – as much as anything can be – that a name or a title is a temporary solution to the question of one's being.' He stopped and looked at Cervantes fully. 'It seems to me folly to try and place a name on the universe that exists within each of us.'

Cervantes had no response to this and asked the old Knight if he had a place to stay. 'Why the very next tree is mine for shelter,' said the old Knight. 'Farewell, until we meet again,' he said, saluting Cervantes. Then he turned smartly and marched clear into the yard of a house, and banged into a hen house, causing a great ruckus of clucks and squawking.

And as far as Cervantes could tell, this is where his new friend spent the night.

The Knight of the Table

The vision of the bad-tempered merchant.

*T*he evening following the famous fight in the tavern, the old Knight returned to find the merchant still unconscious. The candles were burning, tended faithfully by the tavern-keeper, and the merchant still lay supine, eyes closed, with his hands crossed upon his sword. The tavern-keeper had thoughtfully carried the table into the largest of the dining rooms.

The old Knight knelt by the table and prayed. The effect was immediate, for the merchant awoke and demanded in a hoarse voice whether he was dead or alive. The old Knight told him that these things were difficult to tell, but what was certain was that he had been defeated in fair combat. Further, that he must renounce the way of material gain, and place himself in service as a squire.

After a thoughtful pause, the merchant said, 'This is all very well, but I really have no inclination to leave the altar that I find myself on. And surely, as a man of God, you must see that above us, the archangel Michael stands astride me, wielding his sword of retribution, and I feel disinclined to incur his wrath by moving or acting in a restless way whatsoever.'

The old Knight then told him that he was having a foolish delusion from a bang on the head.

'I would have thought,' said the merchant, 'that a man of God would be able to see as I see.'

'You are a little de-arranged,' said the old Knight, 'for if you were seeing the archangel Michael, then I would be able to see him too.'

'Well, I would hate to contradict you so soon into our new friendship,' said the merchant, 'but I have a perfectly clear recollection of the kind of person I was before receiving a bang on the head. Then, I thought you a mad old fool, and now, lying on this altar, I think of you as being the best of men, and that it is not so far from the truth to see visions of angels.'

'Perhaps we should make you a knight, as I am,' said the old Knight, 'and that will either displace your delusions, or confirm that you have the right to have them.'

'That sounds like an excellent idea,' said the merchant. 'Indeed I could laugh at the joy of such a suggestion but for my supine position.'

'We shall keep vigil, according to the style and custom of chivalry,' said the old Knight, 'and we shall call you the Knight of the Table.'

'This sounds very good,' said the merchant, 'and indeed a high honour. But I have one request.'

'It is the right of the novitiate to be granted a request,' said the old Knight, 'therefore you must ask.'

'I do not think that I can be the kind of knight that fights in battles, or travels far on horseback without eating,' said the merchant.

'Well, that would be a shame, for this is mostly the occupation of knights,' said the old Knight.

'The truth is,' said the merchant, 'that I feel a great disinclination to rising from this table. To me, it is like the kind of cushion one might find in heaven. I am perfectly content to lie here and, when I am not encountering my vision, perfectly content to count the spots on the ceiling.'

'This is all very well for you,' said the old Knight, 'but a true knight is wholly given over to a vigorous life of combat and doing good.'

'Perhaps,' said the merchant, 'I can do good from here by keeping watch on the archangel Michael, for his immediate presence here leads me to believe that the division between the temporal and spiritual realms is not as distinct as I had previously imagined. Perhaps I can also recount my vision to people who visit, and collect alms for the church.'

And this was how the merchant became the Knight of the Table.

The Tavern-Keeper

An ingenious solution.

*J*t was not long after this conversation between the merchant and the old Knight that Cervantes entered the tavern and found the tavern-keeper not at his accustomed place, but sitting at a small table, sighing loudly, and drinking heavily from a bottle of dangerous liquor. Surprised, Cervantes asked him why he was unhappy. The tavern-keeper, a usually kind and jolly person, could only look at Cervantes with the greatest distress, and shake his head disconsolately. Cervantes insisted that he divulge his sorrow, for the tavern-keeper to be seen drinking like a man who has lost his favourite dog was indeed bad for business.

'Well,' said the tavern-keeper and sighed heavily, 'my business has suffered from the preposterous nature of recent events.'

'Meaning what?' asked Cervantes.

'And,' continued the tavern-keeper, 'I must hold you responsible for my ill-fortune, for I cannot hold a mad old man responsible, and you were as much a part of this incident as the mad old man.'

Cervantes took hold of the bottle that the tavern-keeper had been drinking from, and said firmly, 'If you drink any more of this noxious brew, you will be mad in a week, and dead within two.'

'It's true,' said the tavern-keeper, 'that liquor makes the best of a joy, and the worst of a sorrow.'

'Now tell me,' said Cervantes, 'what has happened.'

'Perhaps it is not your fault,' said the tavern-keeper, 'but in your light-hearted folly of last night, this tavern has been turned into a shrine, and it is well established that the drinking of liquor and the worship of God do not take place within the same dwelling.'

'How much have you had of this?' asked Cervantes, raising the bottle.

The tavern-keeper became earnest. 'Look,' he said, 'the merchant who knocked himself cold last night has since awakened, and has been prayed over by your friend the mad old man, who has since dubbed him "the Knight of the Table". And now this so-called Knight of the Table,' continued the tavern-keeper, getting agitated, 'has announced that he cannot move from his supine position on one of my best oaken tables because of a vision of the archangel Michael standing at the gates of Heaven. That being said, the old man, no less mad from so much praying, has announced that my biggest dining room is now a shrine, and that those of us ready to pay alms and visit the Knight of the Table can do so at any hour.'

'Is this where all your customers are?' asked Cervantes.

'Indeed, the whole pack of them are in there, looking dazzled and bewildered in as short a time as it would have taken them an hour of drinking ale in my establishment. And that,' said the tavern-keeper, standing and shouting at the general direction of the entrance to the ante-room, 'is my best room for entertaining, and we have had, God can tell, many a good funeral and wedding in that room.'

He sat down again, once more disconsolate, his brief flare of temper gone. 'That room,' he said, 'has the best fireplace in the whole quarter.'

Cervantes tried to console him, suggesting that things may

not be as bad as they seem, for indeed it is an honour that the tavern be considered a holy place.

'Ah,' said the tavern-keeper, 'you forget that God feels differently about drinking than I do.'

'Excess is the sin,' said Cervantes. 'But I am sure that once your customers have seen and heard of visions, they will only be too willing to discuss the matter over ale among their friends.'

Saying this was the cue, for the door of the dining room opened, and many of the tavern-keeper's customers entered, talking in low and excited tones.

Cervantes said to the tavern-keeper, 'Let me discuss the situation of alms with the Knight of the Table. There is perhaps a sound and profitable solution.'

Cervantes left the tavern-keeper, who was eyeing his customers dubiously, and entered the dining room.

Cervantes found the newly christened Knight of the Table lying on his back, candles at his head and feet, holding onto his sword and staring at the ceiling. Cervantes only had to enter when the Knight of the Table said, 'You have come at last, for it has been an age since our encounter and my deliverance into the realms of God.'

'Perhaps,' said Cervantes, 'another knock on the head would re-acquaint you with your family and neighbours.'

'It is good of you to think of me,' said the Knight of the Table, 'but I am sure they would willingly sacrifice my company to God so that they might be removed of the unpleasant and cantankerous person that I was. I also served no useful purpose as a merchant, and my wealth was never used for the benefit of others. In my present position, I feel more than adequate and more than justified in keeping watch over the archangel Michael.'

'And eating and drinking,' asked Cervantes, 'and for other functions by which the body betrays its gross origin, how will these be taken care of?'

'This I have already thought of, as I have a tendency to become hungry,' said the Knight of the Table. 'I plan for my vigil to take place during the day from the hours of noon until midnight, when it most serves the devotional, and perhaps those merely curious, people of the region. After midnight, I will cleanse and feed myself, and prepare for the watch of the next day.'

'As we are talking about practicalities,' said Cervantes, 'I would like to propose a plan for combining the worship of God with a business venture, so that all due respect to God is performed, and that a thriving commercial concern continues to succeed.'

'You have unfailing politeness,' said the Knight of the Table, 'a characteristic that I could not fail to notice, even when I was so angry with you last night. But I am not sure of what you mean.'

'Well,' said Cervantes, 'we cannot determine when and how a person may suddenly become acquainted with God.'

'This is true,' said the Knight of the Table, 'and certainly true in my case.'

'In fact, God could visit you in any given place,' said Cervantes, 'whether you were busily engaged or no. It would be to your inconvenience and not his.'

'Again, this is true,' said the Knight of the Table, 'for God is behind all events.'

'Then,' said Cervantes, 'for the sake of our beloved tavern-keeper and for the trust that you place in your vision, let us discuss the distribution of alms. I have noticed that a plate has already been put out for the purpose –' and Cervantes indicated a plate overflowing with small coins '– and is already brimming with money.'

'Really?' said the Knight of the Table. 'I have hardly had time to think of such things because of tending my vision. Are you suggesting that the alms be redistributed to their previous owners and that the giving of alms be further discouraged?'

'No, no,' said Cervantes, 'for that would amount to a certain kind of blasphemy, for the giving of alms is indeed a token of our veneration for God. If he has seen fit to create a shrine in the quarter's busiest tavern, then we cannot say that God is wrong. I suggest that the alms be collected by the tavern-keeper as a means of providing the upkeep and maintenance of this new shrine. As a good man, he will ensure the cleanliness of the place, and provide shelter, food and drink for the many pilgrims that are sure to come visiting.'

'I can see,' said the Knight of the Table, 'that God has given you an enterprising way of conducting his veneration here on earth.'

'It is only to be wondered,' said Cervantes, 'that I cannot apply the same to my own personal fortunes.'

'You must excuse me,' said the Knight of the Table, 'for I detect that the archangel Michael is stirring, for perhaps I am too taken up with our discussion to pay due attention to my vision.'

'Then I will leave you,' said Cervantes, 'and take this plate of alms according to our new arrangement.'

However, things were not harmonious when Cervantes returned to the main drinking parlour. The tavern-keeper was barring the way out and brandishing a large roasting spit. 'And do you seriously think,' he was saying vehemently to the crowd of customers, 'that you can leave this establishment without paying due respect?'

'This establishment is a house of evil and a den of serpents,' said one of the regulars. 'We cannot live with the shame of being such regular patrons.'

'Shame!' roared the tavern-keeper. 'Why you were raised on beer and spirits, and if that were not shame enough, young master Elvio, then remember when you were so besotted with this place that you undertook to help paint it!'

'The ways of sin are subtle, for this is how I became initiated into this evil place,' said the one called Elvio.

'Aye,' said someone else in the crowd, 'and the respect due is to leave.'

'You are indeed as large a crowd of fools and buffoons as any likely to cross my threshold,' said the tavern-keeper. 'If it were not for a lump on a merchant's head, you would not wish to leave, for he put it in your mind that taverns were a bad thing.'

'He did not,' said one of the regulars, 'although the sight of him and his talk of visions did make us all religious.'

'And since when does that make a man leave a tavern in such a hurry?' demanded the tavern-keeper.

'Indeed, it does not,' said one, 'but taverns make a man poor.'

'Ah,' said the tavern-keeper triumphantly, shaking the spit, 'you were reminded of a sin, for YOU ALL OWE ME MONEY!' he shouted.

'Indeed not,' said the 'indeed' person in the crowd, 'but we paid the little money that we have in alms.'

'Heaven take it,' said the tavern-keeper, becoming more furious, 'that for a few alms, you are unable to buy a drink?'

'Why would we owe you money,' said Elvio, 'if we were not poor?' The regulars agreed in chorus. 'And are you,' continued Elvio, 'determined to make us poorer by the carrying of that spit?'

'This spit,' said the tavern-keeper, 'is self-protection, for if you were to become truly incensed by my pleas, then you might tear me limb from limb.'

'Whether you plead or not,' said Elvio, 'we're bound to leave, for the money that we had for drink we spent on alms.'

Cervantes then intervened to say that he had come to a solution after a discussion with the Knight of the Table. 'Therefore, this plate of alms that all of you so unquestioningly gave to the Knight of the Table shall go to our friend here the tavern-keeper,' said Cervantes, 'who shall then use them to provide shelter, food and drink for the wayfarers visiting our shrine.'

'And would these pilgrims and wayfarers include us?' asked Elvio.

'You are the best example,' said Cervantes. 'Honoured tavern-keeper of the shrine of the Knight of the Table, accept these pilgrim gifts.' He handed the plate of alms to the tavern-keeper.

'Willingly,' said the tavern-keeper, 'and as it so happens, I have on store a great amount of food and drink, immediately available, which these alms will more than pay for.'

So it was that the tavern became a shrine to the Knight of the Table, and alms were collected in a plate just inside the entrance by the tavern-keeper for his customers. It was well known that the tavern-keeper's business thrived, and that many pilgrims came to see the Knight of the Table and talk with him about his vision of the archangel Michael.

The Academy

Whispers, jealousies, and other cultural events.

*T*he Duchess did eventually read the poems that Ongora had left her. The volume was slim, and she was soon finished; their slight taste reminded her unwillingly of, in contrast, her husband's love for epics and martial poems, many of which he knew by heart. He would even recite the bawdy campfire songs of his soldiers, not sparing her delicacy, watching her flinch at the lewd words and phrases. He would sing and recite them in such a way that she would easily divine the meanings of the words. Why, she had asked, are they so foul? 'If you marched through the night in the rain with no food,' he had told her, 'then you would soon find it a relief to curse the hairy behinds of your enemies in song.' Something in her had remained troubled. The efficacy of an obscene lyric for venting feelings, yes. For men, yes, their coarser feelings and emotions needing to be contained, the keg for powder, yes. It was the abusiveness that troubled her, not the coarseness. She had even giggled at some inventive descriptions. But their aesthetic? Using words to attack? Is that necessary? Her husband had perceived her trouble. 'Because you are courageous,' he had said, 'I like to test you with the brutalities of my profession.'

'Yes,' she had said, 'but how is it that you can speak these words to your men, join with them in their sentiments, if you can call them that, and not find yourself reduced to the sensibilities of an animal?'

'I live in two worlds,' he had said, 'and our love is more piquant because of it. I bring the stories of my adventures, my experiences, and each time, it is like another wooing.'

'This does not answer my question,' she had said firmly.

'I was going to continue,' he had said, 'that retelling these experiences, here, with you, in this marvellous mansion, with Heaven knows a marvellous beauty listening, is like telling a story of another man's adventures.' He had paused. 'My men return from campaign to conditions just as hard. They do not love their wives, nor their wives them. They do not like their profession. They are poor. And yet, sometimes, while digging a ditch for their dead comrades, they will burst into song of such lewd humour – and I have protected you from the more explicit ones – that I would not swap their song for dinner with the Emperor.'

And now I am strayed into this retrospection, she thought, Ongora's poems neglected on her lap. She recalled some phrases. Fine, delicate, well-constructed, pertinent, and . . . He had dedicated some individual verses to her, the rest of the volume belonging to the Emperor. Why then, she thought, am I thinking of vulgar rhymes recited by my dead husband? Because it is something I prefer?

She sighed and leaned forward as though correcting her posture would straighten her mind.

She felt obligated by Ongora's gift in some way, and that she had taken so long to acknowledge it was an indication of how unwilling she was to resolve the debt. Her wager with Ongora was another matter. It would be thought of and encompassed in its own ready time. But the gift of the poems, the mention of the Emperor, her duties with the Academy, she found these all unwelcome at the moment. The activities of the Academy might well be suspended in the dusty months of courtiers travelling from Madrid to the new capital. But it nearly being the beginning of summer, visitors would be inevitable. And as Denia had also indicated, the activities of the Academy were likely to become more central to the new court, a thought she hardly relished. Then of course, the new Emperor might, in a brief fit of curiosity, feel the need to visit her. During which, God forbid, she would have to paint Cara like herself, rehearse her with a few polite statements, and leave her nodding to guests while she hid in her apartments. And if her heart were too oppressed, load up one of her husband's pistols, and show the Emperor how quickly death could be produced from it. From all report, the new Emperor would not even know that he was dead. But for now, the hope was that he did not visit.

But this did not mean neglecting the activities of the Academy. A recital of Ongora's poems would repay him and unify the Academy. Ongora, a newcomer, was heartily hated by the resident literati. But that was of no surprise. It was almost an initiation. Would it perhaps reduce the amount of sarcastic pamphleteering that had grown so rapidly? Happily, none of this kind of competitive exchange had occurred within her house. Their rapiers and insults had been brandished in the square, whilst they appeared in the best of smiles and linen at her mansion. They knew she would not tolerate it, and had often reproved some for 'a point of honour that is no more than envy, and hot disputes that are no more than bad-manners'. So a recital of Ongora's poems, to which everyone would be invited. It should be arranged at once. She would draw up a list of guests, and write the invitations herself.

Later, as the list grew, she wondered how her mind could decide on an action which her heart could not support.

Arranging Bucolics

An attempt to force the muse.

*O*ngora received a letter that morning. The crisp waxen folds rattled on his desk as he prodded it. He picked it up again. So formal, he thought, and so pre-emptory in its painful rebuff. The letter had returned with the book of Ongora's poems, the same that he had given to the Duchess. He poked at the letter again. Written, he continued in his mind, by the Emperor's secretary, whom he knew took on the shadow of his master's superiority and used it like a minor bully. He read the polite words, and comprehended the slight beneath them:

> The verses contained in this charmingly bound volume are well scribed and pertinent to their subject. However, they do not move the reader, and their content could hardly inspire anyone to achieve the end of the book. We expect more of our gifted friend, as perhaps he would of himself, were he not committed to the folly of writing prettily rather than profoundly, and we would urge him to remember that the subject of his attention is no less than his Emperor. Poetry in praise of the Emperor must be high praise indeed. Strive towards that end. To do more is your duty; to do less would be treasonable and an insult.

The letter was signed on behalf of the Emperor by his

secretary. But the postscript was a curiosity – it made him suspect that Denia had dictated the letter.

> PS. By the way, yesterday I saw a young student reading a book in the street; he was actually slapping his forehead and laughing in delight. When I enquired the cause of this youth's merriment, I was told that he was reading one of the latest comic adventures of the mad knight Don Quixote, written by Miguel Cervantes. The vitality of his prose is the envy of all, and an example for all writers.

> PPS. Perhaps you can save this beautiful binding for the next book. Until your verses 'ring like a bell in the highest tower', we can only stop our ears to your name.

That day, Ongora found fault with one of the pageboys, and thrashed him.

Ongora's mood changed briefly the following morning when he received the Duchess's invitation to read from his new collection of verses. He was in favour again, he thought. What if news of this should extend to the Emperor's ears; how could this be arranged? Then it lurched into him again that the Emperor's rebuff was not a small poisonous nightmare that he had just awoken from. He recalled the words and the crispy folds of the meticulous note, gavel knocks on his bare, exposed reputation. The note still lay on his desk. He felt contaminated by it, a canker inside and out. It made him vile, spotted with shallowness and inefficacy. And what if Denia had copied the note, and circulated it among the authors of reputation? Perhaps behind the still undrawn window coverings were ranks of mocking authors, pointing out the salient points of ridicule from their copies of the note. Even worse, Denia had ordered it printed, laying it carefully before the eyes of the precise Robles, who in turn would show it to that blonde-skinned idiot, his wife, and explain to her that the handsome, reckless poet was a shallow man with no more reputation than a precocious child.

He prodded the note as though it were noxious. He spied through the window coverings; no-one there, no retinue of ridicule. Why has Denia taken such dislike to me? he thought. How do I threaten him? Well, it will be some measure of satisfaction to destroy this Cervantes, Denia's creature, and to accomplish it through the Duchess. For although Denia has mastery over the Empire, and intends to glut himself with the power, the Duchess is inviolable; she's too popular. Her dead husband had been a hero.

And then perhaps, if the plan went well, and if the Duchess performed her part, then the debunking of Denia's soldier-poet would become the highlight of the year's gossip, and a subject for humour that even the Emperor could appreciate. Some tension between his regal highness and Denia, the royal favourite, is bound to happen, he thought, even as the Marquis's girth and quota of lands increases. To have this delicate deception honed to humiliate Denia . . . This was the aim in view. He could imagine himself, in glittering costume, treading on the face of a somehow older and dispirited Denia, that once smiling chevalier. And the Duchess would be attendant on him. And the Emperor would be smilingly gracious, and have his poems read aloud before banquets. So all would be well. If he was patient and pretended that nothing had happened.

He opened the top drawer of his desk and pushed the note into it with a rod from the brazier.

Perhaps he would go out and appear confidently in the square. Prod people with his rapier scabbard as he was wont, and challenge them to a war of verses (he was quite good at that, and entertaining). But it might be better to have a new poem to brandish. That meant writing it. So . . .

He looked around for inspiration. The villa was rented with furniture, which he disliked, and some faded carpets, which he hated. He rang for one of the pageboys. 'Go and bring some flowers,' he told a sullen youth.

Half the morning later, still in his night shirt and robe, he was fighting an irritation in his nose from the violent perfume of the meadow-sweet and jasmine branches that covered his desk. But there was nothing on the paper. Breakfast had not helped. He might have to rework one of his earlier poems, disguise it a little. He must appear, confident, with a sword and a poem. He bent over the page again.

The Continuing Adventures of the Old Knight

The infatuation of Bucephalus the mare.

*I*n the preparations for his quest, the old Knight had become aware of the demonic forces that were set against him. And so, as he and the love-smitten mare travelled the countryside, the old Knight took measures to ensure that demons did not make off with his armour, his faithful steed, or himself in the middle of the night. They would choose a spot together for the night, eat whatever victuals were to hand, sing a few half-remembered heroic ballads and then settle down to sleep. But not before the old Knight had securely tied the mare to himself, along with other valuable objects. This caused complications when, for example, the old Knight had to relieve himself, or one night, when the mare charged a tree that she saw moving and dragged the old Knight and his utensils for some yards before realising her mistake. There was also the problem of securing their camp-fire because, they had discovered, flames were uncharitable to rope. The old Knight solved this by first wetting the rope and then tying everything together, including himself, in a circle around the fire.

'This means,' he said to the mare, who listened to everything he had to say, 'that any demon trying to steal the fire will have to encounter us, and anyone trying to steal us will be revealed in the light of the flames.'

One night he sat up after a few restless hours and told the mare that he was far from satisfied that they had catered for every contingency, demons coming as they did in all shapes and sizes, and some whose malevolence towards human beings was expressed with subtle skill. He was convinced that a demon could make off with his interior being and leave him 'like a marionette, to continue, unequal and vacant to the task. There must be some way of testing that I am who I really am every morning, and similarly with you, Bucephalus, that you are who you really are, and that your real self has not been stolen, and malignantly replaced with the essence of a baboon.'

It was therefore agreed that before settling down, they were to shake each other's limbs, the old Knight taking the mare's foreleg and finding the mythic golden steed in his hand, whilst the mare would tremble and neigh softly at the odd delight she felt at the old Knight's touch. Similarly, they would do the same in the morning. And so it was that, until now, they have found themselves intact every morning.

Pedro's continuing encounters with both the old Knight and the mare neither improved his opinion of them or his luck.

On one occasion, Pedro met the old Knight, sitting backwards on the mare, wearing a large breastplate strapped upside down to his torso, with the large end of a telescope fixed to his eye.

'What are you looking for?' asked Pedro.

'I am spying out evil,' replied the old Knight.

'Well, it's right in front of you,' said Pedro, slyly.

'Where?' said the old Knight, looking again into the wrong end.

'The nose on your face,' said Pedro, and doubled up in laughter. His mirth increased the more he remembered the afflictions and blows he had experienced in the old Knight's company. Remaining poised at the end of the telescope, the old Knight looked down at him with what was, to Pedro, perhaps the most genial expression he had ever seen. 'You have made a joke at my expense,' he said gently, 'but my affection for you remains unchanged.'

This only made Pedro more sarcastic. 'Why,' he said loudly, 'do you insist on wearing your best piece of armour upside down on your body? Do you have no thought of which direction you are turned? Are you up or down? Tell me, which direction does rain fall to you? Is it the sky that is above you or the earth?'

The old Knight's response was confident. 'Even a chicken knows which way is up,' he said, 'otherwise it would stop its eggs from going to the bottom of the nest.'

'Knowledge that I am sure will make my life many times more interesting,' Pedro said.

'You obviously have no learning in the art of warfare,' said the old Knight, 'because it is well known that surprise is the master of combat. For a man in battle is a superstitious creature, and if anything out of the ordinary happens, then he'll run to save himself from it. Imagine how my enemies feel when I charge at them, roaring like a lion, and they see themselves reflected upside down in my armour!'

Pedro knew there was something wrong with this line of thinking. Eventually he said, 'Why, old Knight, that's ridiculous, because no matter which way a mirror is held, the reflection stands the right way up.'

'Well, there you are,' said the old Knight, 'that proves my point!'

'My guess,' said Pedro, 'is that proving a point is more painful for the meat than the spit. Tell me what it proves, although I feel uneasy even as I ask.'

'Well, imagine their surprise when they realise,' said the old Knight, 'that I don't know that!'

'There, you've done it,' said Pedro, 'you have hurt my brain and there's probably no repair, because as the yolk said to the shell, once you let me out, I'm never coming back.'

The Satire

A dictation from Dulcinea del Toboso, the uninterested
lady love of Don Quixote.

*T*he Duchess applied herself with a customary dedication to the task of writing the satire. Having
had the spark of invention in her discussion with
Ongora, she thought more of the kind of character
Dulcinea would be, and decided that it was time to study the
pamphlet that she had confiscated from Cara.

The pamphlet described an episode in which Don Quixote
and his faithful squire had found themselves at odds with some
muleteers who, angered by the crazed Knight's assertions as to
their character, had thoroughly beaten him and the squire with
large sticks.

The Duchess read the episode grimly. Acknowledging Ongora's
opinion that the work subverted the classical forms of the time,
she was also concerned that popular pamphlets cheapened
literature. If her satire succeeded, then it must point out that
anyone who could appreciate the pamphlet would be better
served in studying the classics. She finished reading the pamphlet
and realised that there had been very little amusement stimu-
lated in her. Why had she not smiled or laughed? Some subjects,
she thought, are too coarse to be amusing. She re-read the
pamphlet and finished with the same conclusion; nothing in
it made her laugh, and therefore, why did it amuse everyone
else, and to what end? She sent for her maid.

When Cara entered, she immediately saw the pamphlet, and her hands twisted anxiously in her apron. Would the Duchess forgive her or chastise her? She was terrified of both outcomes.

'Cara,' the Duchess said to the stricken maid, 'I have read the pamphlet that you appeared to enjoy so much.' The Duchess looked at the pamphlet by her side; was it innocent? She could not tell. Or perhaps, she would not say. Why? 'You will do me the goodness,' she said imperiously, 'of explaining why it is considered humorous.'

Her maid looked at her in real terror, for it crossed her mind that her mistress had begun to rave. Surely, it could not be explained why anything was funny?

'My Lady,' she said inadequately, and stopped.

Her mistress waited.

'The drawings are humorous,' she said. Her mistress said nothing and looked nothing. 'I mean, the old Knight looks funny. Because he is melancholic, and so serious, and dressed in old bits of armour, my Lady.'

The Duchess had not looked at the illustrations; nothing could be learned from them. Thus far, her maid was not convincing. 'Perhaps it is the context that is amusing,' she said, more to herself than the maid.

'Yes,' said Cara, 'it is funny, because he is dressed so peculiar, and speaks very finely, and he takes everything so seriously.'

The Duchess felt a peculiar warmth in her cheeks.

'One time,' continued Cara, 'it rained, and he could not open his visor because it had rusted shut.' She chortled. 'His squire had to bang it open with a stick.'

The Duchess had reddened completely.

Her maid stopped, suddenly aware of her mistress's discomfort and unable to account for it. 'My Lady,' she said in a small voice, 'I have heard some episodes read aloud. In a tavern.' This was difficult to admit for, as the servant to the Duchess, she should have unblemished amusements. But I am still young,

Cara thought to herself. And so is the Duchess, she thought, and wondered anew at the uncomfortable blush on her mistress' cheeks.

'I trust you in the choice of your pastimes, Cara,' said the Duchess remotely. She was caught in the feeling of having been intimately exposed, that some truth had been sounded and she had not comprehended it.

'Yes, my Lady,' said Cara and dipped deferentially.

'Bang it open with a stick,' the Duchess said to herself.

'My Lady?' said the maid, alarmed.

What has happened to me, the Duchess thought privately. Nothing in her maid's remarks had been said to cause harm, and yet she felt scalded by sensitivity. Her maid had merely described the character of Don Quixote as melancholic, and taking everything too seriously. So, she thought, this must relate directly to me, for the saying of it had made me very uncomfortable. 'Perhaps we can arrange to have such a reading of one of these episodes here,' she said absently to Cara, who having seen the silence of preoccupation in her mistress, had already turned to leave. 'Yes, my Lady,' said Cara and slipped out of the room.

I have lost all humour since the bereavement, thought the Duchess.

Having grasped the reason for the discomfort that had so affected her, she became grateful for Cara's consideration. There are so many in service to me, she thought. This affords little opportunity for informality, for any lightness.

I have lost all my humour, came the thought again. The realisation resounded. And then there were the other words that had so affected her; bang it open with a stick. Prising open the armour around a face; the image had swooped in on her like a blade. This meant some shell around her. Perhaps the preoccupation with salting her grief, making it acceptable to the limits of her mind, had made her remote, an uncharted island.

She looked down at the pamphlet at her side, and remembered the sound of Cara's laughter in the closet. It was strange, the maid had hidden herself the better for her enjoyment. And then she remembered the first perception when she had confiscated the pamphlet, how something so crafted could also be so carefree.

She suddenly saw herself as the ghost that haunted the mansion, while her servants and retainers waited respectfully, and from not a little fear, as their mistress paced the floors of her misery. She had thought herself capable of compromising grief by the rational; books, the Academy, her mind. But her mind had become a hollow tower, disassociated from the turmoil of her heart and senses. Thinking herself capable of scouring grief from her soul with the books of philosophy, she had been walled in.

She stood, and as if to compound her painful analysis, her limbs creaked, and she felt light-headed, as though her mind had become vapour. She would write the satire, she decided, for that would lighten this self-imposed, tyrannical gloom. Lighten the mind to ease the heart. The exercise would bring her self-preoccupation from the shadows.

She sat down at the desk. Pen and paper were at hand. An exercise in lightness. She was ready.

The satire opened with some invented remarks of a clerk, who had been bidden by Dulcinea to set down her declaration, for she had not learned to read or write. The clerk had explained the peculiar summons he had received to take the dictation of Dulcinea, and in a small tone of complaint, that little could be done with the punctuation of the piece for Dulcinea had been peculiarly excited. The clerk also complained that he had not yet received payment for his work, and would like the world to know that he was owed money, and that he should not be expected to perform his labours for free. He would have demanded payment of Dulcinea, but that she seemed a large and imposing person, and he had not wanted to irritate her. But the world should know that a professional clerk does not work for free, and should the world require his services, they should come with money, or satisfy their demands by learning to read and write.

The satire, as dictated by Dulcinea, then continued:

As all the people in this region and those beyond have come to know of a certain mad old fool's passion for my person, it has been advised by my own good senses and the good senses of the kin in my household that I should protect my name and my person, not that I need that kind of protection, for I could whack the old fool so hard that he would not be able to rise for an age, no, not even for a month. So being advised, and confident in the strength of my limbs, I have come to say to those reading, that the old fool is an old fool, whose person, being abhorrent, must not be imagined to accompany mine in the marriage bed, the Lord save me, and that chivalry is dead, and therefore a meaningless profession for young and old alike. This last point was given me by my kin, and therefore is not close to my heart, as is that ire and disdain which I feel whenever I see the old fool lurking in my yard, and such shall be the punishment that I will administer on him, that he shall be afraid of pitch forks for eternity. This then is my statement to the old fool, and it shall be published in print, and circulated to the whole population, as a warning of dire urgency, and to keep certain persons like the old fool from approaching my person. Here is the statement.

One, that I, Dulcinea del Toboso, am considered a strong girl for my age, and shall mistreat any that shall attempt to take me with the force of arms.

Two, that I am determined to marry a baker from the next town, who has wooed me from the first, and can buy me a new dress every year, and he does not look like a thing of twigs, as does the old fool, and is fat and healthy.

Three, that I am not one who takes readily to fancies and romances, as I have seen too much of the midden for fantastics to please me.

Four, that I have been angry for a long time now, and were it to be that the old fool and myself should be bonded in a matrimony, I should be hard to live with, not getting over the ire for at least a month or more, which is a misery for any newly-weds, and I say this as a protection against the old fool, although should he come near me, I would not afford him any.

And so the satire continued, with a long list of threats and mistreatments promised by Dulcinea against the person of Don Quixote. Dulcinea finished with a diatribe against all 'old fools' and a recommendation that they be generally inspected and, if found wanting in a certain soundness of the brain, thence exported to the hills, and left to conduct their mad fancies on each other, and any rock, goat, or crag that their illusions take as maidens, dragons, and wizards. She recommends the founding of a community for this purpose called 'Senility', and that villages and towns be guarded against the entrance of old fools from this community, and that if these derelicts should replicate themselves, God forbid, then these progeny should be kept away from the walls of all sane towns and cities.

The satire ended with a postscript from one of Dulcinea's brothers, who promised to stand on guard outside Dulcinea's room, and thwack any mad person who came close.

Having finished, the Duchess had an impulse to send for Cara and read it aloud to her. But then she must protect the anonymity of it, and it would bring some satisfaction in the future perhaps, should Cara discover that her mistress was the cause of a dangerous amusement that, in another moment, she had confiscated. She read the satire over again and experienced a slight savour of distaste; was it her nature to pen something so facile? But then, it was satisfying to have so freely entered the world of buffoons and to have so easily taken command. She would send the satire that afternoon to Ongora, and if anything were amiss with it, he would, she was sure, delicately let her know. But she did not think he would find anything wrong with it. It was a small but definite triumph. Perhaps there was more to be made of her abilities than she had thought.

However, the next day found her with another temperament.

The Evil Poetry Reading

The old Knight's first battle and escape.

*J*t was the day of Ongora's recital, and he had already arrived, a good deal too early, with one of his boys, and was rehearsing in the salon. The Duchess, having received news of Ongora's arrival, sent a message with Cara that she would be attendant, and guests would be arriving within the half hour. Cara left her, and the Duchess, having turned to another detail in her administration of the mansion, thought it better to go down herself and greet Ongora. She would then come back up and dress.

Her timing was acute. She was in sight of the vestibule when she saw Ongora, standing rehearsing his cue to enter the salon, violently slap his pageboy. Ongora did not see her witness this, nor see her turn and make rapidly for her apartment. Once inside the room, she leant against the door and breathed deep . . . It was not the blow, so much, although it had had unnecessary force. True, the boy was mulish, and she might have dressed him with her tongue herself. It was that the boy had expected the blow, that it was inevitable, whether he stood at a point or no. And it was the reason: that Ongora's rehearsed entrance to the salon, to the audience, must be perfect or else someone was to be punished. She had seen that Ongora's blow was not a simple reprimand, but contained a nasty anger. His rage was the living coal of what? I must remonstrate with him, she thought, because it cannot please anyone to see a boy so badly used.

How have I not seen this of him before? she then thought. A light knock on the door, and while her mind still held to this thought, she turned and opened it. Cara bobbed, and said, 'The guests are arriving, my Lady, the kitchen is setting up, and the windows have been opened on to the garden.'

'Make sure the kitchen finishes in good time. We do not want their sound during the recital.'

'Señor Ongora asked me if you would consent to introduce the theme for the recital, my Lady.'

Something in the Duchess darkened. 'I have no answer to that,' she said. 'Go and help finish preparations.'

Cara was no longer surprised by the Duchess's peremptory fits and quickly departed.

This left the Duchess some time to discover what her heart had already divulged. There were now a host of feelings and realisations that had converged on her during this brief exchange with her maid. She had once seen her husband, having received a letter from his company-commander, sit down in his undershirt on the floor of his study and pour forth a mourning, impassioned tirade. Once restored to his usual balanced manner, he had discussed with her the contents of the letter, a report that a number of his men had been caught selling supplies to the enemy and falsifying the accounts. His feelings were not so much that his men would engage in this type of petty crime without any thought to its treasonous results, nor of the inevitable result of being caught, but how their dishonesty had escaped him. 'I know my men,' he said to her in distress. 'I know how they march, carry arms, curse, fight, walk, talk, and think. I know them by name, their age and rank, their aptitude in battle, their reasons – many dubious – for fighting. But why is it that I did not see this?' He was asking her rhetorically. He shook with the paper. 'Many of them are already hanged.'

'You blame yourself?' she asked.

'I do,' he said definitely. 'If I had not believed in their lies, they would be alive and in the service of the Emperor even now.' He leaned towards her passionately. 'They hid themselves from me, and it was easy. I did not see it, because I believed in their flattery.'

So now I have it, she thought, and the lesion between my mind and my feelings can only be healed with such truths. But why truth in retrospect, when truth in advance would pre-empt many mistakes? She sighed. I can only go so deep. And in the meantime, my present understanding is still to be thought out. And her understanding of Ongora? I have not seen his violence, she thought, because he commends me ceaselessly, and I strive not to let his praises affect me. My principles, my desire for nobility, my aspiration to a cultivated and elevated life, all this he can manipulate.

She must dress; guests were waiting for her. And she must find some suitable comment for Ongora's poems, even though her mind had not been able to find a purchase in them. And he was sure to ask her. Listening to the recital might prove them to her hearing. But then the reason for organising the recital now seemed hollow. None would appreciate it, listening in envy, perhaps derision. The thought of the recital was repugnant. She had no desire to attend.

True enough, the salon had filled and Ongora was poised for an entrance. They were all waiting for the Duchess. Cara avoided Ongora, and tried to look busy, even though everything was ready. Where was her mistress? Cara thought she knew. She had seen the lady's last mood. She went upstairs and tapped deferentially on her mistress's door. Nothing. Cara's mind raced and she decided on an initiative that would save the occasion, excuse her mistress, and might only be of small risk to herself. Although given the moods of her mistress, it might be anything from banishment to kindness. If gratitude were earned, then maybe she would be forgiven the pamphlet. Although it was still hard for her to understand why a series of comic adventures should so disturb her mistress. Cara shook her head, and then went to her own chamber. She must dress.

So it was that Cara appeared some minutes later at the main entrance of the salon, and after a whispered consultation with the steward, the doors opened and she entered upon the hushed audience. Although fashionably veiled, Cara knew that everyone could see that she was never the Duchess, but it also satisfied her, as she approached the ancestral chair of her mistress, that the guests remained quiet and her walk did not falter. Once at the seat – there was a slight hesitation when habit nearly made her take the smaller seat to the left of the Duchess's own – she tapped the arm of the chair with her fan. As the doors of the salon closed, she unhurriedly adjusted the folds of her gown. There was a supreme hush in the room. Cara knew that she had a small voice, unlike the contained yet lustrous tones of her mistress. But she used it to good purpose and announced, 'Members of the Academy, honoured guests, and fair friends it is with regret that the Duchess is unable to attend us this afternoon.' She paused. The guests waited. 'As you are all aware, the Emperor, having chosen Valladolid as his new home, has since sent special instructions to the Duchess, begging her attendance on him.' There was a murmur of interest. 'He has heard of the activities of the Academy, and has asked her to furnish him with a list of the artists that are its members.' She thought the lie an adequate one, and was gratified at the murmured zeal from the guests. 'Having finished this urgent duty, the Duchess may well yet attend. Now let us hear from one of its newest members, Luis Ongora.' She sat down, and the guests, relieved that all mystery had been harmonised into the excitement of the Emperor's attention, settled as well. Cara only hoped that the Duchess, if she roused from her mood, would notice the hurried note that she had left outside the door.

Ongora heard all this, stationed with his boy in one of the side entrances to the salon, and found the uncomfortable rouge of his embarrassment hard to bear. He cursed the Duchess; had she forsaken him? A dull report of the members of the Academy? That was imperial rote, a hangover from the Emperor's father who had kept a list of everything. What was she doing? Any fool could compile the list. What had happened?

The doors opened. He yanked the boy and booted him into position. The boy was to lead him in, a conceit of the ancient tradition of a pliable youth leading Homer's blind bard. The boy began pacing forwards, leading him. Ongora smiled at the faces of the audience, his fingers clenched cruelly on the boy's shoulder.

Earlier that afternoon, the old Knight had traced the progress of a placid river and found himself on the Duchess's estate. He had wandered through the game parks and, eventually seeing the mansion, tied Bucephalus to a bridge across the river and prepared himself for what he felt certain was the next adventure. The gardens impressed him with their distant layering of arranged lawns and classical statuary. He found a grotto of small trees, a love seat under the helm of Dionysius. Next, he discovered some secret steps leading to a pool, decorated with Etruscan tiles. Hidden, shadowed, cool, the sun filtered through the green weight of wisteria. In full view of the house again, he marvelled at the beauty of the grounds, and wondered what kind of enchantment had set this place. Was it intended to entrap or delight? He shook his head. No, the genius of beauty that created this had no evil purpose. He came closer to the house. There were large windows, opened out onto the lawn, and for the first time he could see a number of people in the house. The calm of the garden had almost persuaded him that there were no inhabitants. He must see what the denizens of this extraordinary place were doing.

Some yards from the house and the old Knight could hear a voice raised in special tones. He stopped and listened. Something was disquieting about it. It sounded like a strange kind of litany. A few yards later, and the old Knight, now wary, could see into the room. What he saw began to reverse his so far admiring impression of the place. Rows and rows of human beings were sitting facing one direction, as though locked into their chairs, wearing expressions of almost absolute vacancy. The prisoners, as it seemed to him, were doing nothing. They were not talking, eating, or watching a spectacle. The dangerous litany was coming from a single individual, and it seemed as though the prisoners were held fast to it, as though chained. The old Knight turned his attention to the strange warden of these poor unfortunates, and his impression was indeed unpleasant.

Ongora had coiled his hair into ringlets and was wearing a turquoise jacket of iridescent vanity. He was powdered and perfumed, carried a white ivory stick – sometimes to punctuate the rhythm of the verses and sometimes to support a pretended exhaustion from the turbulence of the muse – and he let the pages of his poems drift to the floor when he had completed reading each one. His eyes were shut, but for an occasional glance at the pages in his hand.

The old Knight knew that he had found the chief demon of the area, and that this was a more powerful kin of evil than the buffoonish malignancies of Fabritinex. The demon had caused a spell to be cast on a room full of souls, and had wiled them with a potion of terrible verses. He listened again. Indeed, yes, the blue demon was a superior magician, who magicked his victims with terrible poems.

For Ongora, the recital was going well. Though a hot afternoon, the doors and windows were open on the salon, its classic interior irradiated by the light from the stones of the garden walks. As had been required by the Duchess, most of the members of the Academy were there, along with visitors and those on retainer to the Duchess's household.

Ongora introduced each poem, as was customary, with the cause of its original inspiration. Or at least, he presented an idyllic lie, and to please himself would recall in his mind the real event behind the verse. 'This was composed on a particularly hot day in summer –' an afternoon tryst with Micaela, his dissolute mistress '– when from my window, I observed an innocent maid walking with her basket through the trees of my estate.' They had finished love-making, and were leaning out of the window, looking at the crowded back streets. They could see a girl, reddened from the sun, wringing linens in her porch. 'I had been reading something philosophical –' Micaela commented on the girl's sullen look; perhaps she was still a virgin '– and so the conception of this poem is written in the high style of the early Italian sonnets.' His smile, directed at the audience, was at the thought of Micaela, who had suggested that he seduce the girl.

Ongora did not really read to his audience. It was as if they did not exist and he was talking rather loudly to himself. The pastor drowsed into sleep, lulled by Ongora's affected delivery, and then began to snore. Irritated by the interruption, Ongora signalled one of his pageboys, who prodded the pastor.

At the same moment, the old Knight clambered through the window into the room, ready for an encounter with this new demon, saying aloud to himself, 'I must establish with a touch of a hand the true character and nature of this creature.'

He walked towards Ongora, who was startled by the appearance of this bizarrely dressed visitor. 'For example,' continued the old man, while others in the room watched him with astonishment, 'when I left the asylum and shook the warden's hand, it revealed the character of a playful child. And then, although I was not allowed to touch the hand of the Marquis, I'm sure it would have revealed the claw of some ghoulish spirit.' Ongora could only stand in surprise, snatched from the reverie of memory and the pleasure of his own words. 'Now all I need to do is grasp the hand of this seemingly interminable creature, and it will be revealed that it is a –' and at this moment, he took the tentative hand of Ongora '– serpent!'

The moment was a shock for both of them, and it reverberated through the room. The old Knight actually jumped from the shock of finding the sinister coils of a serpent under the skin of the poet's hand. Ongora jumped as well, for he had already conceived that the old Knight was an assassin, sent by a disgruntled husband, a jealous lover, an envious writer, whomever. His mind was full of enemies.

The moment however was different for the audience. Some attending thought that the old Knight was a diversion, and that Ongora was experimenting with a dramatic element to his recitation. Accordingly, they nodded in polite approval and contributed tiny applause. Others saw clearly what had happened; an old man had climbed in through the window and, talking to himself, had shaken hands with Ongora and concluded that the poet was a reptile. Whatever the condition of the old man's mental state, the manner of his attire, or his unconventional manner of entering the room, they thought him quite correct in his summation of Ongora's character. There began in the salon the unmistakable sound of sniggering.

Ongora stood amazed. Someone woke up and began applauding, calling out, 'Bravo, bravo,' as though condoning the sudden atmosphere of mockery.

At that point, the Duchess entered.

She had heard that something was amiss. A servant had finally roused her from her room. In her mood of reckless despair, she had heard small, deferential tones at the door. 'My Lady, there is a madman in the salon.' A madman? thought the Duchess. 'Wait,' she said. Her body, as she raised it from the bed, was stiff. The faultless pleats of her dress swayed as she recovered, and stood. How will it be, she thought, when the madwoman meets the madman?

The effect of the Duchess's entrance was immediate. The sniggering stopped. The servants held their breath. There has never been anyone so beautiful, thought Ongora. He was surprised at his own absolute statement. Her eyes, continued his rhapsody, her bearing, her sensual figure, her gravity. Somehow, he lost control of the papers in his hand and they dropped to the floor.

The Duchess meanwhile had regarded those in the room, and had already registered that there was a stranger among them, standing close to her. She did not falter and brought her gaze around to whom she already knew was the 'madman in the salon'. Her deliberation was also a moment of savouring for her. What would be in the eyes, she thought, of someone whose interior world had rebelled and was laying siege to reality?

But the moment her eyes came to rest on the old Knight, he bowed. She recognised that the bow was very low, correct, and expertly done. There was a moment of due silence, then the old Knight raised himself and said, 'My Lady.' His eyes are so benign, she thought, there must be a mistake. She nodded politely and said, 'Sir.' He gestured with the salute of a soldier, which surprised her. 'You are very formal for an intruder,' she said.

'It is a rule of chivalry,' he answered immediately, 'to honour the beauty of a sword.'

'And where is this sword?' asked the Duchess.

'You are the sword,' said the old Knight, 'the purest, most finely tempered steel that I have encountered in my long life. God give it to your mind that such a sword be used for the greater glory of God, and not for the hateful ends of a demon's malignancy.' The Knight turned and looked at Ongora. The Duchess followed his look. Ongora smiled deprecatingly. When the Duchess turned again to the old Knight, he was already half through the window. 'Stop,' she said. He turned and looked at her. 'You must forgive my trespass,' he said politely, 'but God has directed me in search of an evil magician, and such matters do not allow for niceties.' He paused, considering her reflectively. 'Were I not on my quest, and were it not for the terrible consequences of Lancelot's love for Guinevere, I would say that you are the most splendid woman I have ever looked upon.' Ongora was startled by hearing his recent appreciative thoughts so closely echoed. 'I must now withdraw to consider how to combat the evil infesting your domain.' The look the old Knight directed at Ongora was almost meditative. 'May your beauty live forever,' said the old Knight to the Duchess, and turning, marched through the gardens.

The old Knight's statement so utterly charmed her, she felt coy, like a girl, and could not think that what he had said was flattery.

Ongora had already left the salon, to avoid the difficulties of his anger with the Duchess, his mind passing swiftly on to plans of retribution against the madman. The old fool had interrupted his recital and called him names. Further, if anyone dared to interfere with his good-standing with others, then let them beware! He had already given instructions to one of his pageboys.

Having left the mansion, the old Knight resumed a careful reconnoitre of the grounds, listening for the sounds of pursuit from the evil magician. He had wondered at the presence of the Duchess within the vicinity of such a deadly influence, 'for beauty has come so close to danger,' and concluded that this was the work of God. 'For how else could beauty become wise?' The old Knight was also enjoying his sojourn in the garden, and it took some time to reach the bridge where he had tethered the mare. Here events caught up with him.

As he stepped on the bridge, he was challenged by a trio of Ongora's servants, breathless after running from the mansion. 'We have been sent to incinerate you,' panted the first servant, 'on the orders of our master.'

The old Knight nodded comfortably. 'You have me at a disadvantage,' he said, 'and without weapons, which was no doubt the intention of your evil master.'

'You are outnumbered,' said the first servant. 'I have a rope, and as you can see, he has a garden rake, and this one is a boxing champion.'

The old Knight smiled at them and rolled his sleeves. 'You shall have to catch me first,' he said. 'I warn you that my right arm is endowed with the strength of God,' and he squared into a boxing stance.

Prodded on by his companions, the boxing champion shuffled a few steps forward and crouched belligerently. They were all on the bridge by now, and the following sequence of events took no more than a few seconds to complete.

The old Knight launched such a scalding left hook, that the boxing champion found himself sitting down on the bridge, holding his bloodied nose, and shaking his head in disbelief. The first servant then charged with his garden rake. At the same time, the servant with the rope tried to lasso the old Knight, but missed and harnessed the servant with the garden rake instead. By this time, the old Knight had taken a serene, vertical dive off the bridge into the river. Overcome by the impetus of his charge and wearing the lasso, the servant with the garden rake, shouting in dismay, followed the old Knight into the river. Shocked by their rapid disappearance, the servant with the rope rushed to the rail. But by this time, the current had already carried the servant with the garden rake down river after the old Knight. The servant with the rope had just enough time to observe this, when the rope tautened in his hands, and with a jerk that he could not resist, pulled him into the water.

Now the mare who, tethered on the far side of the bridge, had watched all of this with equine amusement, decided that as everyone else had gone for a swim she would go also. She slipped the casually tied tether around her neck, and clambered into the water, a little fretful to catch up with the old Knight, whose songs of winged steeds and golden heroes were still vibrant in her ears.

The boxing champion returned to Ongora and stoically reported all that had happened on the bridge. Ongora was enraged, calling him a 'mindless baboon' and declaring that they needed a search party now not only for the old man but for their brains. As the tirade continued, the boxing champion became gloomy. He finally said that interfering with the old man was a sure route to hell, for what did one expect from trying to catch a Don Quixote?

'What do you mean?' demanded Ongora.

'Either the book has come to life, or the living has been put into the book,' said the boxing champion, 'for there's not a pea's difference between them.'

This was a revelation to Ongora, and he could only stand open-mouthed at its implications.

The Poet's Progress

The satire and an anonymous Introduction.

*H*umiliation, anger, revelation, Ongora faced them all the morning following the recital. But there were compensations. He received a package, the loose manuscript of the Duchess's satire. Included was a note in her careful script, which – and he carefully read the note several times – had not the slightest hint of vanity in her accomplishment. The note asked him to read the manuscript and prepare it for publication – if it was suitable – as was agreed between them. He smiled at this, at her trust. He realised that, fresh from his bed, naked under his bed-robe, his casual physical adjunct to her considered lines would be something she could hardly have imagined. He enjoyed this; her Olympian mountain air and bracing winds, his Dionysian reek of cooled heat, the attar of his pleasure. He enjoyed the secret rules of their communication: that while he fed her illusion, she fed his sensuality.

He made it his duty to read the satire that day, and finished that morning, finding the short document as good if not better than he had hoped. He would continue the publication of it as soon as possible, while blemishing it in the mind of the Duchess, probably by praising it too much. It will be sufficient, he thought, to distribute it at the court and have everyone laughing at Cervantes within a month. Everyone will wonder who has written such a well-turned piece. He would then release it delicately, like a whisper in a vault, that the Duchess was the author. With a few phrases written in an afternoon, the Duchess would prove Cervantes' ineligibility at court. And then of course, he would rumour it that the Duchess's mentor in her new found satirical skills was he, smiling in modesty, the best poet in the land, and the soon-to-be Emperor's choice.

Micaela came to him that night, roused from her performance on stage. As the Duchess had been much on his mind, he could not help but make comparisons. His actress, he thought, and his Goddess. It was an irony, he realised, that Micaela was playing a goddess in some brief piece; she was hardly made for divinity, for her particular beauty – the length of her lip, her cruel flirting, the instinctive acquisitiveness of her eyes – had all the marks of danger.

They drank wine, talked casually, disrobed. They enjoyed the hardness in each other. As their ambitions made love, Ongora's mind turned the possibilities of the accomplished satire.

Having finished, with Micaela peacefully under covers, Ongora's mind continued musing in the dark. He knew that the Duchess's satire would, of course, find its mark. But perhaps there was something more. He could write an introduction, as was the convention, write it anonymously, and have them both published as a whole. Once written, the introduction and the satire would adequately prove that Cervantes' prose had no distinction, for anyone could write the same. Cervantes' defeat would be complete.

He rose from the bed, quickly draping a gown about him, and furnished a light for himself at the desk. Now that he had a subject – the humiliation of another – the tongue in his pen was eloquent enough. His introduction was a mocking catalogue; Cervantes' wounds, his sexual inadequacy and inferior social position. The voice of mockery would make the humiliation complete, he thought, and if this did not reduce Cervantes to the status of mud, then he, Ongora, could never bless his own hand.

The work was quick. Ongora was unleashing his own wounds on the page. Let these few paragraphs lie, he thought, for tomorrow's light. He turned back to the bed, the burnished heat of his mistress' breasts and, made languourous by her sighs and the satisfaction of his ploys, he drifted into sleep to dream of laurel wreaths and accolades.

Instructions on Printing the Satire

The commission of an enemy.

*J*t had already been a difficult morning for Robles. His boy had delivered him a number of manuscripts for printing, which were more than usually undistinguished. As he flipped through, he could find nothing that was not either mundane or bizarre. He wondered then if his reputation as a printer hung upon the curious collection of diatribes that he produced, just as his reputation as a man, or rather lack of it, was deduced from advancing age married to a beautiful wife. Just as these pamphlets set out to be serious works and then missed their mark, he thought, so I have married and have yet to win the love of my wife. The sincerity of one's aim or desire does not produce the end.

'Diego,' said a soft voice. It was his wife, and she looked frightened. Before he knew it, she was in his arms and clutching him like a child. 'What is it?' he asked her, as she trembled. 'I rose early. There is much work to do.'

'It was a nightmare,' she said, embracing him hard.

'Maybe you should write it down and print it. It would be better than many of these tall tales,' he said, indicating the manuscripts on his desk.

'A cruel man,' she said into his chest, 'who wanted to scratch me with his rapier.'

'And then you awoke,' said Robles, who was a realist, 'and

discovered a feather in your bed, and thought that it was time to have breakfast, and went downstairs, and were embraced by your loving husband.'

She withdrew and looked at him seriously. You Goddess, he thought.

'Is that it?' she asked.

'It is like one of those curiosities,' he said. 'A man dreams that he is lost in the mountains in the wild snow, and then he awakes and finds the window open and that the rain has blown in.' She was now looking at him with what he thought was her usual childlike vacancy. But then he reviewed this. There was something about her attention – her luminous eyes, her slightly open mouth – that he had missed. He sat on the edge of the desk. Their faces were now level. 'Do you remember that you dreamed of your mother, that she was going away for her holiday. She was dressed in her travelling clothes, and she blessed you and told you to look after the house. She was very happy. Do you remember?' She nodded slowly. 'And then the next week, she died.' Her eyes were wet. 'Come,' he said, 'it's meant to be a curious story, not a sad one.'

'She was wearing her travelling mantle,' she said, 'and her gloves were very fine.'

Robles said nothing for he had just discovered a great secret. He had realised that he knew now how to inspire her devotion. Because love for her was uncomplicated. She would freely give it, he realised, if he only took time to cosset her dreams, listen to her fears, and tell her a few stories. Nothing could be simpler. And why, he thought caustically, none of these erudite and esoteric pamphlets could tell me this is a mystery beyond even the power of God to solve. Although, come to think of it, he thought, why his own brain had not conceived of this was another question. He should reserve this for a private discussion between himself and a bottle of liquor.

At that moment, the door of the shop jangled. Robles and

his wife were in the back of the shop. Having achieved this level of intimacy with her, Robles did not want to forgo it. He wanted to impress on her that this, so far, had been for him the most important moment of their liaison. And he also feared the intrusion of a customer on their private moment. There were further sounds of activity within the shop. He signalled his wife to hush, and then said to her quietly, 'I must attend to the shop. But in a short while, if you are agreeable, let us share breakfast together.'

She nodded her head. 'I always keep a place for you. But you have never come. You are always busy.' She said this without any recrimination.

Robles gaped, which was unnatural for him, then quickly recovered. He was discovering a good deal this morning. He watched her leave, and then went into the main part of the shop.

Standing before him, handsomely dishevelled, was Ongora. Waking from his bout of written invective, and finding the stains of Micaela still on him, he had dressed rapidly, leaving his shirt open, and his hair unprepared. He wanted an animal sheen about him.

He shook a curl from his face, and produced a satchel that contained the satire and his introduction. He placed this on the counter, and then unhitched his rapier and scabbard and laid them across the counter as well. The effect was, as he had calculated, a forceful one. Robles regarded this display with irony. He flicked the rapier with one of the pamphlets. 'It is rare to see the dissolute up so early in the morning.' Ongora leered and took out the manuscripts from the satchel. 'I associate with you because you are a tradesman, and appended to my position,' he said. 'Nothing else distinguishes you. Other than that brown skinned Venus that you keep hereabouts in horribly indifferent clothes. Your wife, as she calls herself. Or is that fantasy?'

Robles then divined that it was Ongora's attentions that had caused his wife's nightmare. Flattery, good looks, a poet's effusion, they could not hide this gentleman's particular nastiness. His wife had sensed the violence in Ongora.

'Do you expect me,' said Robles, 'to do business with you after these insults?'

Ongora dismissed this with a contemptuous gesture. 'I want these two documents bound in one. This public letter serves as the prelude to the main part,' he said holding up the introduction and the satire. 'A thousand printed and circulated by next week.'

Robles continued looking at him coolly. 'I can make you,' said Ongora nastily, 'and it would be better to obey me, than to have someone in power force you. Which I can easily arrange.'

'Money,' said Robles, 'for no power, nor any dignitary with whom you share the same whore, can force me to print without a fee.'

Ongora slammed down the documents and held out a bag of coins.

'You will excuse me if I count the coins, as your last fee was underpaid,' said Robles. He steadily counted coins while Ongora seethed. 'There is more here than is needed for your new project and your previous debt. But I shall hold this on account, if not at least as recompense for your manners, and for the unwanted attentions that you have paid my wife.' Robles pocketed the coins and then looked calmly at Ongora. 'Now, what is it that you require printing?'

'It is a satire,' Ongora said deliberately, as though Robles were hard of hearing and stupid. 'Written by an eminent person, who shall remain anonymous, to which I have written an introductory letter. I am also to remain anonymous.'

'Written by two no-ones,' said Robles. 'This should amount to a large nothing.' He examined the manuscript of the satire. Carefully scribed, legible, which was to be thankful for. 'A satire of what?' he asked.

'You sometimes print the episodes of an ex-soldier and dilettante on the delusions of an old man who fancies himself in the age of chivalry.' Ongora's eyebrows lifted in mannered surprise. 'Perhaps it is a portrait of you.'

Robles ignored this. 'You mean Cervantes?' he said. 'I would be careful. His episodes are popular. If you hope to raise a laugh at his expense, best make your jibes at home.'

'Popular with whom?' said Ongora. 'Illiterates, students, drunks, and the rabble, many of whom cannot even afford to buy his deluded tales.'

'More than that,' said Robles evenly. 'Even the Emperor is aware of his popularity. Recognition that you cannot ignore.'

Ongora turned a discomfited rouge. 'It is fashion, nothing more. It is the latest hair, that is all, of which everyone is aware, whether high- or low-born.'

'I will be interested in how this turns out,' Robles said. 'If the satire is good, it may well increase Cervantes popularity.'

Ongora smiled. 'I doubt this will be the result.' He turned and left the shop.

Robles now wondered what harm the satire intended. Who had written it? He looked through the manuscript, smiling occasionally. Well, yes there was ridicule here. But harm? If anything, this would fuel Cervantes' popularity. He turned his attention to the open letter that Ongora had said that he had written. Ah yes, the poison was here. Here was a sentence that informed the public that Cervantes had been cuckolded. Another phrase ridiculed Cervantes' crippled hand. So if the introduction was taken with the satire, then the attack was monstrous, very uncharitable. Yes, the satire will smart Cervantes like a schoolmaster's lash, thought Robles, but Ongora's introductory letter will prove a real flogging.

So should he print it?

He had no choice. He had already taken the fee. And he had long ago decided that if he formed opinions as to the fine ideals and aspirations of the authors who came to him and their works, he would soon be out of business. And if you take the tongue out of a man's head, then he will come at you with a sword. Unless he could be tried for printing treasonable material, or considered a warlock for printing moon-rites over triple-horned toads, or found blasphemous for printing arguments against the Church, then any madman could pay him money to print their ravings. If he could make a living from the opinions of others, then so be it.

But of course, it would be a disaster for Cervantes, and he had put so much hope into these episodes. If the satire proved effective, its anonymous authors would be famous in a week. The taverns would rock with jeering, theatre clowns would read out the choicest invectives to warm the audience, and gossips would salivate the details in the salons. Ongora had indeed founded a pretty piece of mischief, one that could make Cervantes a pathetic absurdity.

I should tell him, thought Robles. It would at least enable him to prepare a defence. But this again was against his principles. If he took sides in any of the pamphlet wars that raged in the new capital, then his business would be seen as partisan. So he must print these insults against his friend. That would be a private storm, rather than the public quarrel that Ongora seemed intent on producing.

Why is this young man, he wondered, inspired with such venom towards Cervantes? Why can he not be content with his advantages? It cannot come to any good. He thought of Cervantes. The deities of providence have chosen this lanky, unsung hero of the wars on which to practise all their afflictions. It must be that he has such unassailable humour, that he is besieged with so many grievances.

He turned back to the manuscripts. These were now a practical task. He took the pages and began to spread them out.

An hour later, he made a discovery. He searched in a box among receipts and letters requesting his work. It did not take him long to find a paper with elegant writing. The crest was notable. He studied the writing and then went back to a page from the satire; the writing was the same. He knew that all educated hands wrote in more or less the same way. But the writing of the satire was particularly well scribed. So now he knew the anonymous author of the satire. He wondered why Ongora had been careless in protecting the identity of its author. Perhaps Ongora had not been able to wait, Robles thought. Or maybe his primary unpleasantness could no longer be hidden. It was that which could not wait.

The Satire's Effect

Mirth and humiliation.

*A*nd so it was that a week later, as Pedro took his customary walk through the lower quarters, he was greeted with what he thought at first an agreeable amount of mirth and good humour. He did not need his prepared banter for neighbours and various trading partners that morning. A jovial fit has seized everyone, he thought. Look, here is the mistress of the bakery, who has not only started laughing at first sight of me, but cannot stop while I greet her, and is still laughing as she turns the corner. He checked himself cautiously. A funny food stain? His breeches on backwards? No, everything was in good order. He entered the butcher shop firmly, and with a loud good-natured greeting announced his presence. There was an ironic, speculative look from the master butcher and his assistant. He knew both well, and was hoping to trade some nicely rotted pheasant for other meat. But again, he had but to open his mouth, when a fit of giggling passed through his acquaintances.

'Friend Pedro,' said the butcher, 'tell your business acquaintance the author that if any more of his creations come to life and insist on their right to existence, then we shall have to build a new town for them.'

'And call it Imaginopolis,' called out the assistant.

'And that he'll find himself writing for a century to popu-
late it.'

'And that he must write himself another wife and so save
himself a head of horns!'

At this last remark, they fell about laughing so much that
Pedro knew further conversation would be useless. And as
they were determined to be so funny, he would refuse to trade
with them and they would see how amusing that would be!
He backed out of the door and left the shop. Am I in a dream
world, he wondered. Why is everyone so hilarious? In the bread
shop, the baker stopped him before he could utter a greeting
and said, 'Tell Cervantes that he must hurry his book along,
otherwise his characters will finish it for him.' And then with
a seriousness that made Pedro even more puzzled, said, 'Tell
me, is it so easy to write a comedy? Perhaps my second trade
should be writing comic romances. What do you think?'

Pedro demanded what the baker was talking about. The
baker winked hugely and said, 'Now don't try to pretend
that you don't know anything, one who has all the latest
information on anything now and in the future! Here, an
extra loaf if you tell me how to write a comedy and attract
such bad opinion. Come tomorrow and tell me your secrets.
But for now, you must leave my shop, otherwise everyone will
know that you're telling me your merchandising tricks!'

The baker then pushed him out of the shop and closed the
door. Pedro, usually the master of making exits, could only
shake his head and walk on. What was the meaning of this
mysterious mirth and all these curious remarks?

Entering the courtyard of Cervantes' house brought further
confusion. An uproar of loud quarrelling voices and the banging of pots issued from the kitchen. He hesitated before going
in, and then thought that none of the furore could possibly
be attributable to him. Moments later, he was to regret this
assumption.

He was happy to see Cervantes in the kitchen, but his pleasure was short-lived, for as soon as he entered, he became the subject of abuse.

'You,' said Isabel, in a fine glowing fury, 'a Harlequin stick if anything was ever black and white! What brings you here, you fat, lazy, ogling fool!'

'It is hard for me to resist the company of beautiful women,' Pedro said readily. The sneer at this was universal.

'Friend Pedro,' said Cervantes gently, 'as you have never been lynched before, let me inform you that few recover from the experience.'

'Well, I have just come by to greet you this morning,' Pedro said, 'and must now take my leave . . .'

'Do not move,' Isabel said to him.

'Husband, the shame of this can never be countenanced, not even in a million years,' said Doña Catalina.

'Well, perhaps a little less than that,' said Cervantes.

'Your irony is wasted on me,' said Doña Catalina. 'You might be impervious to slander and calumny, but that is more to your disgrace that to your credit.'

'If I am to be kept captive among such fair company,' said Pedro, now a little alarmed, 'perhaps someone could explain to me what has happened.'

'Is your brain still abed?' said Constanza.

'And who shall defend my honour?' Doña Catalina demanded of Cervantes.

'I shall bring this up with Robles myself,' said Cervantes. 'As to honour, we have never had it to our account, so we can hardly feel the abuse of it.'

'He is another enemy,' declared Isabel. 'I shall make a list and attend to them every one.'

'Robles is not an enemy,' Cervantes said. 'He's a printer and a business man.'

'Both of these points I shall discuss with him,' said Isabel. 'Then I shall beat him senseless.' There was loud applause at this.

'Heavens!' said Pedro. 'When did you all become so blood-thirsty?'

'Then we would be missing a printer, and you would be in prison,' said Cervantes to Isabel.

'How can you defend one who has so deeply hurt us?' said Doña Catalina now very angry. 'Are you a fool? The worst of lies and slanders have been reported of your wife and of yourself, and you make this a subject for debate! Why have you not already left this house, without the pain of this discussion, and forced this pathetic printer, whom you would so shamefully protect, into recanting his actions and giving you due recompense? Why have you not left here –' furious, she pointed at the door '– and choked this Robles into an apology and made him pay in blood for his cowardly actions?'

'Because he is not the enemy,' said Cervantes. There was quiet in the kitchen. 'If he were malicious, which I know he is not, and if he were the author, which I know he is not, and if he believed in these lies and slanders, which I know he does not, then my task would have been as you have already said; to punish him and demand redress. But he has done none of these things—'

'You defend someone who is at fault,' Doña Catalina cut in.

'It aggrieves me that someone I thought a friend . . .' Cervantes said.

'You have no consideration for the feelings of your family,' said Doña Catalina in tears.

'But I must find out who is behind this,' said Cervantes, 'not just simply accuse Robles.'

'I am still very much in the dark,' said Pedro to Isabel.

'You can thank your lucky stars that it is not because I have laid you flat,' said Isabel.

'It's too easy for you to find an enemy,' said Cervantes. 'Would you have me declare war on the city, all its inhabitants, and never stop to think what additional harm this will produce, added to our own?'

'If something could happen by the end of this morning,' said Constanza sarcastically, 'that would be good.'

'Someone tell me what has happened!' shouted Pedro.

There was a glaring pause.

'You should know what has happened,' shouted Isabel in return, 'because you are in part responsible for it!'

Some moments later, within the hearing of further disputes from the house, Cervantes and a shaken Pedro exited the courtyard and headed towards the print shop.

'It is an anonymous satire,' explained Cervantes, 'and of itself is nothing more than an amusement. If I were to take offence at it, I would be a fool.'

'Then how is it that your household is armed and ready for war?' asked Pedro.

'Our friend Robles,' said Cervantes with some hurt, 'was commissioned to print the satire and an open letter, which poses as its introduction. This introduction makes the difference.' Cervantes stopped. 'The author asserts that he has cuckolded me with Doña Catalina. He mocks my crippled hand, calls my reputation into doubt, and devotes a paragraph to obscene insults on my pretensions to being a writer.' He shrugged. 'Any more than that and such hatred would have become a subject of ridicule in itself. But the satire is well written. And the introduction has a sneering quality enjoyed by many. As you know, I am seen as an upstart in these circles.' He took a copy of the satire from his pocket and showed Pedro. 'So we must find the author. The ire of my household is their humiliation and their pain for me. So let us talk with Robles,' he smiled briefly, 'before Isabel reaches him.'

Robles knew that his friends were intent on confrontation as soon as he saw them. He shooed the boy from the shop and drew the latch on the door. Cervantes and Pedro followed him to the back of the shop.

'It's a fine day for honest dealings and fairness between neighbours,' said Pedro sarcastically.

Robles lifted his eyebrows. 'And you shall be our guide in this?' he said.

'The day is acrimonious enough,' Cervantes told Pedro. He turned to Robles. 'Explanations are sometimes necessary between friends. We are not so clever as to guess the whole of another's intentions, nor so sufficient in ourselves to be without suspicion.'

'You are talking of the satire,' said Robles. 'You want me to justify the printing of it. And in particular, you want me to remove the hurt that it has caused.'

'A magician!' said Pedro. 'Can you predict the roll of a dice?'

'I cannot help you,' said Robles.

'Well then,' said Pedro, now entirely caustic, 'we can only stand by and watch a gang of women descend on you, burn your shop and your possessions, sell your wife into slavery, and then stretch your entrails from one end of the square to the other.' He nodded enthusiastically. 'I shall be selling tickets.'

'Pedro,' said Cervantes, 'this is hardly the way.' He turned back to Robles. 'Let me demand of you certain things and perhaps we can progress from this.'

'To this I am amenable,' said Robles.

'Did you not think,' asked Cervantes, 'that printing this satire would do some measure of harm to those whom it ridicules?'

'I am a printer of books,' said Robles, 'and not a reader of them.'

Pedro said, 'But this pamphlet, that you have so carefully not read, contains the worst of opinions of your friends and neighbours.'

'Thankfully,' said Robles, 'my opinion of my friends and

neighbours is in no way affected by this pamphlet. I formed those opinions long ago, and without recourse to reading.'

'But you must have read it, in order to print it,' said Cervantes.

'If myself, rather than another here in my employ, had read it,' said Robles, 'it would have been as an editor, not as a member of the public, to see for instance whether the blocking was correct, and the letter spacing was adequate.'

'But the material is malicious,' said Cervantes, 'and persuades others of an untruth.'

Robles gave a look of ironic surprise, and said, 'Are you under the illusion that all books contain the truth? Perhaps you are saying that because the printing of books began with the Bible? It is a faulty assumption that everything impressed on a page is the truth. I would say that the reverse is probably true, and the further something is from the truth, the sooner you will find it printed on a page. And I am sure that you are aware of this irony, Cervantes.'

'The irony is that amid so many enemies,' said Cervantes, 'I find a friend of false coin. Do you not know that my respect for you is an appendage to your profession? You cannot tell me that because malicious pamphlets are in fashion that you must print as many of them as you are able.'

'I see,' said Robles, turning to Pedro, 'that our mutual acquaintance here is angry at me for not having the same set of scruples that he has. By the same token, he would have us all wear the same beard, say the same speech, and expire on the same day. Listen, Cervantes, you are free to have me as a friend and to admire my profession. But this does not mean that you own my treatment of you, or can approve it according to your own dissatisfactions. Our friendship is a business relationship, which to my mind is one of the most honourable that can be had. Otherwise, one should have perhaps a single particular friend, whom one can rouse in the small hours when the moon is full. Let the rest be business acquaintances, and that's the best.'

'Now if I could write and had set that down,' said Pedro, 'it would be enough for a small pamphlet entitled "How to Repel Friends and Make Enemies; a Diatribe set down after the Words of our Illustrious and Exceptionally Wealthy Printer Robles."'

'See Pedro here,' said Robles, unperturbed by Pedro's gibe, 'he has made friends with everyone in this town to further his own ends. It is well known that at the bottom of every business here are Pedro's trades. Here is the man you should study.'

'But you have not traded with him,' said Cervantes.

'Because he does not like me,' said Pedro.

'Like is not a part of it,' said Robles, 'it is merely business.'

'Ah, yes,' said Pedro, 'for there are many times that I have seen a yolk looking for a white, and a king looking for a crown. It is the nature of certain things to be indivisible.'

Both Cervantes and Robles looked blank.

'You cannot separate these things, in other words,' said Pedro. 'Which is, you cannot have business without friends, and therefore you cannot have a business without likes and dislikes.'

'Pedro, you have hit me,' said Robles, 'you have found the mark.' He produced a bottle and glasses from a cabinet. 'My feelings about you,' he said, holding the bottle, 'should have gone unnoticed. I pride myself on the ability to remain neutral to anyone with whom I have business dealings, no matter what their character, from the silliest bride-in-hope to the book worm who has died already and does not know it. If I have shown a small ill-feeling towards you Pedro, it is a reflection of those inclined towards you –' turning to Cervantes '– and that these feelings, like moths in a closet, have gnawed at my respect for you.'

'Me?' said Cervantes. 'What have I to do with your disliking Pedro?'

Robles poured into the three glasses and handed them out.

'As I understand it,' said Robles, 'Pedro prompted you to write this farce—'

'Novel,' said Cervantes.

'—as a means of making money. You accepted the idea, and so far you have had remarkable success. In fact you have made a profit off me. But this does not content you. You have aspirations for a more philosophic work. Your ambition is to be universally recognised. You wish to become known. And now you are incensed because you are attacked for attempting to rise above your station? It seems to me that you must ride the course that you have chosen with good grace, and do not stop to complain against the blows that you receive.'

'Now, Robles,' said Cervantes, 'the truth is that you seem to have many dislikes, and not just one. And that once you have found one reason for dislike, then others breed like flies. Yet you present yourself as a man of complete neutrality. It seems that you are up to your elbows in the bad opinion of others, and not ink.'

'Well you have caught me at my worst,' said Robles. 'Have another drink.'

'Do you dislike me?' said Pedro.

'I punish boys for pranks and on occasion drown kittens,' said Robles.

'Remember that it is me that he dislikes and not you, Pedro,' said Cervantes, 'and that there are many dislikes that he has not even mentioned besides the numerous ones that he has. And now, friend Robles, explain to me which dislike is your favourite, for I might adopt it for my own and employ it at my leisure at some future date.'

Robles and Pedro laughed.

'You are a discerning man,' said Robles, 'and a humorous one. Pray God these qualities will help you on the course that you have taken.'

'In working with God, there is no other course,' said Cervantes.

'But you have not told us who wrote the satire,' Pedro said.

'It is a confidential matter,' said Robles sternly, 'as you well know. I have not blabbed it to the town that you are trading pheasants for hats and telescopes. You should respect the same of me.'

'But this is a matter of pain,' groaned Pedro. 'Can you not relent on your principles a little?'

'What good are principles,' said Robles, 'if they bend.'

'I shall break in and look through your receipts,' Pedro said.

'And I shall be waiting with a hot poker,' said Robles.

'It is an educated work,' said Cervantes. 'Someone who has the leisure.' He thought a little. 'Someone who takes the woman's part.' He looked shrewdly at Robles. 'Someone whom you are concerned to protect, even from your friends.'

Robles said nothing, while Pedro clowned at looking at him closely. 'I saw a tremor,' he said to Cervantes. 'He's bitten by truth.'

'And this someone,' continued Cervantes, now mocking, 'has the money to publish and distribute a satire while keeping their name and intentions private.'

'Isn't it enough that you have an enemy,' said Robles, 'without wanting to know their name?'

'You are very careful,' said Cervantes. 'You cleverly avoided using the word –' and he smiled '– she.'

Pedro spun on him. 'What!?'

'You shall get nothing from me,' Robles said.

'The Duchess of Alcanares, the mistress of a literary salon,' Cervantes said. 'She is the author of the satire.'

'Would she amuse herself so?' Pedro said.

'The satire is a good piece of work,' Cervantes said. 'It seems obvious that the satire and the introduction are a way of dismissing my work as subversion. She is known for her high standards.'

There was a moment as this penetrated.

'Is this right?' asked Pedro.

'What good would it do for you to know?' said Robles.

So it was that Cervantes assumed that the Duchess had written both the satire and the introduction.

A Letter to the Duchess

An assumption and a quick response.

*T*he revealing discussion with Robles, his practical, if at times unyielding honesty, and the spirits that they had all imbibed, all of this created an inspired glow in Cervantes, and formed the decision to write to the Duchess and ask her to explain her conduct. This feeling lasted as long as the walk home, which was not far, and evaporated as soon as he sat down at his desk, and prepared to write.

The difficulty lay not so much in his decision, which, though it could lead to dangerous results, he knew he must follow. And he could not have stifled his urgency for an answer. It was because he could not simply accuse the Duchess of spite. Given the unsettling virulence of the introduction, her power and influence would no doubt hang over him like a malevolent cloud. None would protect him from such an enemy. Therefore, any accusatory missive from him, though the feelings of his heart demanded it, would neither satisfy his need for understanding, nor induce her to be candid about her motives.

Why had she written such a violent piece of prose? he asked himself again. Something must be wrong with the mind to endanger the heart so. Perhaps, he thought, she was keeping company with a corrupting influence.

He had thought of writing a pleasant rebuttal to the satire, playing with Dulcinea's scorn for Don Quixote's ardent love; the crazed Knight would so blithely misunderstand her threatening statements that he would behave exactly contrary to her words. The Knight would thank Dulcinea for her favours, (which were refused in the satire), observe a vigil outside her house (guarded jealously by her family in the satire), and be presently occupied in search of a complete avenue of trees on which to carve her name (when the satire had threatened his demise should he venture near the smallest sapling with a knife). It was in his mind already. It could only serve to extend the character of Don Quixote, and effectively round off the combative publication of the satire into a publicly enjoyable war of wit. This would have been preferable.

But the introduction, with its sexual scorn, the strident hatred of his position, his small ambitions, and his wounds as a soldier, the rancorous tone of derisive opinion, how could this be answered? The hatred of it stuck in his throat like a bone, which would, if the malevolence of the piece were believed, choke the life out of him altogether. It was mystifying, to have unwittingly earned such an enemy.

His letter then had to be polite, observing her rank and reputation, credit her with the authorship of the satire (and, God help her, the introduction), and incline her to a personal discussion with himself on the subject. A petition to her civilised sensibilities. In any event, he thought, I must see her, the better to sound a mind that one must suppose has descended into hatred.

But the letter must have the right tone. Otherwise, it would be easy for her to write a dismissive reply. As a soldier, he knew that some battles had never been fought because soldiers found their friends or neighbours in opposing ranks. Sometimes, the realisation that the enemy is a simple, wretched being like oneself will take the heart out of fighting. Unless the Duchess were far gone in hatred, he thought, if she sees me, she will sympathise. He had already decided that if she accepted his petition, that he would meet her in uniform, and take the recommendations of his bravery that had been written of him by his old commanders. At the top of the letter, he listed his years of service, his commanders, the campaigns in which he had fought, emphasising that the Emperor Philip II had made special mention of his heroism in the battle of Lepanto.

> My Lady, [his letter began] one who would wish to be your servant, greets you and commends you to that benign spirit which governs us all. This letter humbly wishes all respect to your position and to the good name that you have earned with your many acts of kindness.

These lines he could write with ease, the standard considered politeness of the time. Now, how to petition her for an audience.

> It is your fair attention that I would wish, and my request that you grant some amount of your time for a discussion on the origin and authorship of a certain satirical work, recently circulated. As you must know, the satire derided a character of my creating that has recently enjoyed some popularity. As well as the enjoyment from the pleasingly engrossing task of creating my characters, it was a particular flattery that one such character could be so readily taken by another creative spirit and given further life. This is the compliment that I would willingly pay to any who have so pleasingly extended the range of a fiction with their own abilities.

It was then that he had an idea. Perhaps it was good fortune that his character of the old Knight was popular, and that the satire, or more his character of Dulcinea, threatening him from the pen of another author, had also struck a common vein. She must be pleased herself, thought Cervantes, seeing the startling physicality of Dulcinea come so readily to life. They could collaborate, he thought. The episodes would complement each other; Don Quixote could continue his unlucky courtship of his vision of beauty, while Dulcinea would continue her farm-work, issuing inarticulate but serious threats. Their dialogue would achieve a double popularity.

But would she agree to this? Presumably, she had written the satire to expose a fashion in literature that she found unaesthetic, lacking in taste. It had offended the standards of her Academy. So she was somewhat particular, ambitious for the Academy, aware that the new court would elevate her status, make her important to the Emperor . . . But this was guessing. The introduction was the real cause of hurt, that she could write such a deeply personal attack. Then again, and this was another guess, the introduction may just have been a callous joke. Somehow, he would have to find out from her. He continued writing:

> Some elements of the satire were highly stimulating to read. It has occurred to me then that a collaboration, anonymously pursued of course, between the authors in further episodes could only serve the growing popularity of these burlesques for the public, as well as enriching the source of our country's literary heritage.

Yes, well, these were conceits that came readily to the pen, but he did not know if he particularly believed them. But then:

> It would therefore be my honour to discuss with you your opinion of these matters, and how they might be concluded.
> I remain your faithful servant, etc.

He had finished, the fresh ink shining in the lamplight of his room. He sanded the parchment. He felt that some mysterious entity approved this dusting of the message. It would be sent by courier tomorrow. It was clean, as if he had lanced a gross ulcer, the perplexities of the future.

His thoughts returned to the Duchess. Perhaps she had

had the satire written by one of the circle of authors at her Academy? This was not unknown. It would explain its tone, if it had not come from her, but a desperate dilettante.

Well, if he wanted truth from her, their interview might be very difficult. But then, his letter was reasonable, and perhaps their meeting would be more merriment than bile. Perhaps. If the letter ran as smoothly as he wished, and she had the cultivated sensibilities of her reputation (minus the satire, that is), then perhaps he would win her as a friend, as much as her status would allow.

Perhaps.

Cervantes dispatched the letter to the Duchess the next day. It surprised him then that her response was so swift: a letter arrived that afternoon. His nerves jumped as he read her elegant hand:

> Sir, your request is accepted. I shall expect you tomorrow morning. Please present yourself promptly. Your arrival is anticipated.

Well then. Tomorrow is a day of fate.

The Interview with the Duchess

A discussion on muskets and soldiery.

*D*ressed in what remained of his uniform and carrying letters of commendation from his old commander, Cervantes rode out to the Duchess's mansion the following morning. It did not inspire confidence that the mansion was so large and that the liveried attendants were better dressed than he. Well, I am respectable, not impoverished, he thought. He had used pumice on the rust of his infantry blade. But there were the threadbare lesions in the covering of his scabbard. And what of the faded black of his riding boots, his dishevelled cloak? At least his letters carried the royal seal, the imperial favour, which had not faded as had his old uniform. He hoped that he presented a respectable figure, a stalwart, worthy soldier, honoured for heroism, a reminder of all that made the Empire great.

He had not to say a word of greeting or enquiry, for all hands seemed to know and be ready for him. A footman let him into the main house, ushered him into a waiting room, and then shut him in without a word. Inside, a hushed array of family portraits watched him with serious concern. A click and then feminine steps. This was not the Duchess, he thought, too young. Cara did not bow or greet him but showed him into a salon. As he turned into the room, he thought he caught something of a smile on her face and looked at her fully. She had already turned to leave, and thinking herself unobserved, was smiling as she pulled the doors to a close. 'I am to wait here?' he asked.

Cara nodded definitely, and said. 'The Duchess will come and see you immediately.' She seemed on the point of giggling, controlled it and withdrew.

He had only a few moments before the door opened. There was no time to prepare before the Duchess was in the room, the door closed, and he was looking at a force of beauty. He saw her intensity, glowing through the faultless structure of her face, eyes of demanding intelligence, a mouth of sensual compassion. But the intensity? He realised that he was staring at her like a stricken subject, and that the attention she so fiercely directed at him could only mean a passion. Her mind was primed, he realised, because her heart was on fire.

The Duchess walked firmly to him without a smile of greeting.

'Señor Cervantes,' she said without giving confidence to the name.

'My Lady, I salute you,' he said. 'Let me say that it is an honour . . .'

Her gesture of dismissal was absolute.

'What is it that you wish to discuss, Señor Cervantes,' she said with a brittle tone. She remained standing, forcing him to do so as well.

'It is not a great matter,' he continued, feeling the heat of humiliation in his face, 'and as I explained in my letter . . .'

'Your letter explained nothing, señor,' she said. 'Other than that you desire something of me.'

'Then I have not explained myself adequately,' he said, thinking that he had divined her passion. 'I wish nothing of you other than your time and the answer to some questions. The circulation of a certain satire of my work—'

'You will get nothing from me, señor,' said the Duchess evenly.

'My Lady, I do not understand—'

'I shall be pleased to ask my questions first.'

'It is your prerogative.'

'Do not flatter me, señor. Are you married?'

'Yes. But again, my Lady, let me assure you—'

'Assurances are too easy, Señor Cervantes. Do you have children?'

Cervantes hesitated. Where was this going? What had moved her so? 'I do, my Lady.' Would she ask how many?

'And you are a veteran of the wars,' she pursued.

'I have letters of commendation.'

'Which you have very carefully brought with you.'

'Yes, my Lady.'

'Along with an infantry sword and jerkin. Do you have wounds?'

'I would blush to show them, my Lady.'

'Indeed,' she said bitterly, 'and when has that ever proved delicate among men? You are the cause. They are your boast.'

'A boast hides the pain,' he said, for the first time in defence.

'And death? How do you hide that? With a joke?' Her eyes were wide and accusatory.

'If my answers do not satisfy . . .' he said, now bewildered.

'You wish my patronage, which I refuse. It would have taken you little to discover that I do not grant patronage to writers of the Academy, or to any. To attempt to elicit this from me with sympathy is the worst cynicism. You think that you can buy my feelings with the costume of a soldier, and some faded letters of commendation that any might have received after the wars—'

'My Lady, you are in error,' he said.

'Prove me wrong!' she challenged. 'Show me that you are not intending to gain influence, or money, or power, or some such satisfaction—'

But now Cervantes' passion had set in. 'My intention is to satisfy myself of *your* honour!'

She went completely white. 'What did you say?'

He tried to placate. 'My Lady, I require nothing more than to discuss your writing of the satire—'

'The plagiarism gave me no satisfaction.'

'But it is very good.'

'I will not accept the praise!' she said, her voice rising. 'What is commendable in writing to satisfy a trend? It was a lie to satisfy the fashion. Have you not discovered this for yourself? You fought for the lies of an Emperor.'

'You have some conception of me that I cannot answer,' he said. 'I fought for the Emperor and that is my pride. I am a veteran. This I assumed would have given me some respect in your eyes. But as it has won me no sympathy with you . . .'

She was shaking now with rage. 'What sympathy should be given to the gang of murderers who have pursued their lusts across half of Europe!'

'You call them murderers?' he said. 'Then what does that make their mothers?'

There was a moment in which she seethed. She turned and as rapidly as she was able in skirts, dashed from the room.

Cervantes collapsed on the couch, utterly amazed. He could not have imagined so disastrous an interview.

There were voices outside the room, the sound of protesting, a slap, and the voice of the Duchess, insistent, definite. She is so angry, he thought. He stood and prepared to leave. The interview lay in pieces around him, shards of misunderstanding, the private disgust that both felt for their own exposed feelings. Her misconception of him, he thought agitatedly, was astonishing. How had it happened? The truth he wanted of her had no chance of being revealed.

The door swung open suddenly, and the Duchess appeared, surging forward with a box in her hands, Cara following, remonstrating, a scarlet mark across her face. The Duchess stopped short of Cervantes, set down the opened box, and took out a brace of pistols.

'My Lady!' pleaded Cara.

'Stand over there,' the Duchess ordered her. 'Give the signal when I tell you.'

'No, my Lady, no,' sobbed Cara.

'Then get out of my sight!' Cara ran from the room. The Duchess rounded on Cervantes. 'Here is your chance to prove the bravery of which you brag! You shall exchange shots with me, a woman, one of the weaker sex, whose brains are addled so much by emotions, that they cannot be relied to shoot straight!'

'Please, my Lady, I had not intended to rouse your passions, and if anything I have said has caused you—'

'Grief? Why no, grief is secondary, don't you think? It's much better to be able to shoot straight and accurately. Here,' she forced one of the pistols on him, 'it's primed. Stand further off, and pray to whatever military genius has this far kept you living.' She took a stance ready to shoot.

'No, my Lady,' Cervantes said, and put down the pistol.

'Are you a coward?'

'I have stood before God on the battlefield, my Lady,' said Cervantes.

'The height of arrogance,' she hissed, 'to sanction murder as the action of God! Take up the pistol, or you can ask God yourself whether he agreed to your Emperor's slaughter!'

'I cannot,' he said clearly. 'It would not be honourable.'

'Then I force honour on you,' she shouted, came forward rapidly and slapped him hard across the face. She withdrew again and raised the pistol. 'Is it honour that you feel now?'

He felt the sharp iron of blood in his mouth. There were rapid steps through the house. Members of the household burst in and then froze. He shook his singing head. The Duchess stood before him, her eyes as black as the mouth of the raised pistol. He shook his head again, this time to deny her. 'Shooting me will not allay your anger,' he said through sticky lips.

'You might well be wrong,' she said. She raised the pistol, aimed at him, and pulled back the hammer.

'I came in respect, my Lady,' he said quietly. 'Whatever planets have made this interview so misunderstood, let us pray they will not be here tomorrow.'

'Respect? Mere deprecation,' she said. There was a pause. She turned and handed the pistol to Cara. 'Keep these from me,' she commanded. At the door, she turned. 'You are brave,' she said to him. 'Whether that is a quality, a virtue, or foolhardiness, it is hard to tell. Ask that of yourself, Señor Cervantes. And ask yourself why you have had more than most of death and battles.'

The Relapse

Powerful enemies and the failure of Don Quixote.

*A*fter this unfortunate interview with the Duchess, Cervantes rode heavily home on the dusty road, well aware that without wishing it, he had made a powerful enemy. As his horse patiently plodded the route, his mind encountered a hydra of confusion. How had he been so misrepresented? Worse, with such determined and well-connected opposition, was it wise to continue with his book? He might have to leave it for good. How had the writing of a comedy made so many enemies? But then, no-one had the reasons for writing the book as he had. For the characters of his story were a genial reminder of the folly of all humanity, written with a divine spirit that he could not deny, and it would be foolish to try to. There was a pause in the turmoil; this veracity had banished confusion.

'It seems appropriate,' he continued, more meditatively, 'that this portrait of human kind should be delivered by a crippled veteran soldier. After all, the Gospels describe the preaching of a carpenter, a man of the people.' He wondered if this was heresy. But then, laughing at how earnestly his own thoughts were ready to condemn him, he remarked to the horse's ears, 'A book can only go so far. And you can only trust a book so far. There is no doubt, if one reads Christian writings closely, that some apostles were not too right in the head. And I do not choose to be less intelligent, even for God! But then let me reflect on that last announcement. For it seems to me that I have just behaved like one of these foolish apostles by accosting the Duchess in her opulent den, and by thrusting a tender conscience upon her proud mind.' He smiled wryly. 'She almost ate me without garnish.' The interview with the Duchess, her sudden irrational fit, the furore in which he had left her mansion, it was hard to remember these events without flinching. But the common-sense nature of truth reminded him that her actions had been both unwarranted and extreme in spirit. 'Perhaps her heart does not know her mind.' That much had become obvious from her extraordinary outburst. 'She cannot be that unkind! Remember her large and beautiful eyes.' He drew reign, and stopped. Remembering the beauty of the Duchess was something of a pleasure, even though much of her rancour and disdain had been directed at him. She had also listened to him with a fine attention, even if with a closed opinion and an undeterred purpose. 'But look how my perception has changed in her respect. No doubt, because of her lovely eyes.' He urged on the horse again. 'But she must repent her bad opinion. She shall not escape from hearing the truth.'

The Idyll

The site of a proposed idyll.

*T*he victory of the satire prompted Ongora to revive his ambitions for the position that Denia had so mercilessly dangled in front of him. Just think of it! Poet-confidante to the Emperor! He would have the whole cultural basin of writers and playwrights, creatures of words and motives, in which to dip his hands, rinse and scour as he would. Certain poets had taken to using the dubious dregs of their vocabulary for sinister and bloodthirsty characters in plays. He would correct them! Oh yes, a golden rod of high classic verse to chastise the word-mongers. Theatre was for the verbose. But if he could attain this position, and wear the rich gown of influence, it would not be to deny theatre, he thought, but rather to elevate the poets. They would be the first among writers. He would be the first among them.

However, at the same time he knew the position was as far from him as ever because of his inability to handle Denia, the stirrings of this soldier buffoon Cervantes, and the absence of a definitive issue of poems by his own hand. If he could destroy the hobbled run of Cervantes for the position and the influence of Denia through manipulating the Duchess as well as promoting the satire, then surely the stars would allow him the primary inspiration for a collection of poems. What would he have to sacrifice? What was it, he was asking the demons of opportunity, what would be required? A month of celibacy? He would finish with Micaela tonight! His blood? He could get a scratch in some duel! Some immortal part of him? If this were invisible and dispensable to his ambitions, then what would it matter? To wear the silk of influence in the Emperor's presence, to be the royal seal on the Empire's words, to wear laurels in the Empire's Golden Age . . . The tang of this possibility was so strong, that he felt his sex stirring, the chafing halves of desire and anticipated pleasure.

Stratagems were progressing well. He had decided against visiting the Duchess; otherwise he would have to control an eruptive celebration of victory. It was beholden to him to produce another collection of verses: whilst Denia and his veteran author languished, his new poems would fill a vacuum. He now doubted that the Emperor had ever seen the previous collection. With these optimisms at hand, he felt secure in beginning his poetry anew. It would be better, he thought, to find a theme. To reverse the derisory influence of Cervantes' work on the established classical forms of the Empire's literature, he thought it a good idea to execute a series of odes on a pastoral theme. And it might prove something to his name if the poems were conceived and written in an especially beautiful park to merit the theme. Perhaps a riverbank somewhere, under a fated tree, where he could confidently lounge and devise verses that would inspire the nation with the beauties of the natural universe! Something, pastoral, something rustic. Maidens, sheep, the song of birds, dusk, moonlight, green boughs; it would all be there! Now these ideas were simmering, it occurred to him that he could seek out a certain spot for inspiration, and fashion it a little for the purpose. The poems would be entitled 'The Idyll' or 'Remembrances from an Idyll' or something like that. He had to find a spot and make it the inspiration for these poems.

The Discovery of Lancelot's Chapel

The old Knight interrupts some minor demons.

*O*ngora sent out his boys to look for the proposed idyll, somewhere close to the capital with water, trees; he had a list of specifics. They had returned, no doubt via the back entrance to a tavern in the hope of witnessing a hand of cards, and reported on a few likely spots. One interested him, in which there were trees, a hut and it was reasonably secluded.

He went out to visit the hut and found it immediately desirable. There was a hint of wildness about the area. A Dionysius, dragging his rod of chaos, tangling the bushes, spurting the small white flowers, a quick enveloping of potent scent. Running with the fox. A stag at midnight with the glowing moon. A root, glistening hard, driving into the earth. Yes, he thought, if the spirit of riot was here, then so much the better for his purpose. He would need to prepare the area; this was part of the plan. If he could make the spot more usefully pastoral . . . Dress the trees, clear some of the ground. Make the paths less hidden; light them with oil lanterns at night. Then decorate the hut. An open window in which he could pose. A bench outside. A lectern on which he could set a notebook with – he had already decided – very large pages, luxurious to turn, impressive to watch. He already had his costume in mind; a soft hat, flowing sleeves. Then Micaela, dressed not too provocatively, as a shepherdess. She would have lost her flock and be seeking the help of him, a forest philosopher. The conceit of the poems: a philosophical discussion between the maid and the philosopher on pastoral joys and the bliss of the divine recluse. Well, he had it all in mind. Tomorrow, he would return with some helpers and accomplish this transformation.

He was not to know that the hut was also the poacher's stowaway and now served as the old Knight's forest chapel.

The Destruction of the Chapel

A vow of vengeance on the Evil Magician of Bad Verse.

*T*he following day, Ongora ordered his boys to transform the area into a rustic idyll. There was much conveying of decorations and materials, and so it was, in the late afternoon, that Ongora, satisfied with progress, returned home to try on hats. He left the boys to finish, especially a swing that they were hanging from a bough with ribbons covering the ropes, instructing them to clean up and report back to him in the evening.

The boys had discovered some signs of occupancy in the hut. It was puzzling, for there was no sign of bedding. If boys from the town were using it for their hideaway, there should be bits of flintlock and twists of powder for scaring pigeons and each other. Another curiosity was that the hut was uncommonly clean; the floor was swept, a broom of tied twigs set behind the door. There was a plain earthenware jar for water, a carefully trimmed candle and, oddly, the remains of a flag, arranged over the table. The furnishings were simple; a chair, the table, a small bench for the domestic items, and then one other object which roused their curiosity most of all. It was a dummy, a hard stuffed sack of hessian and sawdust, fixed on a pole with a crossbar hitched and tied horizontally for the arms. Another sack uneasily mounted the top of the pole for the dummy's head. The hut had been arranged so that most of the floor space was empty with the dummy set at one end. So the dummy was being used by the resident for fencing practice.

One of the boys ran back to tell Ongora. The other boys, confident in Ongora's response to these oddities, ritualistically disembowelled the dummy, and dragged it gleefully around the hut, letting it bleed sawdust and loll helplessly. Then they set it up outside and took turns lunging at it with their knives, slashing it triumphantly, using the swagger that they had seen in the street *bravados*, splenetic youths, as they cut up their victims. Then they planned a foray, and charged the hut, yelling as they burst in, and dragging the furniture outside like unwilling captives. The slaughter was ecstasy. They jumped on the chair and flattened it. They used the table legs to further abuse the dummy. The flag was slashed into strips. They lynched the dummy, hanging it from the bough where they had just tied the ribbons of Ongora's romantic swing. Then they went inside and cleared out the remaining signs of occupancy, tossing the votive candle far into the briers.

It was into this scene that the old Knight arrived.

The old Knight had seen much of wars and battles and became immediately cool when he saw the delirium of the boys. While he observed their actions, they were unaware of his presence among them, until he had seized one boy, the biggest, and held him struggling by the shirt.

The old Knight knew that the chapel had been invaded; the votive candle had whizzed past him in the briers, and the shouts and screams had alarmed him some way off. He had tied Bucephalus and approached quietly. His silence was camouflage. He was thankful that this minor tribe of demons had not fired the chapel or chosen to ambush him. They were trying their little powers on a small target, roving after dark, sharpening their teeth on the excitement of wrong.

'Desecration is a sin,' he said to the struggling boy, 'whatever the age of the perpetrator. Do you report these acts to an infernal authority?'

The boys stopped their activities and looked at the old Knight with that solemn intensity of animals interrupted in a primal compulsion. The boy held by the old Knight struggled free. The old Knight was surrounded now, a ring of panting dishevelled sprites. He wondered if they could talk. He had decided that, after the successful accomplishment of his quest, he would write a guide on the hierarchy of the infernal legions, recording the powers and characteristics of demons, how they were ranked, what were their duties, and so on. For example, this creature in front of him would be recorded as Type: demon; Status: minor realms; Powers: as yet unknown; Function: petty destruction, desecration, defacement; Additional characteristics: as yet unestablished. 'As a minor demon,' said the old Knight to the boy, 'are you able to converse?'

The boys recovered their cynicism, learned in their service to Ongora. Some of them recognised the old Knight from the disastrous poetry recital. He was their master's enemy and had already escaped attempts to detain him. The biggest boy saw their advantage and said, 'You're the old madman that interrupted my master's poetry of late.' So, thought the old Knight, it can speak. And it came as no surprise that their master was the magician of evil verse. 'Ah, so you are in service to the evil magician,' he said. 'Tell me, are you and the other demons in the pack in full knowledge of the evil extent of your master's powers?'

The boy looked around at the others. 'We know that he's evil,' he said and the boys sniggered, a little uneasily. The youngest were aware that it was fast becoming night, and this talk of demons was beginning to impress.

'And did he order the desecration of my chapel?' asked the old Knight.

'We have been ordered to make the place pretty,' said the boy, and they all sniggered more loudly.

The old Knight nodded. 'Being minor demons, you have no recourse for repentance and so you cannot benefit from repairing the damage that you have caused. In another encounter I had with a senior demon, he was destroyed by a lightning bolt from the heavens, but that seems to be too dramatic on this occasion.' The boys looked at each other; his madness was very convincing.

'We should tie you up and drag you to our master,' said the boy.

'It is inevitable that he and I should meet as it is my task to destroy his invidious power over this region,' said the old Knight. 'So you see I cannot volunteer that you take advantage of me.'

'It would be no trouble,' said the boy, enjoying himself. But the other boys were withdrawing, aware that the discussion was growing too complicated for them to understand. Besides, they did not feel comfortable with this talk of demons. They began to creep away.

'Your companions are withdrawing,' said the old Knight. 'They know the impossibility of winning in any combat with me.'

The boy, startled, looked around and found himself alone. The others, feeling safer in the undergrowth, called out. 'Pablo,' they shouted, 'run! He's mad! He'll cut you into pieces and make you into pie!'

He needed nothing more than this, and ran, not even waiting to curse the old man whose confidence had made them all uncertain. But he ran blindly, and the dummy took revenge. Still hanging disembowelled and maimed from their knives, the boy ran into it, a tangle it seemed to him of hard dark limbs. It fell to the ground with him, and he fought it in terror, some tattered giant spider that was trying to eat him. Sobbing, he fought free, and dived into the bushes. Wailing at the sound of his fear and panicking exit, the boys ran for, at least, the known hells of service to their master.

So it was that the boys appeared to Ongora, breathless, dishevelled, and at length managed to tell him of having been invaded by the old man, who was also resident in the hut. Then the biggest boy arrived, bloodied from his collision with the dummy, and told of the old man's threats against Ongora, as he held his tingling nose. Ongora didn't like the blood dripping on the floor, and would have dismissed them all immediately, but for the story of the old man. He instructed them all to attend him the next morning, and they would all go to the idyll together.

An Evil Encounter

A terrifying report of despicable goodness.

*T*he boys were in a perturbation because they had made a mayhem of Ongora's idyll. Of course, they would have cleaned up their destructive exuberance, had not the old Knight appeared. So it had been privately decided that the destruction would be blamed on the old Knight.

But this was not the scene that Ongora found on his arrival, and at first the boys were delighted. Everything had been returned to the facile harmony that Ongora had ordered. The path was cleared, the swing gently hung from the tree, the area was neat and the door of the hut enticingly open. The remnants of destruction that the boys had left were gone. The hut was empty too, which relieved the boys. But then Ongora found a note pinned on the tree in the old Knight's archaic script. The boys hung back, mute, as Ongora read the note: 'To the notorious and ill-merited magician of bad verse from a humble questing Knight.'

Damnation, thought Ongora. He continued reading:

Knowing your mind to be as fallibly evil as your hide is black, and having seen the work of your demon minions in desecrating this holy site, I am even more resolved in your utter and total destruction. Therefore, on the morning, please it to shrive yourself of your sins, (or ignore this act of contrition as is perhaps the rule of the demon kingdom). Thereafter, I shall arrive and destroy you, to the comfort of the region, the exultation of this great Empire, and the glory of God. Yours respectfully, etc., etc.

And then of course there was a postscript.

It would be a merit in your favour to share at least some details of your existence in Hades before I summarily destroy you. I am preparing a guide book on the habits and customs of the demon race, and demons being boastful, it should contain much useful information.

Ongora's response was to rend the note into pieces and throw them from him. Then he snatched one of the boys by the arm and slapped him repeatedly. Even though the boy struggled and wept, Ongora did not – could not – attend, abstracted by his fury. He kicked the swing, and then turned and dashed into the hut. Nothing was inside for him to destroy, so he emerged again and kicked the outside of the hut. 'Burn it,' he said to the boys. 'Burn it, and do not report back to me until it is ash.' He then turned and left.

The old Knight, finding the hut burned, rode forth immediately to reclaim the sword of Sir Lancelot and challenge the evil magician to a famous duel.

Pedro's Wife's Famous Black Pot

A rivet and the fate of the quest.

*T*hat morning, Pedro's wife told Pedro that if there was one small useful thing that he could do that day, among the many large and useless things that he would certainly do that day, then please to take the best black pot and have a small rivet on the handle fixed at the smithy. Pedro replied sardonically that indeed taking the black pot – and does his wife mean the famous black pot that has remained in the family for over three generations, and is such a pot that even princes could be fed from it – would be a small thing to do in a day filled with very important events, and that it so happened that he, Pedro, has already made an appointment with the smith to fix the shoes of their horse in exchange for a brace of partridge that he, Pedro, had exchanged with the town poacher for an old telescope, for in between giving pheasants sleeping draughts, the poacher liked to watch the stars.

Pedro's wife said, 'You will be watching stars as well if you do not leave this house to the women.'

'Very good advice,' said Pedro, 'for a house with so many women is like a sack of snakes, and you dare not put your hand in. Farewell until this evening, and give my love to all our daughters, however many there are today.'

The Smithy

The black pot and the sword of Sir Lancelot.

*P*edro quickly left the house, taking the pot with him in a sack, and made his way to the smithy.

At the smithy, Pedro was astonished to find the old Knight, sitting attentively by the forge, gazing into the flames. He did not hear Pedro's greeting.

Relieved, Pedro then greeted the smith and asked him what the old Knight was doing. The smith, his leather apron already covered in the splashes of his trade, said that the old Knight had arrived early that morning, and calling him the great Vulcan, had told him that Sir Lancelot's sword would mysteriously appear today, and that he, the Knight, would take it as his own and use it to tame the evil magician of bad verse.

Pedro shook his head, and said, 'It is lucky that such a lunatic can have so noble a bearing. For a man whose wits are completely gone, he makes an occupation of the strangest ideas. This does not seem to be one of his better ones.'

The smith asked, 'Friend Pedro, I am curious why you like this old man so much.'

Pedro replied, 'He is a good person, and he must have suffered greatly for his wits to have turned so. And for this I like him, even though he exasperates me, and has got me into a great number of unpleasant escapades.'

'Many say,' said the smith, 'that madness is contagious,

and you can catch it like the influenza.' The smith pointed a scorched and muscular finger. 'Many also say that you, friend Pedro, have already caught this craziness!'

Pedro laughed, and said, 'It is the envious talking, for it is not craziness, but creative commercial enterprise. Now, to the business at hand. My wife wants this black pot repaired.' Pedro produced the pot from a sack. 'There is a rivet on the handle—' But he got no further, for the old Knight suddenly woke from his reverie at the fire, gasping aloud at the appearance of the pot. He fell on his knees, shuffled to the astonished Pedro and, gazing admiringly at the pot, said, 'Let me behold you, O you finest of weapons, second only to Arthur's Excalibur. Here you are, in the hand of our beloved servant and the choicest of squires. Let me recount your history. You were made in the deepest fires of Vulcan's smithy, and the steel came from the ore of Olympus, and the blade was cooled in the river Styx, and your hilt was crafted from the gold of Helios. And now you appear before me, ready to be taken up in my quest for the Grail.'

Pedro smiled uneasily. 'This is only a pot. True, a very historic old pot, but nonetheless, merely an old pot.'

The old Knight shook his head and patiently said, 'Faithful squire, your senses have been abused by the magician of evil verse who beguiles this region. You cannot see that this sword is the finest weapon that has ever been made. And despite your misgivings, and even if you have a confirmed loyalty in protecting such an object, you must deliver up the sword to my spotless hand.'

'This pot is not a sword,' Pedro repeated, 'but a pot.'

The old Knight said, 'As the Spell of Wrong Appearances is hard on you, we shall have to melt it out of you with sound reasoning.' He turned to the smith who was watching the exchange with dour interest. 'Perhaps, the Divine Mind of Vulcan here will aid me.' To Pedro's astonishment, the smith nodded and said, 'It does seem to present a puzzle, friend Pedro.'

The old Knight turned back to Pedro. 'Now, my redoubtable squire, answer me this. If it is a pot, then why did you come this morning to the smith, when I had dreamt that the sword would be delivered to me this day?'

Pedro said, 'If that is logic, then it is yours and not mine. The truth is that delivering up this sensible pot –' and he emphasised the word '– to you, a crazed old fool, would be sentencing myself to an early end. My wife would never forgive me, though we were married forty times forty.'

The old Knight said, 'Faithful but deluded squire, you must deliver up the sword, and must stand firm against the wiles of evil magicians.'

'And, friend Pedro,' said the smith, 'it does need to be repaired.'

Irritated by this, Pedro said, 'I see that it is of no consequence to you whether or not this pot is a sword or a pot, Master Vulcan Smith.'

'You are right, said the smith, 'whether it is a pot or a sword it is immaterial. For it still needs to be repaired.'

Exasperated, Pedro said, 'Why do you insist on the point? Is it not enough for a chicken to lay one egg, but that she has to lay half a dozen eggs altogether?'

'Señor Pedro the Squire,' said the smith with laconic humour, 'I merely want to repair this pot or sword, or what you will, because it is my business to make and repair items of iron and steel.'

'Is it not enough that I have to go through seven hells just to get the pot here,' said Pedro, now beginning to rave, 'but that I have to be greeted with a foolish old man and his preposterous conclusions, and a smith who does not care about the truth of things as long as he can make a business out of it.'

'Ah now, Pedro,' said the smith, 'if you lose your temper and become any hotter, I will have to douse you in my bucket of water.'

'And,' said the old Knight, 'you cannot call me old and foolish until you have advanced a good twenty tears.'

It was then that Cervantes appeared at the entrance of the smithy.

'Friend Pedro, Master Smith, and Sir Lancelot,' he said, 'how fares the morn?'

'It is a blessed and halcyon morn,' said the old Knight. 'The angels told me last night that I would recover the sword of Sir Lancelot and have it for my quest. And look, here it is!'

Cervantes regarded the pot in Pedro's hand. 'Why Pedro, is that not the famous black pot that has been in your wife's family for over three generations?' he said.

'It is,' said Pedro.

'The same pot that has fed many of your neighbours with delicious stews and sauces?' continued Cervantes.

'The very same,' said Pedro, heartened now by Cervantes solicitous recollection.

'The same pot that now has its own hook, and has held pride of place in your kitchen for these twenty years?' finished Cervantes.

'That is the pot,' said Pedro, 'and yes, it is so respected and venerated, that it has an appointment with the smith here to mend a loose rivet on the handle.'

'Or a loose cross-guard,' said the smith, 'if it be indeed the sword of Sir Lancelot's.'

'Heaven be praised,' said the old Knight.

'This is a conspiracy!' said Pedro, his eyes staring.

'Come,' Cervantes said, and he took Pedro off to one side, 'as the smith has noted, the pot or sword needs to be repaired. And whether it be a pot or sword, then it must be mended this day, friend Pedro.'

'See, the God of Reason under this very roof!' said Pedro to the old Knight and the smith. He turned back to Cervantes and said, 'And then?'

'And then,' said Cervantes, his voice dropping to a murmur,

'you must deliver this sword to the old Knight, for he has better use for it than your wife.'

'What!' said Pedro, now completely exasperated. 'Has the world gone mad in one short night? Has everyone suddenly become philosophers, without so much a care of how to make a living, but rather musing on whether bread nourishes and wine intoxicates? Why, I think I hear God laughing at us right now. This,' and Pedro brandished the pot at the old Knight, 'is a black pot in my strong right arm, and there is the crown of your head. Should one collide with the other, then I think you will forsake the senses that you have, and regain the sensible five that all mortals share in common!'

'Friend Pedro,' said Cervantes, 'it is rare to see you in such a passion, which must mean that you dined on fish last night, or argued with your wife this morning.' Cervantes took Pedro further off to make his remarks more confidential. 'But notwithstanding, and without further trying your patience, which I am sure you will regain, but this honourable old Knight, whose wisdom you have so castigated, has come far and suffered much to be among us and to achieve an honourable end. You have but to look at him to realise that he is one vision away from death, friend Pedro. Look at him! Thin and frail, but with such an aura of lightness and resolve that one cannot think of him as a crazy old man. He is someone who talks to God everyday and will live with him soon. He does not want your black pot to spite you, he wants that black pot to achieve a blessed death!'

'Why, oh why,' said Pedro mournfully, 'do I have a friend who can twist me into kindness? Is it not enough,' and this was more to himself, 'that I have a morning of bad temper and broken handles, but that it shall continue far further than supper, perhaps for a week!' He appealed to Cervantes, 'There will be anger against me for a year!'

'Longer, I would suppose. But friend Pedro,' said Cervantes, 'the good that you do now will help with the bad that follows.'

'Is that comfort?' said Pedro. 'I would rather risk the temper of a viper than my family's!'

'Whether you are in a bad temper or no,' said Cervantes firmly, 'the fate of his quest is in your hands.'

'Why am I supposed to be kind?' said Pedro becoming irritated once more. 'Having arrived in a temper, and having been seen in a temper, and having been seen to have no kindness or perception of the trials of others, I must foolishly hand over the family pot and return dutifully to my house for blows and scorn? Why, I should settle for the lesser sin, and kill the old fool right now, on the spot!'

'Steady,' said Cervantes, trying not to laugh at his friend's wildness. 'Your heart will burst.'

'I do not want to be kind!' shouted Pedro.

'There,' said Cervantes, 'now your passion is over. And the truth is, friend Pedro, that you are kind. Unless you eat fish for supper.'

'I did not eat fish for supper,' said Pedro sulkily.

They both turned to the others, finding the old Knight muttering devotions with his eyes closed, and the smith stoking his fires.

Pedro sighed. 'I had herrings for breakfast,' he said.

And so, after a brief stint of hammering by the smith, the old Knight, wearing the sword of Sir Lancelot strapped to his waist, climbed his mare Bucephalus, and rode forward to fight the evil magician of bad verse.

The Old Knight's Revenge

A challenge to the death.

*T*he old Knight, having followed an inner prompting to Ongora's villa, shouted out his challenge. 'Come out from your dark and dangerous walls, O you scribbler of dread and evil verses. It is I, Sir Lancelot, champion of these Isles and defender of the Holy Grail, who has come to shake the devil by the ears! Rouse yourself from your sty, you stinking guillemot, for your neck shall meet my sword this very day! Ho within! Rouse your dark carcass, thou evil and besmirched buffoon!'

Eventually, the shutters opened on an upper window and Ongora's head appeared. 'You're old and a fool,' he said loudly. 'Please remove that horrible looking horse from the flower-beds!'

The old Knight replied, 'If you will not come out to fight with me, I shall come in to fight with you,' and immediately charged the front-door.

Seeing that the old Knight was serious, Ongora ducked back inside and slammed the shutters closed.

Ongora had one disagreeable thought in his head, and that was to kill the old Knight. He found a rapier and inspected it critically. 'Should a man such as I of important position, of known breeding, allow the invasion of his property and home? And if this invasion is conducted by a crazed old man, only intent on violence to ease the heady vapours of his mind?' A pageboy entered, took one look, and left immediately. 'No, for such a man would defend himself, his home and his honour, even if his assailant is a sadly delusional and weak old man.' He plied the rapier and let it swish in the air. 'Therefore, in a strictly honourable fashion, I will give this old fool a fencing lesson. In the process, I will contrive to become a little wounded, and then eventually, kill the old man. I shall be found, honourably distressed, having defended my honour and my house.' There was a crash from the lower floor.

An anxious house servant had opened the front door just as the old Knight and the excited mare charged through. Ecstatic, the old Knight cantered through the hallway, scattering servants and furnishings, yelling and hallooing his battle cries. The momentum of the old Knight's charge carried him through the door of the dining room, where he crashed into a table, decorously set. The mare skittered on the tiles of the floor and skidded through the doors into the garden.

The poet descended the stairway, carrying the rapier, angrily absorbed in the sounds of destruction from the dining room. A pageboy stood, open-mouthed, at the foot of the stairs. Ongora whipped him with the flat of the rapier.

Out in the garden, the old Knight vaulted cleanly down from the mare like a young man. Ongora emerged from the ruined windows of the dining room, now in a ferret-like rage. He slowly advanced on the old Knight, who was already standing on guard, and said, 'You have obviously intended to do myself and my property great harm, old fool, and to that end, you will find a fitting resolution on the point of my rapier.'

The old Knight bowed courteously and said, 'It is a beautiful morning on which to rid the world of an evil. On guard!'

Ongora needed no encouragement, and attacked.

Ongora was convinced that he could easily defeat the old Knight, who was, after all, armed with only a black pot. But the old Knight was an expert swordsman, very adroit with utensils, and wholly unafraid of the poet's steel. After a few thrusts and parries, Ongora became even more enraged, and recklessly charged the old Knight, who deftly stepped aside and, true to the quintain jousting exercise, delivered a blow with the pot to the back of the poet's head.

The fury of his charge and the impetus of the blow carried the poet far into a bush. Hysterical, Ongora wrestled his sword from the bush and emerged to see the old Knight standing over one of his pageboys, lying prone on the grass. The old Knight said, 'Here lies one of your bad verses who tried to assume the posture of an epic, and fell to the form of doggerel!'

Ongora actually snarled and attacked anew. A mad mêlée began. A dog rushed onto the lawn, barking at the two men. The mare tried to bite the dog. A maid started screaming from the house. A pageboy carrying a stick ran from the house and joined in the battle. Alarm bells began ringing somewhere.

The old Knight fended off Ongora's attack and declared, 'Now you are trying to distract me with noise and clamour. But let your blackened heart melt, because my resolve is to rid the world of your evil verse. On guard, for by this strong right arm and the sword Excalibur I shall destroy you this day.'

Ongora lunged at the old Knight, while the pageboy tried to whack him with the stick. But the old Knight, once more charmed by the gods, side-stepped Ongora's rapier, while the pageboy's blow missed completely and landed with a satisfying crack on the poet's knee. Ongora yelped, and cuffed the pageboy, who dropped the stick and bursts into tears. At the same time, in a parabolic arc that any master builder would admire, the old Knight brought the black pot squarely down on Ongora's head. The pot rang like a bell, and Ongora dropped without a sound.

The mêlée abruptly stopped. Only the old Knight seemed free to move among the others, who were frozen in astonishment. Briefly, the old Knight knelt by the unconscious Ongora, and whispered a quick prayer of gratitude. Then looking up at the crowd of attendants, he said, 'He is unconscious only, and that is lucky, for my sword would ordinarily have twained him, yet for the strength of his ungodly hide.' The old Knight mounted the mare, which had successfully cowed the dog, and looked down at the assembly. 'God puts it into my mind to say that you must not stay in service to such a creature, for he will corrupt your soul. Therefore, and advisedly, you must seek new service.'

And having said this, the old Knight and mare ambled away together.

Ongora stirred and muttered, 'Ah, he has killed me. I shall die of shame.'

The Mystery of the Introduction

The Duchess meets the printer.

A coach arrived at the entrance to Robles' shop and from it stepped the Duchess, veiled as was customary, and with an appraisal that was rare among passers by, she stopped and studied the contents of the shop window. The serenity of her study was far from the nature of her inner world. But this disguise, that had once been automatic manners, was now her shield. Otherwise, the encounter with the grinding busy streets, the colossal energy of the populace, was too great a strain for her. She had privately termed herself 'convalescent', that is recovering from a considerable hurt, although without this being the knowledge of her immediate household, or of society. And so it should be, she thought. I would not have it for public consumption that I am privately disturbed.

But her reasons for being here? These were deep, but their logic was as much to do with sounding a new note in her interior health, as they were to do with rectifying the injuries that her instability had caused others. I am a commodity, she thought, a jewel in the crown of the Empire. Whether by luck, fate, or some design of mine, it is so, and has yet to be discovered by me as a duty or a satisfaction. But as it is, I can be censured for turning the fortunate accident of my beauty and my position into the ugliness of my experience. Anger has whittled my soul. And the

Empire, whose crimes are numerous, and in whose service my husband was expended like chaff, has no more sensibility than a strong box. I break my weapons on an unheeding monster. There are other ways to live.

In the comparative dark of the shop, she seemed a mysterious wraith to Robles. The door opening had alerted him, ruminating in the back of the shop. He had emerged, weary but ready. However the Duchess had more aura than most, and as she drew back her veil, he was removed from his troubles into the experience of her remarkable beauty.

'Duchess,' he said, 'if I had known that you were coming . . .' He shrugged. 'I might have been absent.'

'I know you to be reliable,' said the Duchess calmly. 'I do not intend to take your time, nor is my visit connected with any business. For your last renderings of work on my behalf, I thank you. But my present need is to satisfy my—' she looked for the word '—concern. Here is a letter, addressed to me by one Cervantes, a writer whom I am sure you know.'

'He is a friend of mine,' Robles said.

'Please read it to me,' she said. 'I do not mean to test you, but to make sure that we are both clear on his meaning.'

Robles took the letter from her hand and scanned it. Yes, here was Cervantes' persuasively untidy script. He squinted to concentrate and began:

> My Lady, appearances are deceiving, as it is said, and nothing seems to me to be more appropriate a homily to describe our interview to day. I write this having returned home, stowed my uniform and the sword in the box under my bed, and bathed my swollen face. I shall now proceed to exercise an eloquence on my part that was hardly allowed in your presence earlier. Perhaps anyone in my position would have hoped at least a fair exchange with you, but that was not to be. So having been humiliated, threatened with a pistol –

Robles stopped and looked at the Duchess. She said nothing, so he continued:

> – and having been given no leisure for my voice in your favour, I have decided that honesty can only be my gain. In fact it might be the only profit I have from my encounter with you. Otherwise, our interview was an absurdity, a fiction that I could not have dreamed even with ship's fever.

Robles stopped again, unsure. Once again, the Duchess said nothing. He continued:

> So I shall be plain. My intention in seeing you was to discover whether you had written the satire, for which I would have congratulated you, and then proposed a partnership in which we would have written a series of episodes with these characters at odds with one another. I think these would have been very popular. Supposing I would have thus far achieved my aims, I would then have asked you whether you had written the introduction to the satire. As a marvellous piece of invective, I would have remonstrated with you – but only a little, for you are in the beginning of your craft – that the personal injuries intended by this document are far from the gentleness of your position. To mock vanity is one thing; to jeer at infirmities another. I would have told you that the satire is inspired, while its introduction is heedless and violent. Having established no more than this from you, I would have returned with the satisfaction that the rank nature of the introduction would have been absorbed in the pleasure and results of our new literary partnership. Respectfully yours, Miguel Cervantes.

Robles folded the letter up, and handed it back to the Duchess, feeling that his day had been extended far beyond normal limits, and knowing that the firmness of his business ethic might have caused intricacies far greater than imagined.

'The letter alludes to an introduction of which I have no knowledge,' the Duchess said. 'Please produce it for me.'

Robles was startled, and looked at her puzzled. 'You have not seen it?'

'I have not seen it,' she said firmly. Which was true. The gossip at the Academy hummed with speculation that she had written the satire and, by association, the introduction as well. But she ignored gossip.

'But it was brought to me by –' He paused while at the same time she raised her hand; the name was not to be mentioned. 'I was given to understand that you approved of the satire being printed.'

'I have regretted every moment since it was finished,' she said.

Robles began searching his shelves. 'I must warn you, my Lady, that the introduction is not in the same spirit as your satire.' He found the pamphlet and brought it to her. 'It is not pleasant reading. Cervantes is a generous spirit, and would have forgiven or forgotten these insults, but that his family were humiliated.'

She said nothing, took the pamphlet and began to read. Her concentration being evident, Robles left her and went to his desk to add up accounts, a suitably decorous activity.

After some while she called to him. Her face was white, and he had the impression that steel had entered her. The stiffness, he guessed, was control. Her eyes were pitiless, he thought. 'Destroy this and any that you have remaining. I shall cover the cost,' she said.

He bowed assent.

She was drawing on her gloves. 'I shall discuss this with the person who originally brought this to you.' Her eyes glowed momentarily. 'I shall write to Cervantes and tell him –' The weight in her heart made the rest of her words recede. Robles saw her fade for a moment. What should she tell Cervantes, she wondered; that a scalded cat had raked the nearest face? She finished with the gloves and nodded to him briefly. 'My respects to your wife.' She turned to leave and then said. 'It is of no matter now, but is it not unsuitable that by printing the satire, you should acknowledge the worst in us? I would not like to think that you or any other would form an opinion of me by assuming that I agreed with the contents of this introduction.' She paused. 'But perhaps you cannot afford such principles in your profession.' She lowered her beautiful head in thought. 'But then by your staying neutral, is anything accomplished?' She smiled at him briefly. 'Forgive me, it is my habit to reconstruct everything. Please remember my instructions.' She inclined her head and left the shop.

In the carriage, the Duchess had a mute attack of grief, now common to her, if added to by a deep sense of shame. It was as though she had taken her heart and cast it into a mire. What had she done? And what pain had she caused, driven by a shallow assumption, and some artful cunning of Ongora's? Had she driven herself into this cruelty? Her suffering, her loss, was not meant to turn her bestial, ignoble. Ah yes, and here it is, a stark contradiction. Suffering so nobly and yet the instrument of torture for another. How had she been employed? Because of her bitterness. Denia had unearthed her so easily it was like turning a pebble. And Ongora? He must have found it in her as well, she thought grimly. And then played on her with a handsome set of false aesthetics. Protecting the Golden Age of the Empire, fah! That had all been nonsense. He has the cunning of a dozen snakes. And how she had been manipulated! Had he heard of the inglorious interview with Cervantes? And if he had, was he sleek with good humour at the success of his designs? And her humiliation? Yes, an afterthought, with the tinge of truth. It had been his ploy, she realised, that had she discovered his designs, she would have discovered her own humiliation as well.

It was then that she broke down in the carriage and heartily cried.

Robles was also left with a rift in his feelings. Something in the Duchess's remarks had made the difference palpable between his business principles and the hurt of his friends.

Another Letter

The Duchess decides on her friendship with the poet.

*O*ngora's charm was a mask of the bestial in his nature, and on occasion and to his private satisfaction, he was able to exchange one for the other, like Janus faces. But the bestial invaded his handsome features on the following morning when he received a letter from the Duchess. It was brief, polite, even showed some respect for his position and talents. But it was an execution. Having discovered his manipulations, and his dishonesty with respect to the introduction, she was removing him from the Academy, and from her society altogether. The tone was remarkable for its simplicity and directness. There was no hint in it of any purchase for discussion, nor of any reprieve. He was banned.

He cursed himself for not spending more recent time in her company. He may have been able to prevent her from discovering too much, or have found such room in her affections that remonstrations with him over this latest might have been enough. But the tick of hatred began in him, hot blood in a narrow vein, clicking in his temple, and he bared his teeth at the thought that if she had allowed him to *have* her, then this might not have been the result. After all, she was no longer a virgin. So what kind of preciousness was she protecting? It was her fault then, to be so manipulated, and so humiliated.

She should suffer, having denied him.

But now this was not the issue. Banning him was just high minded on her part, but it meant ruin for him. Unless he pursued his ambitions even more strongly, extended them. If she made friends with Cervantes, then she could share his downfall. Her banishment will relieve me, he thought, of her sycophantic crew of pallid versifiers, and the intolerable duties of flatteries and thanks that one has to endure with aristocrats. No, the best thing is to continue, and make her dismissal his advantage, and something that she will one day bitterly regret.

His plan was simple. He would buy all of Cervantes' episodes, bastardise them, and have a printer in Madrid set them into a book. Included would be his introduction, and he would phrase it so that the whole book was a satire of Cervantes. No doubt, the book would prove very popular and make the stories of Don Quixote seem like weak scribblings. He had other plans. There were many avenues for revenge. The days were long. There was time for all of them.

The Bribe

The printer and the bag of gold.

'This is ironic,' Robles said. 'This is the first time that anyone has tried to pay me not to publish another's work.' He looked at the vain figure of Ongora, detecting a tremor of the poet's mouth muscles. 'But you must know that Cervantes cannot publish his book.'

'Indeed?' Ongora said, trying to keep the leap out of his voice.

'A simple business arrangement,' explained Robles. 'The pamphlets pay for themselves, for so many buy them, and they are inexpensive to make. But a book is a different matter. It is much more expensive, with the gold-leaf on the cover and illustrations. It is something I will not invest in. It is a great deal of work. If Cervantes wants to print his book, he will have to pay for it.'

'Ah,' said Ongora, 'and he has little money, I take it, for such a project.'

'He has too much debt,' said Robles. 'This he well understands, for we came to the arrangement of the episodes, because it would not cost him, or me, anything.'

'This is very satisfying,' said Ongora.

'To you maybe,' said Robles, 'but not to Cervantes. It is no fault of his that he has no money. So if you *were* to succeed

217

in preventing the publication of his book, it would cause his greatest sorrow.'

'If that were a concern of mine,' said Ongora, 'which it is not, then I would say that his sorrow is deserved, for he has striven to cheapen the best of all arts in Spain. His work is lower than a tradesman's.' This startling rudeness was followed by a brilliant smile; Ongora was trying to punish Robles as well. 'He has none else to blame but himself. It is fortunate that it is not within my calling to challenge him to a duel, otherwise, on a glorious day in our history, I would skewer him like a rat.'

Robles could only wonder at the hatred issuing from this beautiful youth.

'I assume then that you will withdraw your –' the pause was deliberate, as Robles looked at the bag of gold dangling from Ongora's hand '– offer.'

Ongora came forward, and dropped the gold onto the counter.

'Destroy the book,' said Ongora, very quietly.

Robles blinked. 'Destroy?'

Ongora's gesture was impatient. 'Burn the blocks. Make some excuse. Force him to find another printer.'

This was too much for Robles. 'Your sense of judgement must be entirely decayed if you think that I will provide the means for your envious revenge.' He pushed the gold away contemptuously. 'Hire someone else. Hire an assassin, for you will not stop him writing by destroying the book.' He laughed harshly. 'God's truth, but you are a monster of envy! Have you no other thought than his destruction?'

Ongora took the gold and smiled, suddenly calm.

'None,' he said briefly. 'And to that end, I shall remain resolved.'

And in a moment, he was gone.

The Plea

The printer refuses to publish the book.

obles could only wonder at the vicissitudes of fate, when, after the vengeful poet had left, he had but a few minutes before Cervantes and Pedro arrived. Both were genial, although Cervantes had that air of fragility about him that many of his friends knew. Overwork made him ethereal. He hefted a large manuscript and placed it proudly in front of Robles. 'My business partner has a few words to put to you,' he said and bowed in an exaggerated fashion towards Pedro, who cocked his leg and tried to bow in return, so low as to scrape his head on the floor for comedy. 'Friend Robles,' he said, 'there are many days. Not only the many days in the year, and the many days in the world, and the many days of a life—'

'No,' Robles said.

'But there are also bad days,' continued Pedro because he was enjoying himself, 'and good days, hard days, long days, and—'

'No!' repeated Robles, irritated. He did not like it that he should give ill news. Both of his friends were startled.

'Our friend is having a bad day,' said Pedro to Cervantes, 'on our good day—'

'Hush!' Robles said to him. He then turned to Cervantes and looked at him directly. 'Cervantes, you seemed to have finished your book, and have brought it here to me because you want me to print it. Let me tell you, and do not misunderstand me, that this may not be. It is impossible. I cannot print your book.'

Both looked at him with the incomprehension of children.

'We're supposed to be the funny ones,' said Pedro.

'I am not joking,' said Robles.

'Why don't you try, it'll make things better,' said Pedro.

'Look,' said Cervantes, 'Pedro is just being funny. It's not against you.'

'He's a clown,' said Robles, 'but that is not the reason for my not printing your book.'

'There are no debts between us—' said Cervantes.

'No—'

'No arguments—' said Cervantes.

'Except this one,' said Pedro.

'No,' said Robles.

'No lack of thanks or gratitude—'

'If you stop spinning, I'll tell you.'

Pedro clapped his hand over his mouth and his other over Cervantes'.

Robles shook his head in irritation at his antics. 'My reasons are part political, and part personal. And do not think that you can argue.'

Pedro groaned and said, 'Well, how can we argue anything or not if you do not tell us anything.'

'This I am attempting to do,' said Robles.

'He'll publish it in a pamphlet and we can read it tomorrow,' said Pedro to Cervantes. 'Isn't that it,' he sneered at Robles.

'Political?' asked Cervantes. 'This book contains nothing of heresy or treason.'

'I cannot publish it,' said Robles loudly, 'because of your enemies!'

His friends protested. Robles cut through this. 'You have too many enemies,' he said.

'Is that my fault?'

'Is that his fault?' said Pedro, indicating Cervantes.

'Yes,' said Robles.

'He said yes!' Pedro shook Robles hand. 'Congratulations! That was your first yes today. Do you feel better?'

'If it is a reasonable yes, than I would like to hear it argued,' said Cervantes.

There was a moment's silence in their sparring. Cervantes and Pedro waited as Robles composed himself.

'Ah, Cervantes,' said Robles, shaking his head, 'you live a charmed life, as I have heard. And as I have also witnessed. And that being so, you also live a dangerous life. Can you not see that your so-called comic episodes are anarchy?'

'There is nothing sacrilegious in them—' broke in Cervantes.

'Let me finish!' interrupted Robles. 'Listen. You write to charm the poor, you give the needy a caricature of aristocracy, you consolidate all the roustabouts of the taverns through the Empire with your seeds of irony, your sowing of mockery. And as many friends you make of the illiterate, you lose among your peers!'

'That is not my intention.'

'Then it is the spirit in you.'

'That I admit to.'

'Then it is a path that you must follow. And it is a path that I cannot tread with you. It is not my business to carve up the belly of the Empire with humorous paradoxes. Neither is it my desire to direct a fart at the literary gentry of the day. They are my business after all. I am a printer. Blocks, print, ink and no pretensions beyond that of my craft. You cannot complain then that if I see your work as seditious comedy, then how might your contemporaries see it? They see it as venomous. These are your enemies.'

'You're trying to protect me,' said Cervantes suddenly illuminated.

'Heavens above!' said Robles and slammed a ruler down

on the desk. 'I am telling you that if I print your book, your enemies will destroy me and my business! Humorous pamphlets are forgotten in a day. But a whole book! And who shall cover the expense?'

'Farting at the literates is no bad thing!' said Pedro.

'Try and make a living at it,' said Robles dryly.

'It is a strange world,' said Cervantes, 'that it should want so badly to destroy a comedy.'

'You have made him sad,' said Pedro to Robles.

Robles remained hot on his theme. 'Not an hour ago, one of your enemies tried to bribe me *not* to print the book.'

'Who?' asked Pedro innocently.

'If I tell you,' said Robles savagely, 'will you buy off his assassin?'

'Can it be wrong that my work,' said Cervantes, 'only serves to lighten?'

'This world,' said Robles, 'is not an answer for that question.'

There was a pause.

'Take the bribe and we'll print the book and say that it was printed elsewhere,' said Pedro. 'You'll be richer, innocent, and we'll have the book.'

'You need a surgeon,' said Robles, 'and so would I if I followed your suggestion and this gentleman found out that I have betrayed him.'

Pedro suddenly became angry. 'Well. He has finished the book, you are a printer, and because some poxed-up writer cannot see further than his own quill and wants nothing better than to make his ambitions political, and because you have no more temerity than the heart of a mouse, then we can go no further! All you have to do is—'

'Pedro—' said Cervantes.

'—put all the episodes that you have already printed between covers along with a few more! Now, is that a strange idea—'

'Pedro, stop raving!' said Cervantes.

Pedro gulped, blinked, and looked at him. 'He is scuttling my best business venture,' he said.

'Small boats sink in large storms,' said Robles.

'You have put us in a difficult situation,' said Cervantes to Robles.

'Me?' Robles said. 'Any printer would tell you the same. It's because of your writings. How difficult is this for you to understand?'

'Well, the last time we had a difficult discussion,' said Pedro, 'the resolution seemed to come from a bottle that you keep hereabouts –'

The tension in Robles broke. 'This is not the time for celebration, and I do not intend to play host to the naive delusions of a veteran and a facetious farmer!'

The hurt felt by this was palpable.

'These days,' said Pedro wearily to Cervantes, 'everywhere I go, and with whomever I speak, there is nothing but spite.' He turned to Robles. 'Before we leave, let me say that I hope your hair falls out, that you go blind in a day –' Cervantes began to push him out of the shop '– that your wife sleeps with a bear, and that we print the book elsewhere, and that it is such a great success that our reputations will be made, that you will be ashamed, and this poxy enemy writer will be humiliated into oblivion.' The door crashed after them.

Robles could only shake his head and remonstrate with himself. Even with the practised neutrality learned from his business experience, he would not have wished for such a strained encounter with two of his friends. He did not take Pedro's insults seriously. It agitated him more that he had to speak painful truths to the already disadvantaged. Whereas with Ongora, whose envious ambition had forced the situation, truth could not be phrased in any form. It was an evil world, he thought, and he wanted to retire from it.

After evicting themselves from the shop, Cervantes and Pedro were now quarrelling with each other.

'Is your friendship with me,' said Cervantes, 'no more than an excuse to insult my neighbours and acquaintances?'

'You may have noticed,' said Pedro at once and very roundly, 'that talking with this particular acquaintance has not improved your thinking. If you see me as no more than a fool, who thinks of nothing but his belly and his hearth, and has no more creative spirit than a dead dog at midnight, then you make less of me and rob yourself at the same time.'

Sincerity and ire made the air hot between them.

'There have been enough insults for one afternoon,' said Cervantes. 'It is not right to deal out so much disrespect.'

They paused, looking at one another.

'How do we persuade Robles to print the book?' said Cervantes. 'Perhaps not even money will persuade him.'

'I already have it,' said Pedro. 'I am so angry that it has fertilised my brain! He *will* print the book! And he will do it as a trade for the latest fashion in boots for his wife!'

Cervantes laughed. 'And so we shall both prove victorious over him! But why these items?' he said. 'How will new boots persuade Robles?'

'His wife, whom you know is more gorgeous than God should allow, has often confided in me. She is my ally in the enemy camp, for Robles is a profound money man and cannot see me as an equal in business. But I know that she is a mere whisper from being as complete a wife as any could wish, but that he is melancholic, and cannot see himself as ever pleasing her, and frets on the numerous shallow boys that follow her with silly eyes and terrible poems—'

'Remember to breathe,' said Cervantes.

'—and that all that she would require is a gift when it is right and his steady avowal of his love. And she particularly craves new boots, even though they are an extravagance for which Robles has no budget.' Pedro winked. 'It is an idea that was simple enough to plant in her head, and has been suggested to Robles on a number of occasions—'

'Upon which he shows you the door,' said Cervantes.

'—upon which he shows me the door, but with the idea lurking in his head like a fox around a hen house.'

'Then we have a plan?' asked Cervantes.

'Like a dog with fleas,' said Pedro. 'I shall immediately contact my business associates in order to find these boots. And this, being a supreme effort of will on my part from enduring many conversations and consumption of much ale, shall so impress Robles that he shall find it astonishing, along with other signs, divinities and God knows what else appearing from the air.'

'And I shall begin writing a mock introduction to the book that will poke fun at all those erudite introductions that no-one can read,' said Cervantes. 'It will divide the world between humour and its detractors.' He bowed to Pedro. 'Farewell, thou incomparable trader, hero of poachers and of the have-nots!'

Pedro bowed in return. 'I salute you as the best worst qualified writer of the era! May my praise stink in your nostrils as you set your quill to paper this evening!'

So laughing, they left each other for the day.

Cervantes Renewed

The patroness.

*P*edro was returning to see Cervantes after a one-sided conversation with the sleepy poacher, whose best wits were nocturnal, when he saw a carriage draw up in the avenue. As he drew closer, the driver leant over and said, 'Do you know which house belongs to one Miguel Cervantes?'

'Why, that's easy,' Pedro said, 'listen for a lot of quarrelling and banging of pots, and you'll find it straight away.'

'Do you know him?' said the Duchess from inside the carriage.

Pedro was enthralled. A mysterious carriage, with a mysterious voice! He tried to peer inside but the driver pushed him away with the whip, saying, 'Behave yourself!'

'I hesitate to give any information, my Lady,' Pedro said cleverly, 'unless I know the nature of your request.'

There was a rustling of skirts inside the carriage. 'And why should it concern you?' asked the Duchess.

'I am Pedro, Miguel Cervantes' business partner,' Pedro said, and glared at the driver.

'This is a fortunate meeting,' said the Duchess. The door of the carriage opened.

Pedro clambered in with enthusiasm, displaying a confident ebullience, where others might experience uncertainty. His mysterious voice sat opposite, her rich skirts arranged on the seat. 'You must be aware that as Duchess, I am the hostess of a literary Academy of which your business partner Cervantes has no doubt heard.'

Pedro gaped. She extended her hand.

'If I kiss your hand,' said Pedro, 'it'll come away dirty.'

'Your choice,' said the Duchess. 'I am wearing gloves.'

Pedro kissed her hand and admired the lace of her gloves. 'When you have given me my hand back,' said the Duchess, 'perhaps we can talk of your friend Cervantes.'

Pedro let her hand go and said, 'The last that I heard, you are his enemy, and opposed to him, and so it might be better to tell you nothing. Had I known who you were, I would not have entered your carriage—'

'The reason for my anger with him,' the Duchess said, 'has passed, and my own irrationality as well. I have understood much of the situation since seeing the printer Robles.'

Pedro snorted. 'You would have found out more by talking to a gargoyle,' he said sourly. 'There are bats who are better human beings.'

The Duchess laughed. 'Your business relations have been strained.'

Pedro shook his head mournfully. 'He will not print the book, just out of obstinacy, and he makes his excuse by talking of an assassin.'

'I perhaps might help,' she said, 'by meeting with Cervantes.'

He looked at her clothing and said, 'He should come to you. Otherwise, if you enter his courtyard, the whole neighbourhood will be stirred up, the dogs will bark, his household will wrangle with you, and it will take a deal of noise and distance before you find him.'

'I am glad of your delicacy,' she said. 'Why don't you bring him here.'

'If he's awake, because usually at this time of the day, he's asleep. Although to my mind he does not sleep. He dies every morning after writing through the night. He only wakes up if the muse prods him and says, "Up, up, and get to work!" Or if I visit him and bring him money.' He leaned forward confidentially. 'Do not mention money to him! It shames him.'

She smiled. 'On the contrary,' she said, 'I am the one to be ashamed. I will at least dismount to greet him.'

Pedro clambered out first and then stood by to help her, although the driver took up the best position, jostling him in the process. For some reason, rather than rushing off to the house on his errand, Pedro watched her dismount. She held the hand of the driver, hoisting her skirts at the same time. Her gaze on him was neutral. He turned and made for the house.

It was not Cervantes that first appeared, but his family, curious to see such a powerful lady in the lower quarter as they hovered in the entrance to the courtyard. Eventually, Cervantes came through, said a few words to them, and approached the Duchess. She looked at him with a new appraisal. A tall man, the trained stance of a soldier. Every man I see, she thought, I compare with my husband. Or at least, every man whose dignity and bearing might emulate his vigorous poise. If he stood, she recalled of her husband, he was ascendant. Either astride his charger, or pacing out the scaled length of their orchard in the library, or stepping up onto a wall in the garden and pulling me up after. Something of grace, she continued, in a man whose life was action.

Cervantes stood before her, head already bowed. The Duchess had thought that this moment would be her deepest shame. She found, however, that her heart was expanding with an accelerating sense of pleasure. From what? She was becoming unveiled, came the thought to her; how ironic a description. And why should this exhilarate her so? Now she was trembling. 'I have come to say something to you,' she said in an odd voice.

'My Lady,' he said quietly, 'perhaps we can talk inside your carriage. The curiosity of my family, and probably soon the whole neighbourhood, has certain weight. It's like being watched by the hungry while you eat.'

Pedro had joined the audience in the courtyard and was telling them that he had seen nothing like the quality of her lace.

'I have just come from inside there,' the Duchess said, hearing herself sound like a child.

Cervantes took command, his hands helped her into the carriage and then he sat opposite. The Duchess breathed deeply once, and looked at him. 'I received your letter,' she said, and it was almost incidental. She was looking at a painting. She could step in and fathom this mysterious soldier, this man of weapons, and flags, and quills . . . There was ink on his fingertips. This perhaps moved her more than anything. She remembered that her husband would sit for dinner with charcoal from a sketch on his hands. However this was not her husband. And she was here to atone. But was there not the possibility of extending her finger, touching his mouth, and saying, 'Look, the world is here, and from the bubble of our attention, we do not disturb it. It sleeps like a rare jewel, and wakes when we wear it, for pleasure, or to show what beauty means . . .'

'Your visit encourages me to believe,' he said, knowing that her state was delicate, 'that we might start again, as friends.'

'I thought it diffcult to see you,' she said in a half-tone, 'but now I find it much more than difficult.'

'My Lady?'

She shook her head. 'But then it is much easier than difficult.' She looked at him fully. 'I have recovered my life.' Her eyes were glistening.

'I am glad of it, my Lady,' he said, comprehending immediately that she had escaped the violent prison in which she had been dwelling.

She took a shuddering sigh and steadied herself into business. 'I have seen Robles, and the satire will be taken from circulation. The work of the introduction did not come from my hand.'

He nodded slowly in comprehension.

'The envy that manipulated me will be dealt with and it shall no longer trouble you,' she continued. 'Having been –' she paused '– unsound for many months, I was the foil for a disagreeable plot. This is over. And to redress all wrongs that I have performed with respect to you, I shall deliver money to Robles for printing your book.'

'That is not necessary,' Cervantes began.

She waved him down. 'As you like. The money is a gift. Neither myself nor the Academy is to become your patron, nor is it required that your work be dedicated to me as a show of gratitude. I would feel unequal to it.' She sighed. 'The Academy and its activities are now suspended, as I do not intend to cater for an illiterate court, nor subject myself to the petty passions that fuelled our disagreement.' He could now see in her the imperious beauty for which she had once been famous.

'It would be a loss to the court,' he said politely, not really believing it.

'As far as I know,' she said, 'the Emperor cannot read or has forgotten how. Unlike his father, who was the patron saint of lists. An Academy does little good for the Emperor. And I suspect that the taste of the self-appointed minister of culture,' she said, meaning Denia, 'is bawdy and runs to political portraits and history.'

'You would elevate the standard,' he said, politely.

'My use of standards has led,' she said gently, 'to violent intolerance.' She thought a little. 'But I must say that even though I have lost my sense of humour,' she said, 'I think that your work is too amusing for my taste.'

'Now you're being funny, he said.

'I find it alarming,' she said, 'that my assistant Cara has to lock herself in the closet to control herself.'

'My Lady,' he said, 'the harder the cruelties, the larger the laughs.'

She changed the subject. 'I hope you do not feel,' she said earnestly, 'that I have brought you nothing.'

'Indeed, no,' he said, 'it will take me a week to overcome your generosity.'

They laughed.

'Are you ending the Academy?' he asked.

She nodded. 'I shall close up the house. Then I shall look for my husband.' She smiled at his expression. 'It is not ghoulish. His family is from Parma. They have beautiful estates. There is a house with some masterpieces and the works of the ancients that I can study. And it is a country that especially knows how to live.'

He nodded.

'I will help you in any way that I can while I am here,' she said.

It was a dismissal. 'Thank you,' he said. The atmosphere changed abruptly; perhaps she could not sustain this kind of talk. He prepared to leave. Her hand caught his arm. 'Do not think me too precipitate,' she said. 'There is much for me to think about. And it is perhaps a little inappropriate . . .' She signalled with her head at Cervantes' family who were still waiting at the courtyard entrance. 'I am forever in your debt.' With this, she closed the carriage door after him.

Then her head emerged, her vibrant eyes glowing at him. The leave-taking had transformed her. 'Come and see me,' she said. Again the imperious tone. Her head withdrew into a mysterious shadow, an oracular retreat. He stood, knowing the unmistakable delight and terror of having been summoned for sensual company.

Not wanting to discuss all the details of the conversation with his family, he told them briefly that she had apologised graciously for her conduct and had agreed to pay for the printing of the book, without thought of any return. His family became exulted, and Isabel all but carried him into the house. He told them that he must busy himself with finishing his introduction before printing the book, and then the real celebrations could begin. 'Remember,' Cervantes said, 'money will not help in printing the book. But we already have a plan for that. And the money will help, in other ways.' He and Pedro winked hugely at each other, which would normally have irritated his household, but for the indulgence of their present good news.

'A patron,' Pedro said in wonder, 'or shall we say in this case, God saving her veil and lace gloves, a patroness!'

For Cervantes, her summons had been clear. And he knew he would answer it.

The Shortest Love-Affair in the World

Mutability and mutuality.

*C*ervantes knew that the summons of the Duchess was immediate. The day already being mysterious, his journey that night proved more than magical. Nothing hindered his ride to the mansion. Doors were opened by deferential servants. And as though it were the most natural thing in the world, he found himself within the private wing of the Duchess's apartments. There, with the instinct of Eros, he paced through the rich corridor and found her in the library, sitting on the floor surrounded by maps.

For the first time, he saw the girl in her. Her eyes brought him over and then her hand, taking his, pulled him gently down beside her . . . Well, I can only tell you that the tender acceptance of her touch removed, with lightning ease, the weight of their first encounter. And further, as he sat by her, admiring her extraordinary and graceful profile, he felt like a child in front of some pleasurable enormity, for she was to confide in him.

'Here are my husband's campaigns,' she said quietly, indicating the maps. 'He marched far north into the Lowlands.' She looked at him fully. 'You must understand that the inspiration of our –' the pause was full of unqualified daring '– friendship has revived all my pains.'

'The signs of life,' he said immediately, his voice low.

'Indeed,' she said, her eyes growing larger, 'so you must not think that I have summoned you simply to talk of my husband.' This statement banished his doubt, even as it had entered his mind. Her hand took his, and in a movement that would stay with him always, took his finger and began to trace a campaign's northward route on the crackling parchment.

'He was a great commander,' he said.

She stopped moving his hand and looked at him, her beauty emergent as she slowly took in his battered, genial face. 'I loved him as my husband. Because of you, I can love him as a soldier. Even though, when we were first introduced, I could ride and shoot better than he.' She stood, the reminiscence beginning to fill the room, and went over to a cabinet, returning with wine for both of them. 'He was so full of life, that I had to challenge him. After a day of riding, from which he complained that I had given him more saddle lumps than a week of campaigning, and after I beat him at shooting plates in the garden, he conceded to be my prisoner, the prize of my campaign. My ransom demand of him was to marry me.' She moved to his side. 'Do not let these reminiscences hurt you.'

Feeling that all his emotions were being announced, as if by a superior steward, the moment they appeared, he said. 'We had a woman in our tercio who was pretending to be a man. She was undetected for the whole of Prince John's campaign against the Turk. She was under my command for a little time.' He acknowledged her amused expression. 'Well, she was scrawny, like many of the boys in the camp, and she had red hair and a redder temper, and everyone knew that she was dangerous.'

'Then how was she discovered,' she asked.

'In the camp games, when she was tickled, she became breathless and hysterical, that gave her away.'

She laughed. 'Very definite evidence.'

'Indeed, although it was said that her discovery was more because of a jealous lover, than because of her sensitive ribs.'

There was a silence, for the word 'lover' had caught them by surprise, and they were looking at each other, very openly.

'Señor Cervantes,' she said in as soft a voice as she was able, 'making me laugh is another sin against you.'

'Then I must make you as sad as possible,' he said, his heart in his throat. 'I shall read you an episode from my book and you will be crying for a week.'

She smiled and looked steadily at him. 'Tears and laughter we already have. Argument, injury, these we have passed through. Now what remains for lovers to demonstrate their passion?' Although her tone was light, her heart was thudding inside her breast.

'I dare not say it,' he said sincerely.

'Then,' she said, with a woman's triumph, 'as a master of action, you must perform it.'

As the sensibilities of the reader have been more than exercised throughout this story, then let us allow the intimacy of these new lovers to prevail. And if you find this interruption too abrupt, then take comfort in the maxim that when imagination and experience travel together, then imagination is king. It remains only to report briefly on a conversation between them some hours later, when still entwined, the dawn was fast advancing on them.

He woke because the room had become chilled, and their lovers' heat had cooled also. His heart ached, and he did not know why and he rubbed his chest to ease it. The customary onset of pain from his fractured hand was in abeyance for some reason. But these were only half-ignited curiosities compared to the sense of wonder that inhabited him. She was not at his side, but even as he discovered this, she appeared in her robe, carrying a bowl and a towel, helped him wash his face and gave him mint to chew. These were small glories, for she was so beautiful in the pre-emergent day. But then his heart was seized again, and he leant back to find out what this meant, even as she eased herself into his arms. Their silence was full of thought.

'Señor Cervantes,' she said, 'your book is finished and the relief of delivering it must equal a year of Sundays.' She raised herself up and looked at him. 'It shall take some weeks to pack up this house. Then, according to my plan, I shall travel to Parma. If you are ready . . . when you are ready, come with me. Or come to me there.'

His heart lurched and he knew that it had anticipated the pain of the present moment. His blood failed at the generosity of her offer. He looked at her, and wondered if it was for the last time. 'Extraordinary beauty,' he said, 'my heart is too big to say what is in it, and the words are far way.'

'You must find them, señor,' she said tenderly, 'for we are on the threshold of a new life.'

'Your station is more than mine,' he said in discovery, 'you have more to lose. Others would always see me as –' and he knew this to be the triumph of insufficiency, even as he said it '– a patched soldier in your company.'

'If you are finding excuses,' she said, 'then that is a poor one.'

'I must protect your generosity,' he said, 'from those who would hate you for it.'

'Señor,' she said, and she had not lost her equilibrium, 'I do not require that kind of armour for my soul.'

'I am obligated,' he faltered, 'my family . . .'

'If you had not come here,' she said quietly, and the hurt made her face even more enthralling to him, 'I would have understood *that* to have been your choice.'

'Then I have deceived you,' he said in real sorrow, 'for although it is a marriage without love, I cannot let it founder.'

She smiled, joyless. 'And I cannot play an illicit mistress. Let us remember,' she said, 'that we have never deceived one another.' It was an open moment in which they both recovered. 'You thought too little. I expected too much.' And she looked at him with the tears of a child. His eyes also flowed, and they gazed at the trembling images of each other through tears. 'You knew this when you awoke,' she said.

'My heart ached with the presentiment,' he said.

She nodded, and a glitter of her tears fell on his hand as she held it. 'Mine too. I saw it by looking at you as you slept.' Her eyes gazed at him wonderingly. 'I have slept with war. Small wonder that my morning should be turbulent.'

This made them both smile. 'Indeed, my Lady, he said, 'war has tattooed me with its kindness.'

'And are not these injuries,' she said, raising his hand to her lips, 'answered with love?'

'Love is not an answer,' he said, 'but the legend of wanting.'

Then they were interrupted. 'My Lady?' It was the voice of her maid outside. She touched his hand again with her lips. 'She will guide you, a path to the road where you will be unobserved,' she whispered. She was suddenly merry. 'Last night, my man with a cloak and hat like yours rode away from the mansion so that all eyes were appeased.' She faced him fully, holding her hands in his, and her gaze was a frank avowal to him, the heart in her eyes, the qualities of her bosom. 'You see, I was prepared for a soldier in my bedroom, and if he had so chosen, for him to be the master of all that was mine.' She let him go, but her eyes were steadfast. 'Quickly, the house is waking.'

Cervantes escaped, even as he yearned to return immediately and catch the creature that had intoxicated everything in him, even to the dregs of his life. He knew that love had lanced him more effectively than the best marksman. His insomniac hours were to be kept more effectively entranced with his expanding heart than by all the flowers of opium in the east.

The Duchess paced her apartment, threw open the shutters, watched as the sun grew. As her maid dressed her hair, she thought of love as the enhancement of life, even though it meant more than was fair of pain. She was delighting in that nothing had finished between them. They had opened a book together and read the first page. Putting down the book for a while was the hardest thing.

The Vigil

The olive tree in the courtyard and the Holy Grail.

*H*aving destroyed the magician of evil verse, the old Knight had set himself on achieving the Holy Grail. It was, he knew, the final task before his spirit would finally revoke all association with his body, and depart to some blessed realm where sins were forgiven, memory restored and he could have fine conversations with some of his friends. Or at least, that was his hope. But he knew that there was some final great effort required of him before he became invisible to the world, and it to him.

But where was the Grail? If there were such an evil magician in the area, then surely the Grail was imprisoned close to hand. A conversation with a particularly sagacious looking tree confirmed this. He must travel again to the metropolis, where he had already met with a few adventures, to accomplish his quest.

And so he gracefully returned Bucephalus to her astonished owner and said farewell. It was not an easy moment. The mare, who after the old Knight's kind words and their victory over Ongora, was so much in love with him as to be coy. She became very sad. The driver could never be as affectionate, and tell her that she was the golden son of Apollo, or take her on such adventures. As he left, she was eating the driver's hat, caught between her disdain for having to return to her old position, and her yearning for the old Knight's kind words and confidences.

The old Knight then made his way on foot to the capital. A true Knight would clear the roads of minor demons and monsters, and achieve as much good as possible. But then the old Knight realised that he must not be distracted from his quest for the Grail. And so, having benignly saluted the capital gates, to the mystification of the guards, and having attracted a solemn pack of beggar-children, he wandered for a day into the business of the city.

The adventures that befell him that day would fill the contents of another comic romance. But because his purpose was the discovery of the Grail, we shall keep with him, and leave the telling of these adventures to another. The beggar-children left him after his adventure with the Society of Thieves. He had now reached the toiling market of the lower quarter, the narrow cobbled streets, full of pushing arguing traders. He reached a square at the end of the market, walked further, turned down into an avenue, and stopped, arrested by the sight of a small courtyard.

The quietness was the first attraction. But also, in the centre of the courtyard, circled by a small wall of bricks, there was an olive tree. But he saw something else. He saw a tree breathing with a mystic significance, an ebb and flow of trembling gold. The roots, he saw, plumbed deeper than the earth, the giant waist and trunk a footstool for God, the branches expanding the limits of the sky. And as he looked, he heard a music that evoked all the glories of the earth, the inside heart of the ocean, its glistening companion the sky, and that humble strip of loam, suppliant to the corrosive wisdom of crags and mountains. And under this he heard the rhythm of a beaten measure, the dreadful pacing of time. He was transfixed and stood in the entrance to the courtyard, knowing that here was the end of the quest. He realised that even time's dreadful tyranny was prisoner to the tree. Here was the end of his journey. All journeys, all roads and highways, were resolved in this courtyard, here before the mightiest of all altars, the heart of all mysteries. He knelt as tears melted from him, and prayed before the end of his quest, the Holy Grail.

It was Isabel who told Cervantes that a crazed old fool was muttering and staring in the courtyard. Cervantes did not have to look to know who it was. He came down however, to alleviate the anxieties of his household, and found the old Knight kneeling in the courtyard. He touched the old Knight's arm gently.

'I have not seen you for an age,' he said.

The old Knight opened his eyes, nodded, and said, 'Your relatives think me mad. But that is good. If they think me mad, then they'll leave me be, for this is the end of my quest.' He looked up at Cervantes with intimate wisdom. 'It is a wonder that I had not guessed that you, Galahad, would of course be the guardian of such a treasure.' He turned back to the olive tree. 'Now I must return to my vigil. Let me be undisturbed.'

Cervantes let him be. He found the old Knight's attention to the olive tree oddly comforting. He returned to the house and found Isabel holding his infantry sword, her eyes wide and black. 'Well?' she said interrogatively.

'He's an old friend,' he said, taking the sword from her. 'He lost his wits in the wars. He's had a long journey and thinks that the tree is holy.'

'All of your friends,' she said, 'are touched or disturbed.'

'Make up a bed for him,' he said.

'You're going to let him die in this house?' she demanded. He was startled at her brutal intuition. 'Off you go,' he said to her, 'and ask Doña Catalina to prepare some soup.'

'Soup is all we have,' she said.

'And be kind.'

She stuck her tongue out at him and disappeared.

The Retirement of Robles

The monstrous fad of pamphlet publishing.

*R*obles had not seen his friends for some days, which in no way surprised him. But the interval was depressing. And the last words of the Duchess, her neutral riposte to his business principles, returned to his thinking continually. He honestly did not know what he would say to Ongora if he saw him again. Added to this, there was a pause in the usual amount of work flowing into the shop. Some caution, he supposed, as a result of the printing of the satire and rumours of Cervantes' discomfort. Or maybe more of Ongora's plots. How had the printing of pamphlets become a war, he wondered. There was this silence, he knew. But he was under no illusion that nothing was happening. It was the interval between skirmishes.

The door clanged and Robles suddenly had his first customer for a day.

After a few minutes, he was once again alone in the gloom of the shop. The customer, a regular, had left him with only a deepened sense of dislocation. The customer was a pamphleteer who found a new subject every month and would print something on it, whether there was an audience for it or no. Robles looked over the pamphleteer's newest effort. He became instantly melancholic. 'Has the world gone mad with pamphlets?' he said to himself. 'Not a day goes by when another ridiculous tract isn't submitted for printing.' He rummaged on the desk. 'Here's a list of some titles.' He read from a list. ' "The meaning of moonlight"; "A variety of recipes for turnips"; "The cause of limping"; "A new practice for deploying a platoon over rough ground".' He put down the list. 'From the subject matter of these pamphlets and frequent conflicts that I have witnessed between their authors, I am sceptical as to the progress of knowledge in the world. Knowledge appears to degenerate with every pamphlet.' Now he went to the shelves where old copies of pamphlets were kept. 'Look here, a description on the turning of base metals into gold by using dew and the sweat of a corpse.' He looked up from a memory. 'Even my wife wanted to publish the suggestion that the curious men who congregate at the carriage stops to see the ankles of ladies should rather step up and help the ladies, and so leave time for the footmen to take down the luggage. There was a time,' he continued, 'when the only printing was the notices for a marriage, a christening, or services for the departed. And although I have plenty of business, and this has made me a relatively wealthy man, I am not happy. I have read so much nonsense and lunacy that I rarely feel aroused by new knowledge, or the excitement of fresh news.' He paused. 'Recent events have made me more than think that perhaps a printer *should* control the meaningless flow of babble that is printed every day. If I were to announce that I could only accept the finest and most literate, the most well reasoned and thought-provoking materials for publication, then at least I would prevent the world from being smothered in paper! But that would never work, to set myself up as an adjudicator of quality. And neither would I make any friends, for authors have the thinnest skin of any, and they would quickly revenge the refusal of my services with a mean rhyme on my appearance, or a bit of gossip on the difference in age between myself and my wife. Why don't you retire, friend Robles, you say, sell your shop, take your fortune and retire. Yes, I reply, and very quickly become too old and tired to enjoy the active life that I have now. No, I would rather breathe my last with my head on a printer's block. And this I promise. That the ceremonies for my funeral shall not be printed, but written in hand!'

The door clanged again and Robles turned to see his wife, unattended by any ardent boys, and with a particular coy smile that he knew was for him, but for which he did not know the reason.

Moments later, Robles knew. And no further customers were allowed that day. The door was locked while he jubilantly drew up plans for selling the print shop, and retiring with his wife to a house in Madrid. But retirement was not the right word. He would be more than creatively busy, while his wife pursued her languorous existence. He would certainly learn more than from the endless rota of pamphlets. Fatherhood was to be his new occupation.

The Rogue from Madrid

A fortune from piracy.

*W*hen Cervantes entered the tavern that night, the tavern-keeper called him over and pointed out a large, overdressed man, very drunk, carousing with the regulars. Cervantes asked who it was. The tavern-keeper said, 'He boasts of being a printer.'

'A curious profession to boast about,' said Cervantes. 'I shall go and meet him.'

The tavern-keeper, knowing the ill-fortune that Cervantes had experienced with printers, kept himself within hearing of the ensuing conversation.

'Welcome, sir,' said the drunk, seeing Cervantes appear at his table. 'I presume that you are a familiar of this place.'

'A familiarity which I extend to you,' said Cervantes, 'if you will accept.'

'You are polite,' said the drunk. 'Will you share a drink with me?'

'I never accept a drink from a newcomer, until I have learned something of their trade,' said Cervantes.

'An interesting policy,' said the drunk, 'although I am not sure I understand it.'

'I would rather,' said Cervantes, 'drink with you on good terms. Once I know something of your profession, then we are likely to become friends. This is better than just taking money from you.'

'Well,' said the drunk, 'here is money on the table for that eventuality. And now I may tell you that I am a printer, and that in a mere month, I shall have already made my fortune!'

'Now that is interesting,' said Cervantes, realising that the drunk was already obnoxious. 'How will you manage this miracle?'

'I shall tell you,' said the drunk, and he waved at the tavern-keeper. 'I live in Madrid, where the craze for printing is like a plague. Pamphlets sell faster than hot bread. I decided to invest in the printing business for I have a rare talent for enterprise.' The drunk tapped the side of his head and winked at Cervantes. The tavern-keeper put pitchers in front of them. 'Where was I?'

'A talent for enterprise,' said Cervantes.

'Ah yes,' said the drunk, and turning to the tavern-keeper said, 'another drink.' He turned back to Cervantes. 'A certain acquaintance of mine, a gentleman of this town –' he began to whisper in a tone that everyone could hear '– a certain elegant poet has proposed a splendid enterprise to me.' He smiled gleefully at Cervantes. 'It was a miracle! Ah, I bless my enterprising blood and the foresight of my brain!'

'And if only bragging were an art!' said Cervantes. 'What is this enterprise?'

The drunk continued proudly. 'The printing of a new comic romance with illustrations and a highly unusual introduction by this aforementioned poet.'

This was becoming tedious for Cervantes. 'Well, you are fortunate,' he said. The drunk grabbed him by the sleeve. 'I have not told you the motive for why the book is to be printed. You must guess,' he whispered loudly.

'For your profit,' Cervantes said.

'That's by me,' said the drunk. 'But what is the motive for the poet? And you'll not guess it! It's the strangest motive! And I shall make money from it!'

'For his satisfaction,' said Cervantes.

'Come, that's too broad,' said the drunk.

'To please a patron,' said Cervantes wearily.

'Nothing so simple,' said the drunk. 'I am playing a game with you!'

'The answer must surely be delightful,' said Cervantes.

'For revenge!' hissed the drunk melodramatically.

There was a silence. Those in the tavern who had been listening surreptitiously since the drunk had started whispering, now turned and watched him intently.

'And why should printing a comic romance,' Cervantes said, feeling that his words were fated, 'be a revenge?'

'Because the poet has stolen the book from someone whom he hates!' The drunk giggled and wiped his mouth unsteadily. 'He has stolen the book, rearranged the chapters, added in some extraneous matter and has written an introduction that mortally insults the original author.' The drunk found this so funny that he began to laugh uncontrollably, wheezing and brushing away the tears. 'And I shall make money from it!' He collapsed, helpless.

'How wonderful,' said Cervantes sourly, 'and the original author?'

'A resident of this town,' whispered the drunk. 'Most likely a fool in a garret somewhere who has no idea that his book is about to be published.'

'And this is your enterprise?' said Cervantes. The violent charge in the air was obvious to everyone but the drunk, who rolled helplessly in his chair. 'It will be the trend,' he gasped, 'and many will practise it.'

'And so you have come here,' said Cervantes, 'to reward the author?'

The drunk gaped. 'Who?' he said. 'The author?'

'Yes,' said Cervantes, 'the one who wrote the book.'

'Not at all,' said the drunk. 'I will take all profits. I have come to meet with the poet, my client, and have him approve the draft that will be published a week tomorrow. Now, are you not satisfied with my little game of guessing?'

Cervantes leaned forward over the drunk.

'Now I shall play a game with you,' he said evenly, although most of the regulars knew that he was very angry. He held out his hand in a gesture mysterious to the drunk. The tavern-keeper was ready, and having already returned from the bar, handed Cervantes his famous more-than-regulation-length sword. 'If I do not guess in one the name of this author that you have so abused, then you may leave with the wits that God has given you still intact.' The sword hovered over the drunk. 'And if I *do* guess in one, then you must run. For I shall pare your wits like kindling and your head and limbs as well.'

The drunk was petrified with fear. 'An acquaintance should not speak in such a way.'

'Our meeting was not so accidental,' Cervantes said evenly. The tavern was very still. 'The name of the author that you have so abused is –' and the sword twisted in Cervantes' grip '– Miguel Cervantes.'

The drunk gulped, lurched up, terrified, and ran for the entrance. 'Help!' he wailed.

Cervantes tossed the sword back to the tavern-keeper. 'He'll die of fright first before murder,' he said, and ran after.

Outside the scene was so absurd that Cervantes almost immediately stopped being angry. Pedro had tripped up the drunk, was sitting on his back, and while hurling inventive abuse, was hitting him with a large cheese.

'Help!' cried the drunk, 'Demons!' His eyes were tight shut.

'You heard?' asked Cervantes as he and Pedro lifted the drunk by the arms and legs.

'Piss-pot!' shouted Pedro at the drunk as a reply.

They carried the drunk to the water trough and threw him in. There was a sustained cheer from the regulars who had followed outside. Bubbles rose in the trough but the drunk remained submerged. Pedro dragged his head to the surface. 'Demons,' gasped the drunk, his eyes still closed.

'Cervantes!' called the tavern-keeper softly. He pointed at the torch-lights of the Watch some streets away.

Cervantes and Pedro ran, hearing the scurry of pursuit behind them.

'He's mad,' said, the tavern-keeper, showing the drunk to the Watch. 'He's from Madrid so it's no surprise. He had one drink, when his conscience erupted, and he took himself outside and threw himself in.'

'Demons,' said the drunk from the trough.

The two friends recovered in a doorway. 'Usury and disrespect have brought this on him,' said Cervantes.

'Agreed,' said Pedro, 'although it would be a little difficult to explain how he brought himself into that trough!'

'But this is now not the emergency,' Cervantes said. 'We have but a week to print a book!'

Interlude

The printer's holiday, a gathering of plots and other items.

*A*nd that was not the half of it. Robles was nowhere to be found. He had decided on removing himself and his wife, before any more mad pamphleteers decided on his services, and taken something of a recuperative pleasure trip to the old capital. This suited his wife as well, as in her present condition she was finding everything a cause for tears, had forgotten how to brush her hair, and was eating too many confectioneries. He had packed a few bags and left that morning.

The Watch reluctantly released the drunken printer from Madrid, even though he continually talked of demons, and made incoherent claims that he was on the Emperor's business, a thought that had been fed to him by Ongora and which he had only too readily adopted into his array of boasts.

Ongora stood his bail, approved the proof copy of the pirated edition of Cervantes' work, and without losing his incendiary temper, arranged for his co-plotter to return urgently to Madrid. The pirated book must be printed and circulated immediately. Still drunk, half-raving and in half-shame, the printer returned as ordered. Ongora watched him go, and having acknowledged that he had found someone suitable for the piracy of Cervantes' work, he also regretted not foreseeing that their scheme and the excitement of imminent profits should turn the printer's predilection for drink so rapidly into a vice. He calculated that the printer's shame at revealing their designs to the one person that should remain ignorant of them, the uncomfortable interlude in the trough, and the willing threat of the Watch to consign him to an asylum, might steady his toxic nerves. He would visit in the interim and check the progress of their piracy. It made him privately glow, the thought that within the week Cervantes' book would be upstaged by a clever parody, and the insults that he had barbed in Valladolid would become the gossip of the nation. Cervantes' life would be dregs.

No-one had information on the disappearance of Robles or his wife. That he should disappear without a word became the real mystery. The two friends found themselves meeting outside the door of the print shop, as though a daily pilgrimage would bring back the acerbic printer. They had been foiled by the unforeseen. And after having so clearly gained the support of the Duchess, it was cruel to lose their ally, whom they felt would have been comforted by the news.

Having nothing to do in a state of emergency made them both sleepless, and while meeting almost on the hour at Robles' shop, they could not think of anything better to do. The manuscript was tied and ready. News was already out in the city, and excited people would stop them in the street and ask them for the release date. His family were agog with excitement that finally fame might be coming to them. The only person who remained consistently unaffected by this mixture of tedium and turbulence was the old Knight, who remained transfixed by his vision of the Grail in Cervantes' courtyard, whilst any number of attempts to shoo him by the family or scent him by the dogs of the quarter affected him not at all. It gave Cervantes something to think about when Isabel demanded that the old man be bodily removed from their property before the regional carrion thought him dead and tried to chew him in place or carry him off in pieces. 'Did you prepare a room for him?' he asked her.

'And where is this mysterious room?' Isabel said sarcastically. 'Have you forgotten how many daughters and nieces you have, both legitimate and bastard, and that a war exists between them, and that the matron of the house, your wife whose name you probably no longer remember, has her own room in which she lives most of the day, which means there are no rooms but yours which you use like a barracks, neither for sleep nor recreation, but for scribbling and fits of unconsciousness—'

'My daughter, the tirade,' Cervantes said. 'He can have the hut in the courtyard—'

'Which is the other thing, if you had let me finish, that I was about to tell you,' Isabel continued, her wide black eyes fixed on him obdurately. 'The old fool will not go to bed, and has stood there since last we talked of him.' She paused, as this seemed to her triumphant news. 'His legs must be made of wood,' she finished.

That night, Pedro came to fetch Cervantes with news that Robles had returned. Together they went immediately to the print shop, where they could see the faint glimmer of light. They banged for a while, until Pedro decided that he would gather all the possible items of barter to sweeten Robles, although this probably meant his being bankrupted. Cervantes should write the notice of distribution, something that Robles would normally do, so that all effort could go into printing the book. They decided that Pedro would return at dawn the next morning to rouse Robles for work.

They had both forgotten that the next morning was Sunday.

Work on the Sabbath

Fine boots from Madrid.

*R*obles had ignored the banging on his door the previous night; drunks, he thought, who don't know how to go home and to bed. His days away in Madrid had been productive; the good news shared with the family, a house selected for purchase, and an increasingly rewarding bond between himself and his wife. She knew nothing but him, a dependency that moved him oddly. His plans on their return were simple. To sell the shop and return to Madrid. No more mad pamphleteers, or the welter of words and ink that engulfed his wearied sensibilities. A note to the Duchess, thanking her for her custom. And some kind of resolution with Cervantes and Pedro. Although this was a little hard to think about. His feelings in this area had receded a little. Now he was no longer sure who was beholden to whom. But now, their journey over, safe in bed, he warmed to the pure sensual trust of his sleeping wife, and dreamed of a daughter, crisp curls . . .

The next morning, he rose and prepared for church. This meant dressing in something formal, good linen and a stick appropriate to a wealthy tradesman. His wife felt too sick and stayed in bed. He went down to attend to some small duties in the shop, even as the cathedral bells began to announce their summons to worship.

Disturbed by noises suspiciously close to the door of the print shop, Robles went to find out the cause. He opened the shop-door to find Pedro, smiling cheerfully, while he struggled with the wiles of a goat, which was trying to back out of a rope halter. 'Pedro,' said Robles in exasperation, 'this is Sunday.'

'The best day of the week,' Pedro said as the goat butted him, 'for praising God, doing good deeds, and for miracles.'

'You must be confident indeed of my friendship,' said Robles, 'to be visiting on a holy day with a yard of useless items—' indicating Pedro's trade items on the stones '—that beast—' nodding at the goat '—and its mess in my doorway.' There were hard pellets and a distinct fetid odour.

'I am confident in two things,' said Pedro, shaking the goat to keep it still. 'The first that it is good to so resolve our business arrangement. And second, that because of your upright character, God himself will scour the doorstep for you.'

This upset Robles; he felt that Pedro's humorous flattery belittled God. 'Stop this useless bantering!' he commanded. 'Go away, and take that market place with you.' Robles turned to enter the shop, but another exasperated thought held him. 'Do you not recall the parable of the money-lenders in the temple!'

'Why, it's my favourite parable, and I have used it many times with my creditors,' Pedro said as the goat circled his back in obstinate cunning. 'And as for taking these items back, that is not part of our business arrangement. They are yours, as much as if they had taken root.' The goat crashed into the back of his leg. 'Except for this goat. Which is anxious to be your friend.'

Robles became still. 'Business arrangement?' He looked at Pedro hard. 'What business arrangement?'

'These items are peculiar to an oral contract in which it was agreed that they would be exchanged,' said Pedro politely, as the goat hammered his legs, 'for the printing of our friend's book.'

He barely had time to finish before Robles, now very annoyed, interrupted him. 'Nonsense! We had no such arrangement.' He pointed at Pedro. 'Go away, it's Sunday. Get away from my doorstep, and make a good Christian of yourself.'

Whether it was from the goat's relentless attacks, or Robles' fierce indignation, or from both, but in this next moment and for the following few hours, Pedro became inspired. He looked at Robles and said with best sincerity, 'Printing the book will be the most Christian act that you will have done in all your Sundays.'

Robles shook his head indignantly. 'Get off the doorstep, and take all this rubbish with you.'

Pedro said, 'How can you call this goat rubbish, or this best lace, or those sausages—'

Robles interrupted, 'I have a goat, lace is out of fashion and there are sausages in the pantry—'

'And boots?' Pedro said quickly.

There was a pause.

'Yes?' said Robles, a little interested.

Pedro nodded encouragingly at him, bidding the memory.

'A pair of boots was mentioned,' said Robles. He looked at Pedro thoughtfully. It was true that his wife's pregnancy was as strong an intoxicant as could be had from any bottle. But it was prudent to be cautious. A new pair of boots would consolidate her new warmth. In fact, she had remarked recently that new boots would be useful because she could look at them whenever she felt weepy. He coughed. 'And these boots, as I remember our discussion, are the best in Spain?' Pedro wide-eyed at the implication of his interest, nodded in assurance. 'Of finest leather, and certainly made in Madrid?' Pedro nodded again. 'Where are they?' asked Robles.

Pedro stared and said, 'Bringing them here would bankrupt me!' He fended off the goat. 'Consider all of this as more than enough for a pair of boots.'

'I will take all of this,' said Robles hard, 'and the boots.'

Pedro looked at Robles and knew that no persuasion was possible. 'Without question,' he said, thinking desperately. 'Wait here. I will fetch the boots,' he said, and then quickly ran off down the street. The goat, now free, immediately butted in through the door of the shop. Irritated, Robles shouted, 'I will wait no more than an hour!'

Hearing this from Robles, Pedro sprinted faster towards to where he hoped was the solution to his dilemma, the cathedral.

Meanwhile, the goat had entered the print shop and proved a diverting problem for Robles. The animal was a master of evasion. He considered locking it in but the animal had already taken a liking to vellum.

Santa Maria la Antigua was only half a cathedral, still in construction, but every Sunday and on all other religious occasions, it drew everyone. Pedro's inspiration was this, that the whole city would be attending Mass. He was running by his neighbours and business associates, who called out to him cheerfully, and wondered why he didn't stop and discuss trades.

He desperately tried to think as he ran. Inspiration was one thing, he thought, but resolution was another. And his mind was full of ifs. His inspiration was a memory of the Duchess descending from her carriage outside Cervantes' house. Had she not, he recalled, in the small hitch of her skirts revealed a very fine and expensive-looking pair of boots? *If* this was a real memory (and this was his best certainty), and *if* the Duchess was at the cathedral, and *if* she relented of her boots, and *if* Robles accepted them for his wife, the book could be printed. 'Those are the ifs,' he panted to himself, 'and here is the cathedral, and here I am running up the steps. *If* I get through this today, I shall lie down for a week.'

The stairs were crammed, and the cathedral square filled with carriages and horses. Inside, Mass had begun, but although the congregation was solemn, and a large attentive circle had gathered around the distant ornate glare of the altar, the noise of conversation was louder than the singing. Pedro ran around the gallants, who were hoisting their swords and hissing at the minor clergy. He risked assuming that the Duchess would have a reserved box towards the front. She was probably a devout one, he thought, and dodged a neighbour who wanted advice on a business negotiation.

The Duchess was devout, but not in the way that Pedro conceived. The nation's God – one for whom she had crossed herself every day – had become a distant avatar of harsh laws, a God of wars, battles, loss, and terrible ironies. She had gravitated to her own powerful proofs of the divine. These she found in books of the ancient philosophers, in Greek statues, rendered by supreme tacticians of stone. Or in the turning leaves of the garden, the studious containment of certain trees. The tender furl of a rose.

But in the suffocating dark of the cathedral, there was something in the swirling musk of the incense, and the dense animal press of the congregation; it was a curiosity. Their devotion, she thought, was the curiosity of a child's sensory exploration of the world. No wonder that their God has become an army of spears, pushing the land mass into dominated territories, wrestling forests into ships, turning knowledge into law, and law into books. Her husband's finest victories had been in the Netherlands, a land hauled up in lumps, reclaimed by its people from the ocean. What was their God like? A serious, sober engineer, no doubt.

That was to be her last thought on the subject. It was the main part of the Mass, and a quiet was growing through the cathedral. Even for the roughs, it was the height of the day's entertainment. The communion bell rang, the priest's voice became the sole sound as he intoned the lines of the communion. Candles on the altar and in the side-chapels were a blur of steady fire.

This common moment of attention was interrupted by an intense whisper.

'Your highness!' It was Pedro, peering into her box.

She looked up, startled. He entered the box rapidly, and knelt by her, crossing himself, which was unnecessary as he was not really thinking about God, and if he was trying to look normal, then this was far too late, as he had already attracted the attention of much of the congregation.

'Your highness is fortunate,' he whispered urgently. 'Today you can perform an act of kindness that the people will never forget!'

'Is that Pedro!' came a voice from the altar.

Pedro stood up rapidly. 'Bless me, but it is God calling me!' He waved at the altar and then winked at the surrounding congregation.

The Duchess smiled privately.

'Pedro!' said the voice, 'stop your nonsense! If you have other business than worship, then remove yourself outside.'

There were wardens bearing down on him, carrying batons.

'God is good,' said Pedro in a loud conciliation, 'and should be obeyed. But it must be told to you that I am conducting a holy act of business with her highness the Duchess!'

'Pedro!' said the voice sternly, 'if you do not withdraw, I shall have you removed!'

The Duchess stood and addressed the wardens. 'That will be unnecessary. We will withdraw together.'

The sigh of wonder that accompanied this statement echoed through the cathedral. The Duchess picked up her skirts, handed her prayer book to Cara, and stepped through the door of the box. Together they walked through a path cleared for them and, as they reached the vestibule, Mass resumed behind them.

'Now Heaven help me,' said Pedro before the Duchess could say anything, 'but is your highness wearing a pair of fashionable boots from Madrid?' He closed his eyes in preparation of the response. The Duchess looked at him closely, and saw the sweat of haste and concern on him; he had a particular mission, she realised. 'I came out here with you,' she said, 'to save you. You risk excommunication.'

'It will not come to that,' said Pedro, 'not as long as I keep the priest provided with meat for his dinner, and bottles of some southern wine.' Then he took an even larger risk than excommunication by taking her wrist and saying, 'Now as your highness is as good as she is beautiful, and as you have lately made a good pancake from all the broken eggs with Cervantes, that is you are his patroness, then you must help me as fast as you can, and listen to explanations later.'

She listened expertly, and found his flattery wholesome. 'You are shrewd to rely on my kindness. But I have paid more than enough money for the printing of Cervantes' book.'

'Only the boots can save us,' he said swiftly. 'Yours will fit. I must have them. If you give them to me, I shall be away like lightning, and then return with as many explanations as will satisfy you, and all of them true.'

'You must be a master thief,' she said lightly, 'to divest me of my boots in the middle of the cathedral, and during Mass too!'

Pedro no longer had time for humour. 'We must go in your carriage to Robles. He is waiting.' He helped her quickly down the steps.

Ongora's carriage was positioned outside the cathedral so that he could watch society leaving after Mass had finished. He did not care to go in. The incense made him ill, and he feared too much gossip. He was lying sprawled in the carriage with his eyes closed in a half-doze when he heard Pedro's urgent tones. He spied through the carriage window and saw the Duchess being helped into her carriage by someone very inept with his hands; it was a wonder that she did not slap him.

Inside the carriage, the Duchess was listening to Pedro describe his instincts for her footwear. 'It is my business to know about your boots,' said Pedro. 'I have an inventory in my head of every item in this county that is likely to become marketable. If I see something that could be involved in one of my trades, I say to myself, "Pedro, remember this item, and call it by name occasionally, and one day, it will come to you." But we must hurry, my Lady, otherwise that stubborn fool Robles will close everything up and all will be lost!'

The carriage arrived while Robles was negotiating the goat through the door. His wife had woken up, hearing the commotion, had dressed and come down. As Pedro climbed out of the carriage, the goat, encouraged by seeing his old enemy, immediately charged. Robles intelligently let him go, and while Pedro distracted the goat by offering it his hat to eat, Robles greeted the Duchess and helped her down.

At that moment, Robles' wife appeared at the entrance, and the two women had first sight of one another. It was a curious moment of instantaneous liking, and Robles later wondered why he had not thought of them as connected before. There was the blonde glow of his wife's skin, the sensual honey of her face. And there was the stunning moment of looking at the Duchess, her perusal from Mount Olympus, the eagle-messenger of her eyes. One terrestrial and one astral goddess, he thought.

Pedro was more prosaic. 'You cannot choose between them for beauty,' he said to Robles, as though the women were deaf children.

'We are not chosen,' the Duchess said severely, 'we bestow.'

'The lady Duchess will bestow her boots,' Pedro said to Robles. 'As fine a pair as can be had between here and Madrid.' He looked at the Duchess to show them. Robles was more sensitive. 'I believe her at her word,' he said. 'But this is not a matter for the street. Please, my Lady, go in together.'

'I have some news,' Robles' wife said to the Duchess. 'Something imminent.'

The two women held arms together and entered the shop.

'Something imminent? What does that mean?' Pedro asked.

'If you're too stupid to guess,' Robles said, 'then I'm not going to tell you.' He began to strip his coat. 'My boy is not here to help me, so you'll have to do.' Pedro gaped at him. 'Close that door in your face,' Robles said, 'and help me prepare the press. Then you can go and tell Cervantes that a miracle has happened and his book is printed!'

Celebrations in the Tavern

The Invisible Knight.

*T*hat night, the heroes of this new comic romance celebrated in the tavern, along with their neighbours of the lower quarter, and while the tavern-keeper poured his best ale, Cervantes read out some of the most humorous episodes. During an interval, it occurred to Cervantes that the old Knight would be welcome, and perhaps persuaded to attend. He asked Isabel, who had developed for the old Knight that rough acceptance that passes for kindness, to go with a very specific message. She was to step gently up to him and say, 'Greetings from Sir Galahad, and would he kindly consider deferring his vigil and attending a celebration of some note at the shrine of the Knight of the Table.' Isabel looked at him with disdain. 'You expect me to speak this foolishness, in a public place, to an old man who has no more wits in his head than a lettuce! Why don't you go and babble to him? Or send that clown trader –' she said, pointing at Pedro '– to give him a dose of one of his tirades!'

'It would be difficult to persuade Pedro to go,' said her father reasonably, 'because whenever they meet, something unfortunate happens to him. Pedro is convinced that all the bad-luck in the world reserved for him is pent up in this old man.'

'He deserves it,' Isabel said nastily.

'Return quickly,' Cervantes said. 'I'm interested in what he'll say.'

She did return quickly, but without the news expected. The old man, she said, was nowhere to be found.

The Poet's Revenge

The choleric assassin.

*W*hen the news was relayed to Ongora that the book had been printed, a fit of rage almost made him faint. He felt rancour consuming him like a rapid wasting disease. It occurred to him, with a sudden certainty, to murder Cervantes. He did not have to do it. It could be expediently done by any footpad or night villain, for Cervantes lived in the capital's darker district. If only he could murder the book as well, smother it before it grew in reputation. But to murder Cervantes while celebrating his achievement. Catch him as he staggered en route between the tavern and his home. A mysterious assailant. All evidence swallowed by the night. The thoughts followed rapidly, drops of poison.

Ongora could not see that in the last months, the bestial Janus face had consumed him completely. His convoluted plots, the defusing of the satire, and the humiliating duel with the old Knight, had degenerated his normally quick mind and fluid thinking – in so much as they served his selfishness – into corrupt anger at the failure of so many of his projects. Perhaps, given time and opportunity, he would have found reason to murder the Duchess, as she had never acknowledged the possibility of becoming his mistress, or Denia, who had mocked him so openly, or the Emperor, for favouring an old

264

soldier before himself. He could not see that ire had replaced all superficial marks of his being a gentleman. Had the Duchess seen him, she would have immediately realised how his charm and cultivation had worn from him, like the scattered remnants of plate gold, and that he was no longer a man, but a creature of unremitting revenge, a Hydra of retribution. The blood scalded in his veins, a fever that could only be eased by the point of a knife.

He knew that the theatres and taverns would provide him with the engine for his revenge. Muted in dark clothes, and wearing a hat to shadow the handsome face, it did not take him long to find someone who for money would ply his weapons wherever instructed.

Ongora overheard this particular gentleman in a tavern close to the quarters of Cervantes' house. Turning about, he saw an angry, florid face, with small, light eyes, and a disaffected way of expounding loudly whilst looking bored at the same time. Ongora, seeing this man's lethal-looking sword, half a metre more than regulation length, and hearing the following brash conversation, knew that he had found his man. Ongora found it amusing, with what little lightness was left in him, that this gentleman, in his quarrel, was arguing on the efficacy of confession at death.

The gentleman was saying to a glazed pikeman, 'Shall I kill you then, and give you a quick blessing in your ear, and there you are, a new arrival in Heaven, with Jesus and the saints all welcoming you and showing you the sights of paradise, and you, having no more virtue than a cloud of flies on a dung-pile!'

The pikeman said faintly, 'Aye, maybe I am a bad man, but that I believe in the goodness of God. That shall save me.'

'Ah, you are talking through your cod-piece, for why, when a man is taken suddenly in battle, if a cannon-ball hits him and blows him into a thousand pieces, which piece would have the wit, aye, and the time to confess? It is foolish to think that confession gives anything to a man in the soldiering profession! If a soldier collects an Emperor's pay, what currency is that in Heaven? Can the soldier, aye, all those bits of him stand before God in Heaven and say, please it, sir, your honour, but slow me down that cannon ball a second and I will dash off a quick account of my sins before the blasted thing hits me! And it please you, your honour, to excuse my appearance, as that iron ball has made me all of a hundred pieces, and certainly, none of them can remember a sin without the company of the other.'

The pikeman was slow, but his knowledge of theology was sure. 'Why, are not the lot of you, those soldier friends and you, all shriven at one time? That is before the battle starts. See, that is the solution.'

'Solution!' said his friend. 'Piss-water! For again, if you think it through, then it is all kind of nonsense! Take tomorrow and think it through, and you'll see that if some are dead and others not in the regiment, and they turn up in Heaven, and God says, being a sharp one and on the side of the priests, "Where are the rest of you?", and you say, "Why, sir, your honour, some survived", and he says, "Well, you cannot enter for it was a collective shriving", then you are lost.'

The pikeman could only look humble at this logic.

'Confession,' continued his friend, 'is for fools who could not find their way into Heaven if it were set in the side of a barn and an elephant could pass in comfort!'

Ongora saw his chance. He adroitly turned the pikeman from his position and lightly shoved him away and, taking his place, said, 'And should confession be the same for all men, no matter what they are?'

The pikeman happily wandered off.

The choleric gentleman, easing his clothing, barely blinked at the sudden change in his conversation partner.

'I shall die in the good conscience,' he said, already bored with the subject, 'of my own devising, not in the choosing of a stinking priest with a thousand bastards, and a box of bribes under his floor!'

Ongora knew then for certain that he had found his murderer.

'And what if you had committed a crime,' he said, 'how would you account for it in your own conscience?'

'And what is crime, your gentlemanship?' said the choleric gentleman sarcastically. 'If the Emperor has me kill on all of the days of the week but the Sabbath? And if I shall be flogged for stealing the sheep of a farmer, when my army has burned his village? Conscience? Why, ask the priest for a conscience and he will sell one to you! And now,' said the choleric gentleman, suddenly violent, 'what are all these questions, God curse your unknown hide!'

'Perhaps I can provide the gold that will buy this conscience for you,' Ongora said quietly.

'Shit in my shoes and I'll piss in your hat!' said the choleric gentleman foully. 'Come with gold and I'll buy what I wish, and a conscience shall be the last thing! Now, you cursed, mangy, rotted maggot turd, deliver me your business, or I shall fillet you as you stand!' He had very swiftly drawn his cloak up with his hand to Ongora's shoulder and an overly sharp dagger with the other. As he smiled with false geniality and kept the dagger low, none could see the threat to Ongora.

Delighted that his research should bring such effective results, Ongora held steady and placed a bag of gold in front of the choleric gentleman. The gold clanked on the board of the table. He resumed a steadfast gaze at the hostile countenance before him.

'A reward for a small service rendered, simple for one of your arm and your choice of principles, and with no questions asked,' he said softly.

'And what shall it be, this small service?' said the choleric gentleman, now quiet.

'The ridding of this world of my enemy,' Ongora said rapidly, 'and you shall know whom it is, and then it shall be your choice whether to take his confession or not!'

Ongora's humour escaped the choleric gentleman. 'You have enough spleen,' he said, 'and why not that you rid yourself of this enemy?'

'I must be seen in other places,' lied Ongora quickly. Since losing his duel with the old Knight, his fretful nerves would not allow another encounter in which he had not previously determined the result.

'Then it is known that this is your enemy,' said the choleric gentleman, 'this is good for me.' The dagger disappeared, and just as quickly, the gold as well. 'When shall this be?'

'Now,' Ongora said, trying to control an exquisite trembling that his plots should be moving so quickly, 'this night. I shall take you.'

A Duel in the Dark

Treachery and rescue.

*T*he murderer-for-hire was called Gaspar. Ongora took him quickly to the road of Cervantes' favourite tavern. Cervantes would have to pass by where they waited on his way home. Ongora described him, a tall man, affable in countenance, usually full of bliss and ale. Had Ongora thought about his description, he would have realised that there was little in it that could cause hatred to anyone. But he continued in a soft voice of meditative menace, and warned Gaspar that, although his intended victim was genial in appearance, he always went armed, as was his right as a veteran, and he knew how to use a sword.

Then Ongora left. And Gaspar, as the street torches faded, found himself a stealthy shadow to wait in.

But Ongora had not really left. Unknown to Gaspar, Ongora found himself a doorway not ten metres away. The other half of his plan was to ensure that Gaspar really did kill Cervantes. And also, once Gaspar had fled the crime, make sure that his tormentor was a corpse. Ongora's arm twitched and he touched the dagger in his belt. He imagined smiling in triumph into Cervantes' dead face. Kicking the corpse, treading on the creative ambitions of this once-writer now-carcass.

He wrapped himself up close and waited.

And so it was that two murderers waited for Cervantes on the night of his triumph.

However, it was not Cervantes that arrived, but the old Knight. Obeying an inner summons, he had broken off his vigil with the Holy Grail and gone in search of what he conceived as a serious danger to his friend, Sir Galahad.

It was to the old Knight's advantage that without the light of torches in the street, or from the lantern that the proposed victim should be carrying, there was nothing for Gaspar to see. He only heard the strange clanking of the old Knight's footsteps before a voice, startlingly close, declared, 'Oh, enemy, you who crouch in these noisome shadows the better for your evil deed, come forth!' As ever, the old Knight's tone was cheerful and ebullient. 'Come forth, thou wolf of sin, and try your horrid weapons on your challenger, a humble knight, servant of the most high!'

Gaspar, already knowing his challenger to be utterly mad, unable to see anything, and yet unwilling to leave his duty unfinished, stepped bravely from his doorway and drew his sword. He hoped that this action would give him new eyes. As it was, it merely placed him within the circumference of the divinely aided swing of the old Knight's pot, which as you may recall, also served, in a double existence, as the sword of Sir Lancelot. The pot rang in triumph on the assassin's skull and Gaspar dropped without a sound. His sword clanked on the cobbles.

Ongora, crouching in a miserable doorway, knew immediately what had happened, having recognised the old Knight's voice and, of course, the pot's particular sound from its impact on a skull. The cursed luck of it, that the old Knight should appear once again to thwart the simplest of plots. It made him bite his lip. He crouched closer and listened.

Which, unknown to him, was also the action of the old Knight, who knew with inner certainty that his real enemy had not yet appeared. Gaspar was obviously a minion, a *sanglier* with a single tusk. The darkness was pricking with a different kind of danger. As the listening pause grew, the old Knight knew irrefutably that it was his old enemy, the evil magician of bad verse, who waited in the disturbing shadows. The old Knight chuckled at this twist of events. 'Come forth, thou evil guillemot, thou spawn of hell. What, will you have further punishment?'

Ongora, quivering, crouched lower.

And into this newest challenge came Cervantes, carrying a lantern, having already heard the old Knight's voice and eager to meet with him. The lamp-light swung on the calm face of the old Knight and the fallen figure of Gaspar, lying prone on the cobbles. 'Greetings, noble Knight, and fair son,' said the old Knight.

'You have found an enemy, I see,' said Cervantes.

'He was thine and was waiting for you,' said the old Knight. 'But the Holy Spirit prompted me of the danger to yourself.' He looked down at Gaspar. 'He is a minion of the real enemy, whom my senses tells me is haunting us close by.'

Cervantes controlled his feelings of alarm at the night being so full of dangers for himself and his friend. 'I see that the sword of Sir Lancelot has proved its worth on our enemy.' He also scanned the dark avenue, then looked down at Gaspar. 'What shall be done with this unfortunate?' The unconscious Gaspar stirred at the sound of conversation.

At this moment, the old Knight, sensing the cogitation of evil, sniffed like a hunter, and grasped Cervantes' arm. 'Look, there he is!' he said, pointing.

For Ongora, this was the most horrible moment in all the troubles that he had encountered with the old Knight. As he crouched, closeted in the doorway and the blind blue of the night, Cervantes lamp had revealed the prone figure of Gaspar, while the two figures of his enemies discussed his presence close by. And then, the old Knight called out and pointed directly at him, when no senses, however trained, should have been able to see through the dark, barricaded, as it were, by the lantern in Cervantes' fist. His fear increased as Cervantes, guided by the old Knight, gazed in his direction. Cervantes said to the old Knight, 'Your senses are inspired. I cannot see anything.'

Ongora took this as his cue, and fled, scrambling down the slippery street, aghast at his astonishingly bad luck, hopeless at his fate, shrill with fear at the possibility of receiving harm, once again, from an old man, yes, an old man.

Cervantes, startled at the sound of someone fleeing, said, 'Who is it?'

The old Knight said, 'An old enemy, whose quarrel was previously with me.' And he took off in pursuit of the hapless Ongora.

Cervantes watched the old Knight with an ache in his heart, for seeing him in pursuit of an invisible malignancy, he felt a premonition.

But then suddenly Gaspar came round. Finding himself on the ground, and assuming that the blow that had knocked him down had come from Cervantes, he made a violent swing with his sword.

Cervantes, astonished, parried with the lantern. Gaspar shouted, 'Come, take out your own weapon, for you have damaged me already, and I shall run you through a dozen times for the insult and the unfair surprise. I shall take as much pleasure in killing you as in my fee.'

Gaspar lunged, his portly belly belying the agility of his legs. In the lantern-light, Cervantes could see the pale, berserk anger in the eyes of his assailant. Puzzled by this homicidal irrationality, Cervantes was also too much the soldier to let this attack affect his already jumping muscles. But he was at a disadvantage, with the lantern in his good hand and unable to draw his sword. It was not a time to panic. He parried again with the lantern, threw his cloak over Gaspar's head and pushed him firmly away. Then he swiftly placed the lantern down on the street, and turned ready, sword in his good hand, while Gaspar struggled from the cloak.

Gaspar's head emerged, choleric.

'Now God give you calm this night,' Cervantes began. But his assailant was too angry to listen. 'Dog's blood, you bastard, I shall be rid of you!' said Gaspar, and lunged forward.

Cervantes parried calmly. 'Who sent you?' he asked.

'I shall tell you,' Gaspar said sarcastically, 'after I have run you through!' And he lunged again, relying on the illegal length of his blade to find a mark. Cervantes, himself holding an extravagantly long weapon, let the sword run past him, and then, as a warning, scored Gaspar on the thigh.

Gaspar's response was, in retrospect, predictable. He howled in rage, and threw his sword to the ground. 'Damn you, you pox-ridden cur, for you have hurt my flesh.' He looked at the wound on his leg. 'It's bleeding, you whore! Why, give me a pistol,' he shouted to non-existent attendants, 'and I shall fix him with lead on the spot!' Not even waiting for a response, which would not be forthcoming, he snatched up the sword by the blade, his heavy gloves protecting him from the cold sharpness, and swung at Cervantes' head.

Gaspar's rage and desperate behaviour might have proved amusing, but that Cervantes knew this was the most dangerous point of the fight. He also knew that Gaspar was beyond a steadying resolution to his anger and would not be stopped without being disabled. Hopefully not killed. He could run, but then Gaspar would catch him, shouting all the while. So, as clinically as he could, he tripped Gaspar, and then ran an inch of his sword into his assailant's abdomen.

Once again, as Cervantes recalled later, Gaspar's response was predictable, for he sat on the ground, holding his stomach, and with the rage of a bawling infant, hurled insults and imprecations at Cervantes. 'Why, you midden-faced, garbage-eating, pox-swelling, turd of hell! You have hurt me AGAIN!' Grabbing at whatever rubbish he could find about him on the ground, he hurled it at Cervantes.

By now, the neighbourhood was roused, and voices joined in the medley. Soon, the Watch would arrive. Cervantes took another look at the wounded assassin. Gaspar was lying back on the cobbles, holding his stomach, and complaining. Cervantes was more concerned about the old Knight. Gaspar sat up again and shouted, 'You damned, plague-ridden, bug-faced wretch, you have killed me!' and then fainted.

The old Knight had given chase but Ongora was quick; he knew that total flight was his only hope. He ran and turned through the intricate streets, and in his panicking fear, slashed at any that crossed his path. The streets became an outcry of wounds, and Ongora a shadowed libertine of violence, even as he scurried from whom he misconceived as the real enemy.

For the old Knight, he did not have to give chase at full speed; all he needed to trace the escape of the evil magician were the wounded, staggering strangers crying for help in the mad lanterns and shadows. The Watch were on full alert, running in squads of bristling pikes and truncheons. And the neighbourhood, heads hanging from windows, shouting out to whomever they saw in the street.

Ongora was crying, crouched in a doorway, and tried to control his fear, biting his hand. His dagger was streaked and there were images of terror in his mind, those whom he had slashed, lantern faces that had startled him. He slashed at them again in his mind. Fools, he thought hysterically, no-one had the right of such innocence. They should be punished.

Mysteriously, the Watch arrived and ran through the alley in which he hid without even stopping to check the doorways. Their sound ebbed and he realised that they had missed him. He supposed that the old Knight had been with them. They would never catch him. Sitting on the ledge of the doorway, with his hand over his mouth, he laughed in exhaustion. Relief made him jubilant, but he tried to control it. He still needed to find his way back, clean himself up, disassociate himself from the evening's alarms. There was Gaspar, his assassin, whom he supposed was in the hands of the Watch. What if Gaspar identified him? He winced at the thought. The evening's events had become labyrinthine, while he had writhed to his course of revenge. The possibilities of his being discovered were real. It might be better to leave for Madrid this night. He would force the drunken printer to lie for him. The printing of the pirated edition would validate his being in Madrid.

Shaking delicately, he stepped quietly from the doorway and made his way softly in the opposite direction to the sounds of the Watch.

The old Knight had not given up on his pursuit, but then the Watch had stopped him briefly, and questioned him on what he had seen. His explanation as to the appearance and motives of the evil magician they accepted, for his madness they reckoned was benign compared to the murderous exit of their fugitive. The old Knight had urged them in the right direction and they had thanked him and left. Knowing that these constables of chivalry had been ordered to apprehend the evil magician, he thought himself relieved of the task. Galahad was safe. The minion subdued. And the evil magician would be apprehended. He did not need to know the punishment that was planned for his enemy. He returned to his vigil.

Ongora knew that he was entering the area where he had planned Cervantes' assassination but it was a good risk; the Watch were still chasing him in another direction. He had not realised his proximity to his chosen enemies, until he crept passed the entrance to Cervantes' courtyard. He was careful, because lights were on in the house. Then his heart was seized with panic when his senses told him that someone was in the courtyard. He flattened himself against the wall. He listened for any sounds of urgency, whether he had been seen, his dagger ready. There was nothing. He peered cautiously into the courtyard. In the half-defined gloom of the night and the lights from the house, he could see a single figure. It was strange, but the figure appeared to be kneeling. He listened hard, trying to peel away the indecipherable shapes of the courtyard. He was trying to hear and see through his own loud panic and the throbbing of his blood. Then a light flared briefly from one of the windows of the house. And he saw clearly the enemy of his nightmares, the mad old fool who had bested him every time, had caused this night's terrified retreats, had foiled him in everything. He saw that it was the old Knight, kneeling in some pathetic religious rite, his eyes closed and his lips moving. A babbling prayer, he thought, that is appropriate! Because I shall kill him and he'll be dispatched to some incoherent heaven where God and the angels will be brightly painted paste puppets, speaking in the mock high language of the carnival. He was terrified, but his resolve was certain. He was of shadows. He quickly stepped in and shoved his blade into the old man's warmth. After all, he thought, as moistness slowed his hand, he is Cervantes' fame. To kill him will end all of that. The old Knight did not falter or cry out, and Ongora did not wait to see the end of his single blow. Once again he took flight, but this time with a final sense of fulfilment. He had achieved his revenge at last.

The End of the Vigil

The collapse of the old Knight.

*C*ervantes arrived, having been released by the Watch, who had discovered enough from the enraged Gaspar to fix firmly the suspicion that the poet Ongora had engineered the attempted assassination. He found the old Knight, lying prone in the courtyard, and thought this a further effort in his quest for the Grail. Then he noticed blood seeping from a wound through the old Knight's eccentrically sewn jerkin. The old Knight was breathing, but the signs were faint. His heart seized by this new cruelty, that his protector and friend had been wounded on his behalf, Cervantes summoned help from the house. This time, there was no question from the family about whether the old Knight should be allowed inside. It was he and Isabel that carried the old Knight up into his bedroom. The candles were lit, the bed that was generally used to collect manuscripts cleared, and the old Knight was stretched out on his side, so that Ongora's conniving wound could be dressed. Isabel went to fetch bandages. Constanza went for the surgeon. Cervantes sat blankly down by the old Knight.

The old Knight opened his eyes at one point and whispered, 'Victory, Sir Galahad! We have won a great fight tonight. The enemy is routed.' Then he fainted. The real enemy is death, thought Cervantes, looking at the delicate happiness on the old Knight's face.

Death

A final farewell.

*T*he surgeon's prognosis was not encouraging; the stab wound had punctured liver and lung. Even though the old Knight's eyes were clear when he woke the following day, and he kindly and immediately greeted Cervantes, he could not move his limbs in any way, and he had the air of tranquil exhaustion. He told Cervantes that he had been stabbed by the evil magician. This being known from Gaspar's account as the poet Ongora, a constable was summoned and given this information. News was that Ongora could not be found, and orders had been given to extend the search outside the capital. These arrangements had no effect on the old Knight. He was confident, as he said to Cervantes, that having defeated the magician in a previous combat, it had merely been his shadow that attacked him, and this would wither in the normal light of day.

The family had quickly used up any initial sympathy for the old Knight, and now they wanted him removed from the house and taken to hospital. Isabel and her two half-sisters, who were only united in their arguments with others, were forceful in their opinions, and Cervantes had to move himself and them outside the bedroom.

'And who will pay for everything while he is ill in the house?' demanded Isabel.

'He's dying,' Cervantes said. 'All he needs is company.'

'That still costs money,' Constanza said. 'And if he's dying, I hope you do not expect us to pay for the funeral?'

He tried to shush them. 'These are particulars that do not need to be thought of now,' he said.

Isabel wagged her finger at him. 'You are trying to shirk the responsibility of making the decision, and then you'll foist the cost of it on our household and hope that we won't notice.'

'Fair daughters of Albion,' said the old Knight. His clear tones could be heard through the door. 'I cannot hear the birds singing for your arguing. Go further off. There are plenty of dogs in the neighbourhood if you want to bark.'

This did not please Isabel, and she immediately re-entered the room followed by her sisters. 'If you're so lively,' she said to him, 'perhaps there are some chores that we can find for you around the house.'

'Although my senses are clear,' he replied, 'some demon of weight has me pinioned to the bed.'

Pedro entered. 'Daughters of Venus,' he said as a placatory greeting. He could see that Isabel was incensed.

'Faithful squire,' said the old Knight, 'have you fed Bucephalus, cleaned my armour, and fixed the missing rowel on my spur?'

'All this and more,' Pedro said readily. 'But I have come to report that there is no sign of the enemy.' He looked at Cervantes. 'I told them of the printer in Madrid.' Cervantes nodded.

'It was a wraith,' the old Knight said.

'A wraith cannot make holes in you,' Isabel said pragmatically.

'True enough,' said the old Knight reasonably, 'but I believe it was the dagger that made the hole.'

'You're mad,' she said.

'Isabel,' Cervantes said, 'let it be.'

'He is having fun at my expense,' Isabel said hotly.

A constable of the Watch arrived with the news that Gaspar

had died. 'A fit of anger,' the constable said, 'carried him off.'

Cervantes felt some sadness. Even though it was clear that he had wounded the choleric assassin in self-defence, there was something so unkempt about his departure, that he wondered at the waste of it.

'As you know,' continued the constable, 'he was continually angry, and he kept bursting his wound.'

'He was a minor demon,' the old Knight said. 'Tomorrow, he will be a toadstool.'

The constable stared, and there grew in the room a definite feeling of unease at the old Knight's pronouncement. 'This is a raving person,' Isabel hissed at Cervantes. 'He should be in the asylum!'

'Well, he is here,' Cervantes replied, 'and we cannot move him, otherwise it will make things worse.'

'Why do you talk about me,' the old Knight said, 'as though I were not here?'

This time, a priest entered. The room was now full of Cervantes' family, Pedro, the constable, and the new arrival. Everyone was therefore startled when the priest drew back on first sight of the old Knight and grabbed Cervantes by the arm. 'Is it awake?' he asked, holding onto Cervantes for support.

Cervantes tried to disengage himself. 'What do you mean?'

The old Knight saw the priest and looked at him sternly. 'I banished you once before. What are you doing here?'

The priest clung to Cervantes arm. 'He beat me once before,' he said miserably. 'Do not let him do it again.'

They were all astonished.

'The reason for beating him is obvious,' the old Knight said. 'As he is hollow, he makes an interesting sound. Added to which, I found him in the street reading a book of profanity, disguised as a holy text.'

This pronouncement was too much for the priest, who had since become aware of the constable and many other witnesses in the room. He made a sound of panic and scurried from the room.

'You had met him previously?' Cervantes asked.

The old Knight nodded. 'I had to knock him on the nose for his lack of spirituality.'

'Are you always merciless with men of the cloth?' Pedro asked.

'Learn from me, my noble squire,' the old Knight said. 'For it was a piece of hollowness disguised in holy vestments, a frequently used ploy of the demonic orders.'

'He was supposed to shrive you,' said Isabel, 'and prepare you for the next world.'

'I am going there now,' the old Knight said. 'Nothing else needs to be done. Farewell to you all.' He nodded to everyone in the room, arranged his hands by his sides, and closed his eyes. In a few seconds, his breathing had ceased.

His departure was so swift and confident, the occupants of the room felt that it was not death that had played the final surprise, but him. In small moments, the room emptied without further words, leaving the corpse of the old Knight and Cervantes sitting by the bed.

Nothing had prepared Cervantes for this moment. He sat blankly. As his mind grew numb, a desolate silence grew in the room. A primary thought scored him deeply. They could not have more inopportunely handled the old Knight's last moments. Had he been bleeding to death in front of them, they could not have wrangled louder. And had not his mortal wound proved his deepest loyalty? It beat on him that they had made a domestic dispute out of the old Knight's exit, a graceless fumble out of the ultimate tragedy of every human being.

But then to be angry for a friend who had died? It divided him from the sorrow, the tender acknowledgement of his feelings for the old Knight. His sadness at the death of Gaspar, his feeling of responsibility in it, that had been immediate. He had kept himself steady through the irrationalities of the last few hours.

Triumph and disaster had washed in on equally strong tides. The book had been finished and printed. The enemy revealed and destroyed. But then his newest friend, the old Knight, proving his loyalty, had been mortally wounded and died as gently as a babe.

'It does little good,' said a voice, 'to have such a clamour going on during one's final moments on earth.'

Stunned, Cervantes looked over. The old Knight was looking at him calmly, with an expression that he had already recalled with affectionate memory. 'Why,' Cervantes said, 'there's nothing dead about you at all.'

'It's a deferred moment,' the old Knight said. 'I could not die with all those demons in the room. Their anticipation of my demise would have irked a statue of patience.'

'You seem much stronger,' Cervantes said.

'The flame burns brightest,' the old Knight said, 'before it goes out.'

He leaned up and held out his arm to Cervantes. 'Help me up,' he said. 'We'll go and sit by your tree in the courtyard.' Cervantes helped him, thinking that perhaps the old Knight had recovered some terrestrial sense. 'Although,' said the old Knight immediately on this thought, 'it should be obvious that it is the Holy Grail and worth a lifetime of vigils.'

Cervantes helped the old Knight downstairs, encountering no-one from the house. They sat together under the tree. The old Knight held his hand. 'Two old dogs,' the old Knight said, 'enjoying the evening.'

Cervantes nodded and smiled, while words choked in his throat.

'I cannot see it entirely,' the old Knight said. 'There is a glimmer, but it is indistinct.'

'What can you see?' Cervantes said.

'The holy city,' the old Knight said. He sighed and then said, 'God has it in mind to invite me from the pleasure of your company.' The old Knight's hand slackened in his. He felt the weight of the old Knight's head on his shoulder increase softly. His breathing, this time Cervantes knew, halted without pretence. The sun had set around them. Dusk had turned the strident commerce of the city into a silence. A breeze touched them delicately, the fingers of a redemptive spirit. As the old Knight's weight hardened against him, Cervantes' tears, his private emblems of struggle, quietly streaked his cheeks. In the half-glow of the burgeoning evening, his face glimmered into the studied, remorseless mask of tragedy.

Fame Secure

Books of ill-repute.

*O*ngora had done his best to purvey the ruin of Cervantes before the authorities could slow his plans. So it was that numerous print shops across the country produced spurious editions and imitations of the adventures of Don Quixote. Meanwhile, with both Gaspar and the old Knight dead and unable to give further evidence, the constabulary could find nothing more against him. They had to let him go. But what could not be proved was counted as absolute truth in the capital. His reputation was ruined. No shop or trade would accept his custom. He was frozen out of public appearances. If he went to the theatre, the curtain would not go up until he had left. His mistress had used his downfall to feed the satirists various intimate details about him. Even though profits were substantial from the imitations, they would probably have to finance his voluntary exile. Otherwise, some gentleman poet, hungry for reputation, would challenge him to a duel. He would have to fight every hour of the day. He was making preparations for departure, when a large parcel was delivered to him with the following letter:

> To the honourable, etc. Please you to accept the books accompanying this letter and these very special instructions. Although these books are unworthy, they are the children of

my brain, for as it has pleased God to represent my duty here on earth by rendering the first of all Comic Novels, so he has shown a divinity that shapes all ends by blessing me with these bastardisations. Even Kings were born at the other end of the house, as the proverb goes, that is illegitimate, and these mockeries reveal the quality of the original. Keep them safe, not to read them, as this would be a dismal and tedious duty, but because so much of late has been stolen from me – even something as invisible and insubstantial as my 'reputation', which God be praised has never been as far from me as the length of a breath – that it would be prudent to protect these signs that God has bestowed me. Keep these editions for me, not in a very prominent part of your library, but at least in a glass case with a lock, so that when you have visitors, you can show them this case and say, 'These are the imitators of Cervantes that made his fame secure.'

The letter was signed by Cervantes and the parcel contained numerous pirated copies of *Don Quixote*.

The Return of Denia

A letter to the Emperor.

*B*ut then Ongora was banished completely, this time by the Emperor. Denia, if you remember, had been so intrigued by his encounter with the old Knight, that he had made extensive efforts to find out more about him. His ambitious knowledge of the crests and emblems that marked all the royal houses of the Empire, and his recalling that the old Knight had mentioned being a royal favourite had been his starting point. And while he sent out his secretaries to find out what information they could, that is, without interrupting the building of the new historical library dedicated to his name, he arranged for daily reports to be made to him of the news and gossip from Valladolid. He would have the report read to him while his hirsute chin and jowls were being shaved for the audience of the day. So he knew much of what had happened, including Ongora's spiked intrigues and the printing of *Don Quixote*. And what he didn't know, he shrewdly surmised. After all, there was much in common between his conniving brain and that of Ongora's. But he was the lion of the court, and Ongora the strange cat looking for territory. But like some predators, he thought, I shall break his neck while he is a kitten, and before he ever grows to threaten me.

And so it seemed fortuitous that a connection became

established between the eccentric old gentleman and Ongora; news of the duel between them in which Ongora had come off the worse had delighted the gossip-hungry court. The assassination attempt on Cervantes had been reported to Denia, and he had made it privately clear that Cervantes should not be detained nor charged for Gaspar's demise. He knew of course that the envy behind the attempted murder was Ongora's. And he felt, with his political instinct for traps, that the future was a garrotte for Ongora.

Then one of his secretaries provided a definitive proof of the true identity of the old man, a favourite of the dead Philip II, and the special assistant to that great old general of memory, the Duke of Alva. Well, nothing could be more satisfying! A highly connected veteran, maddened from the distress of the wars, fighting his deluded monsters of chivalry, and defeating a reputedly vicious swordsman like Ongora with a pot! Delicious!

Denia then wrote a letter to the Emperor. Normally, he would have informed the Emperor of all of this in person, as he generally spent half the day with him. But he wanted this to be formal and as close as it could possibly be to a written order for Ongora's destruction. The letter informed the Emperor that the Empire had lost a favourite son, one whom the Emperor's father had cherished, and that whilst this favourite had lost his wits in the wars, his spirit had nonetheless shone bright and, were it not for an envious and murderous plot, would have been welcomed and reinstated at court. The letter then named Ongora as responsible for the favourite's death.

The letter was clear, and for once, the Emperor was definite in his response. Ongora was banished from the Empire, without hope of return.

A Wreck

The poet's ruin.

*O*ngora boarded a merchant ship for the colonies, but like many of the armadas that had sailed, bad weather foundered it on the shores of Britain. Fate assigned him to the country of the Empire's enemies, where he was washed up on the gravel of the Dorset shore, and like many other half-drowned Spanish, adopted by the family of a fishing village. His artificial blood and good looks seeped into a family enamoured with the exotic, the ascendants of the present author. Many generations later, and their stock of blue eyes and fair skin is still surprised by progeny bearing his olive skin and irises of Mediterranean brown.

And his psychotic ambition? His prickling sensitivity? The deep ocean salted it out of him.